TARNISHED COPPER

By

Geoffrey Sambrook

T F
CP

Published in Great Britain by Twenty First Century Publishers Limited,
in conjunction with UPSO Limited.

A catalogue record of this book is available from the British Library

First Edition: August 2002

ISBN: 1-904433-02-2

To order additional copies of Tarnished Copper and other books by
published by Twenty First Century Publishers Limited please visit:
www.twentyfirstcenturypublishers.com

In memory of Doctor Andrew Ball, one of the smartest of the traders, and one of the best of friends.

TARNISHED COPPER

Acknowledgements.

Many people – wittingly or unwittingly – helped in the writing of this book. Particular thanks are due to Adam Esah, Michael Hutchinson, Fred Piechoczek, Les Brazier, Sally Hemsley, Andrew Suckling, Simon Grant-Rennick, Matt and Sarah Gillie, Ellis Moses, Ian Runcie and Hazel Adams. And of course to Jenni, Rebecca and Victoria.

Lyrics from "Money for Nothing" (Knopfler) © 1985 by kind permission of Rondor Music (London) Ltd.

Prologue

March 1988

The group of graduate business students were welcomed into the London Metal Exchange boardroom by one of the Exchange's marketing staff; he was a young man, well-dressed in a stylish German suit and Italian silk tie, but also with a rather pompous air to him.

"I'm pleased to see you all here," he said. "Welcome to the LME. I'm glad you took advantage of the opportunity to come and see our market, because sometimes we feel we're a bit of a cinderella amongst London's Exchanges, one that most people are not really aware of." He leant forward, to emphasize his point. "And yet, we're one of the City of London's success stories. We are the premier global price setting mechanism for primary base metals, that is, copper, aluminium, tin, lead, zinc and nickel. These are all essential products for an industrial society, and they are mined and smelted all over the world. However, when it comes to establishing the price for them, there is no competitor for the LME. Later on this morning, we're going to go and look at the open outcry market, where the dealers make their trades. You'll see how they scream and shout at each other in what we call the Ring. They trade each metal for a five minute Ring in turn, four times a day. The final bid and offer price in the second Ring for each metal in the morning session then becomes what we call the day's official price." He paused for effect, and looked appraisingly round at the fifteen or so students. "This is the price which is used by producers and consumers worldwide to make their purchases and sales of metal." He paused again, to look meaningfully at the faces in front of him, "That gives us a unique position as the only Exchange in the United Kingdom with such a global reach."

One of the students leant to whisper in the ear of the attractive girl next to him, in a Michael Caine voice, "And not a lot of people know that." She tried to hide her giggles, earning a censorious look from the LME spokesman, who continued, "But we'll see that later. First, we're going to go next door, where we've set up a question and answer session for you about futures and options pricing. So if you'd just like to follow me...", and he led the group of City University Business School finance majors out of the panelled boardroom and into a smaller conference room, set up with chairs, tables and an overhead projector.

Meanwhile, down at the other end of Fenchurch Street from the LME, one of the dealers the spokesman referred to was having a rough morning. Jamie Edwards was accepted by his peers in the market as one of the most talented dealers in the business, but he was getting a serious dressing down from his boss.

"Jamie," said Terry Prichard, managing director of Myerson Brothers, "your performance is not up to standard. You've been losing money too often, and you know why. I don't want to do this, but my co-directors have left me with no alternative." He tugged to loosen his already slackly tied tie. "This is an official warning. Unless you pull yourself together, you're going to leave Myerson's." He held up his hand, as Edwards started to object. "For God's sake, Jamie, you know what the problem is, and you can't expect me to go on making excuses for you if you won't help yourself. It's the drugs that do it. Just get yourself under control."

Edwards left the room. He knew Prichard was right - at least, right now he did. But when he craved the cocaine, his whole perspective was different. He sat down at his position on the dealing desk, and mechanically worked through the morning, making prices for Myerson's customers to trade.

Back at the LME, one of the students put up his hand. The LME official nodded for him to ask his question. "You've explained about pricing deals, but it seems to me that it only works during the open outcry market, down on the Exchange floor. What happens for the rest of the day - like now, for instance? How does it work if I want to buy some copper now?"

"OK," said the guide, "that's a good question. The way it works is that the dealers will be in their offices, and they trade with their customers and with each other over the telephone - just like they do in the foreign exchange market. With a Japanese, for example, you've got a big time zone difference to accommodate, so if he wants to buy or sell copper, he can call his broker/dealer, and ask him for a price. If he then trades, the broker has the opportunity to ask for a market from one of his peers - so in a way, they are all working together, even though they have different clients. Although some of the clients will trade with more than one broker." He paused, and then added, "That's what's going on at the moment, in the brokers' offices. Then, late morning, they will come down to the Exchange, and the day's official trading will begin. The volume of trades is about evenly split between the office market and the floor market."

So, at about half past eleven, it was time to head down to LME floor. Jamie Edwards took the lift down to the ground floor, and out into Fenchurch Street. He followed the street along, past the various office buildings and shops, pausing to look at the jewellery and watches displayed in Mappin and Webb's window, and arrived outside the door of the Wine Lodge, a pub popular with the market traders. In he went, and one of the group of London Metal Exchange traders standing by the bar thrust a pint of beer into his hand. "There you go, Jamie, get that down you", he said.

"Thanks, Ferret", replied Edwards, "Anything interesting happening at your place this morning?"

Ferret - Peter Bantry - was a small weasely looking man of about thirty. He was the senior copper trader at Union Metals, one of the larger and more flamboyant broker companies on the Exchange. It was owned by one of the major Wall Street investment banks, which gave its traders a lot of support in running big, risky positions.

"Nah," he replied to Edwards' question, "not really. A bit of a rumour from the Tokyo boys that somebody over there wants to get this market up. I don't think there's much in it, but I wouldn't be too short at the moment. 'Ow was your weekend?"

They made a strange pair, but they had struck up an immediate friendship when they first went onto the floor as junior clerks. They came from totally different backgrounds, Edwards the son of a successful surgeon, educated at an (admittedly minor) public school, and Bantry, whose father was a cab driver and who came from the more traditional LME traders' heartland of suburban Essex. Nevertheless, they had discovered soon after they first met standing in neighbouring booths on the LME floor that they shared common interests in drinking and gambling.

"Weekend was alright, but I got another bollocking from Prichard this morning", replied Edwards.

"Same old thing, yeah?" Edwards nodded his agreement. "You got to get your brain in gear, Jamie. You're too old for all those games now. You have to learn to be serious about it now, if you want to carry on making money in this business. You get enough orders from Phil Harris to keep you in profit. Just settle down for a bit, execute those orders and don't give them any more reasons to have a go at you."

"Yeah, I s'pose so", said Edwards. "Come on. Drink up. It's time to go."

They both finished their pints and followed the general movement out through the door and across Fenchurch Street.

Walking through the doors of Plantation House, they turned to the left into the foyer of the London Metal Exchange. They passed the display cases containing samples of the various metals traded by the exchange, and walked through the single door in the corner out on to the trading floor. In front of them was a circle of red leather seats, and behind these a rank of booths whose walls were festooned with telephones. In the gap between the two, various clerks and dealers stood chatting, seemingly aimlessly. In the Ring, as the circle of seats is known, about eight or ten young-looking men and women sat, staring down at the notebook they each held in their lap. The clock on the wall above showed 11:53, and in the illuminated panel immediately below it the alchemists' symbol for tin was lit up. The clock flicked over, and the dealers started to come to life. Tin was not a busy market, but nevertheless some bargains were struck before the bell rang as the clock moved to 11:55, and the symbol switched over to indicate the beginning of the aluminium ring.

Up above them, shielded from the market by a glass wall, the students were shepherded out into the viewing gallery by their LME guide. "What you can see in front of you," he began, "is the Ring, where the open outcry trading takes place. That symbol on the wall over there" - he pointed - "tells you which metal is being traded. At the moment it's aluminium, which is probably our second most important commodity. When this finishes, then we'll move into copper, which is our flagship. You can see the dealers sitting in the Ring, and you can hear through the microphone relay what they are saying."

The attractive girl spoke up, "What are all the other people doing - the ones round the edge? They look as if they're just chatting."

The guide frowned at her levity. "They're not just chatting. They are the clerks, and their job is to record the deals their dealer makes in the Ring, and then to agree them with their counterparties. It's a very important job, and all the dealers began their careers as clerks, before they were allowed to sit in the Ring. And the ones standing half in and half out of the booths are on the phone giving a commentary on the action in the Ring, either to their own office, or directly to clients. Some of the bigger clients prefer to listen straight to the floor, rather than go through an account executive up in the office. They'll also be trading currency hedges, because the LME still trades in sterling, whereas the majority of the brokers' deals with their customers are in US dollars. So when the dealer trades in the Ring in sterling, his clerk will immediately convert the currency into dollars. They call the dollar/sterling exchange rate 'cable'."

Meanwhile, Edwards had walked round the outside of the Ring to his company's booth, and punched a code into one of the phones. He got through to Phil Harris, an American who ran a highly successful metal broking operation in Munich on behalf of the U.S. bank Macdonald and Thompson. "Hi, Phil, off we go for the ally ring."

"I'm not too concerned with ally this morning," said Harris. "I'm gonna have some things for you in copper though. The Japs have been trying to buy from me for the last half hour or so" - this was the time Edwards had been in the pub - "and I'm getting a bit concerned that I need to get it back. Something is beginning to look a little like there's big buying out there."

"Yeah," said Edwards, "one of the boys at Union was just hinting the same thing. What do you want me to do - start buying the three months?"

"Yeah," said Harris. "Cable's going my way at the moment, so you can pay up to £985. Trouble is, I need to buy around four hundred lots by no more than that price."

"Christ, Phil, there's no way you'll get that much in. The last offer on the screen was £975. Four hundred lots in this market is worth more than £10." One lot of copper was 25 tonnes, so Harris needed to buy 10,000 tonnes. Every pound the market rose above the level where he had sold meant a loss to him of £10,000.

"I know. So why don't you see how you go in the first ring, and we'll have another look afterwards. But don't panic it, Jamie - there's other buying out there. I'm trusting you. OK?"

"Alright," said Edwards. "I'll see how I go. I'll give you Stumpy for the ring." He handed the phone to the clerk who was standing next to him. "Phil Harris for copper, OK", he said. "He's already given me some orders, but there may be more, so give him a good commentary."

In the background, the clamour from the ring was rising. Aluminium was an active market. Edwards stepped up behind his company's seat and leaned over the shoulder of the dealer sitting there. "Rumour is there's copper buying around. Why not get a bit of ally in, in case it moves with it." The dealer nodded, and Edwards moved back. His dealing skill was respected by his peers, even if his wild streak had created problems for him with his various employers throughout his career. They all agreed, though, that he dealt better in the mornings than after a good lunch - but that hardly made him unique on the LME. He was in his element down on the market floor. He was good at it, and he knew it. That's why he suffered the frustration he did. His current employer, Myerson Brothers, was one of the smaller brokers, owned by an industrial holding company that was highly risk averse, and therefore unwilling to allow its subsidiary to take much of a proprietary trading position. Edwards had last worked at one of the larger houses but had been summarily fired after his cocaine habit had become too obvious to the management. He owed his position at Myerson to an old friendship with Prichard, and to the fact that Phil Harris liked to do his ring business with him. That generated enough commission to make Edwards valuable despite the other considerations. Of these two factors, in the harsh, money-dominated world of the LME, Harris's patronage was the more important.

The bell rang, ending the aluminium ring. It was time for copper, and Edwards moved into his position in Myerson's seat. As ever, he had some minor date adjustments to make, to square up some of the positions on his dealing card, but apart from that Harris's buying was his major concern. Clearly from what Ferret had implied, Union also had some buying. If it was coming out of Japan, then Metal Trading - Japanese-owned - and Commet, with a strong Tokyo presence, would likely also have it. And how much had Harris put elsewhere? Edwards was well aware that his friend always hedged his bets by spreading his business around. One of the problems of being one of the smaller brokers with one of the biggest customers was that it was difficult to hide anything. As soon as he opened his mouth and started bidding, the Ring would put two and two together and guess it was Harris buying. Knowing he was a big player, any sellers would then back off and wait to see how high he pushed the market before they executed their selling. Edwards sat, looking disinterestedly down at the card and order book he held on his lap. He was waiting for someone else to start the market. Around the Ring, there was a constant to-ing and fro-ing of clerks relaying orders coming in from the phones to the dealers.

Ferret looked up, in the Union Metals seat; "Four I'll give, six I'll sell three months," he called across the Ring.

"Twenty I'll buy at six," from the Metal Trading dealer.

"Two lots," replied Ferret expressionlessly.

"Six I'll give," again from Metal Trading. As always, the dealers only used the last figure of the price, the rest - in this case nine hundred and seventy - presumed understood as a continuation of the last trade in the previous session. There were a few more small trades at six then at seven, and then the sellers stopped. Metal Trading bid the price up pound by pound to nine eighty-two, without buying anything more. It did not bode particularly well for what Edwards had to do. The clock flicked over to 12:04 - one minute of the Ring left.

Stumpy leaned over Edwards' shoulder. "Phil says have you done anything yet?" then as Edwards gestured at him in irritation, more urgently, "Pay up to seven, but get something in."

In for a penny, in for a pound, thought Edwards. "Five I'll pay."

"Yes," from one of the other brokers.

"A hundred lots," said Edwards.

"Twenty," from the other broker, as he was obliged to do, having yessed Edwards. No more was forthcoming. Only a few seconds to go.

"Give seven," came from Ferret and suddenly as the bell began to ring, the noise level rose, and all the brokers were screaming to pay seven. No sellers, though.

As the sound of the bell faded, the dealers stood up and left the Ring, to be replaced by the lead traders. Edwards stepped back into the shelter of the box and took the phone from Stumpy. "Phil? All I got was twenty at eighty-five. At the end, everyone was bidding. Looks like the whole market's short. Do you want me to try and get some in round the back or from the customers?"

"Yeah. As long as cable stays around here, you can pay up to ninety if you have to. Let me know how you go, and get me for the next Ring." Edwards was left holding a dead phone as Harris hung up. Punching another button on the board, he connected onto the loudspeaker system up in the office. "See if you can buy any copper up to eighty-eight. Any offers at nine or o - tell me. I may need them." The account executives up in the office would now call their clients and see if they could try to get them to sell anything. It was unlikely, since given the strength of the close of the first Ring, they would more likely wait to see if they could get a better price in the second one, at 12:30. Edwards leaned against the side of the booth for a moment or two, musing. What was all the buying? Who was so keen to get the copper price up? There had been rumours for some weeks of a big Japanese player flexing his muscles, maybe trying to dominate the market. But why now? The fundamental picture was not particularly bullish - demand stagnant, and supply if anything looking as if it was going to increase over the next few years as the Chileans once more cranked up their seemingly inexhaustible production.

"Jamie!" It was Stumpy, holding a phone out to him. "Phil wants to talk to you urgently!"

Edwards took the handset. "Phil, what is it?"

"You're gonna earn that big salary of yours now, boy. We - sorry, I - need that second ring close up above 1020." It was the first time Harris had ever let slip that he might be working in concert with somebody else. "I'm going to give you 2000 lots to buy, to start with. See if we need any more after that. But - and don't let me down - I don't want to pay more than 1020. The close must be up there, though. Just for your guidance, I'll be putting bits and pieces with some of the others, to see if we can't get it moving for you."

"What's going on, Phil? That's a hell of a lot of copper to buy. Who wants it up that desperately?"

"Jamie, just do the order, alright?" There was a hard edge in Harris's voice. "You don't need to know why. If I need to buy more, I'll give the orders through Stumpy during the Ring."

"You're the boss." It was a huge order, even by the standards of Harris's normal big trading. If he got it right, and managed to hang on to the American's coat-tails and buy some for himself as well, Edwards could probably turn around the losses Prichard had been complaining about this morning.

A couple of minutes before the start of the second copper ring, Ferret and some of the other dealers saw Edwards coming up the stairs from the toilets down below the LME. His nose was tinged red, and his eyes had a diamond-bright glitter to them. As they walked through the doors onto the trading floor, Ferret said quietly "For Christ's sake, Jamie, isn't it a bit early in the day for that, even for you?"

"Don't worry, man, I know what I'm doing. Big business for the big boys today."

Ferret shrugged, and turned towards his own company's seat. One thing he had learnt from his friendship with Edwards was not to be judgmental. As Edwards had implied, he was a big boy now, and should know what he was doing. Such a waste of talent, though.

Up in the gallery, the students had been watching the succession of Rings. Nothing had so far really grabbed their imagination, and they were beginning to chat amongst themselves, rather to the chagrin of their guide, who would have preferred a bit more respect for his market. He spoke to them again. "Now we're coming into the second copper Ring, which you will recall is where the daily official price is derived from. That price governs worldwide copper trades done today. I should say that the market is fairly quiet at the moment, so although this is important, I'm afraid we may not necessarily see too much action. But keep your eyes and ears open as we approach the close, that's when the dealers will try to get the price they want for their clients."

The bell rang. The second Ring was the most important of the day, the last price quoted in it becoming the day's official price, the formula on which ninety plus percent of the world's copper was priced. Forget the Zairean or Chilean labourers sweating in the mines, what the international mining companies received for their products was decided by these twenty-odd young city dealers screaming at each other across this circle of seats.

Edwards bought steadily through the ring, and with less than a minute to go, he had got the price up to a thousand and ten. It was an impressive performance, his controlled aggression frightening the sellers into holding off to see when he would stop. He felt good, but the chemicals were beginning to take over. He was the King of the Ring. He could do anything. His voice became more strident, as he bought more and more, pushing the price closer and closer to his target. The clerks behind him recording his trades began to look concerned as the tonnage increased. Somebody had some selling, and Edwards was just soaking it up. On the phone, Stumpy said "Phil, he must have bought more than yours already, and we're still only at seventeen. Do you want to give him some more to keep him going?"

The voice coming back from Munich was dry and hard. "He's doing a good job. I don't think I need to spend any more money."

Edwards was screaming now, buying, buying, buying. Finally, as the bell rang to signal the end of the session, he did it, and the closing price was there - £1020-1021.

The whole Ring was staring at him, red eyes and running nose now, but a look of sheer exaltation on his face. Already, though, his senior clerk was tapping him urgently on the shoulder. "Jamie, do you know how much you bought? About four thousand lots." That was a hundred thousand tonnes of copper, over a hundred million pounds worth at the price he had just established for the metal.

"Never mind, I did my job. Phil's got the price he wanted. He'll take the tonnage." Edwards walked back to the box and took the phone from Stumpy.

"Congratulations, Kiddo," came the American voice. "I guess I bought my two thousand lots."

"A bit more than that, Phil, and most of it was between seventeen and twenty. I'll work it out and give you the final fill, but I reckon I had to buy upwards of four thousand lots to get it there. You should have seen the others, Phil, they couldn't believe I had the balls to keep going. But we all know I'm the best. None of them can stay with me. Your business and my talent - unbeatable!" He was still flying from the chemicals pumping through his blood. He had not taken much, but it had had the effect he wanted.

Harris's voice was flat. "I bought two thousand, Jamie. That was my order, and what you chose to buy is your own affair." The phone clicked and went dead.

"Jamie!" It was one of the clerks, holding out another phone to him. "Prichard wants a word. He thinks you've gone crazy."

"I'll call him back. Stumpy, what did Phil say during that?"

"He hung you out to dry, Jamie. I told him you needed more ammo, but he just said you were going well and he didn't need to spend any more money. What were you doing? Didn't you know you were way over-buying? You're going to get crucified on the Kerb. As soon as you start trying to get out of it, they'll see what's happened, and all pile in ahead of you."

"Jamie!" one of the other clerks pushed a phone into his hand. "Prichard says he's got to talk to you."

"OK," then into the phone, "Terry, yeah, what's the problem?"

"The problem is I think you may have gone crazy. How much copper did you buy, and who's it for?"

"Relax," said Edwards. "I had a big order for Phil, and I bought a bit for us on the back of it. We should be able to get out of it on the Kerb, and hopefully make some money. There's some big buying around, seems to be coming out of Japan." He sounded a lot more confident than he felt, as the buzz from the drug was wearing off.

"I hope so, Jamie, I hope so. Otherwise remember what I said this morning."

"Yeah, yeah," mumbled Edwards as he hung up.

The students in the viewing gallery were enthralled. "Woooow," breathed the attractive girl, "if that's a quiet market, how loud is it when it's busy?"

The LME guide frankly didn't know what to say. He had never seen a dealer perform like that before in his relatively short time in the Exchange. "Well," he began "that was a pretty busy Ring in the end. The dealer who seemed to be doing all the buying is a chap called Jamie Edwards, from Myerson Brothers. If you remember when we went through who the broker companies were earlier, they're normally regarded as one of the smaller ones. Obviously, today they had some very big orders. As you saw, virtually all the other brokers were selling to him." It wasn't his fault, but he didn't really understand how the dynamics of the Ring worked: he was an administrator, not a dealer, and now he wanted to get his charges away, before they started asking questions he would struggle to answer. Jamie Edwards had a reputation he didn't think good for the image of the Exchange. He explained how the next trading would be the Kerb, where all metals were traded simultaneously. "It can get quite noisy," he said, "but we're not going to see that. We've got lunch now, and then some of my colleagues will explain something about our warehousing system."

He led them out of the gallery. As they left, the attractive girl cast a lingering look at Jamie Edwards, standing in the huddle round his company's phone booth. She would have liked to wait and see how the next session was.

In the background, trading in the other metal rings had been carrying on. Now, the LME official was standing at the podium ready to read out the official prices of the day. Most of the dealers ignored him, as his voice droned through the prices, cash and three months bid and offer for each metal in turn. They were all still watching the group around Myerson's booth, waiting to see what Edwards did when he stepped into the Ring for the beginning of Kerb trading. Eventually the official read the last price, three months nickel, and the dealers stepped back into the ring. There was a brief pause, then Ferret offered copper at 1023. Nobody took it, and he offered 1022, 21, 20. Still there were no bids.

Others started offering as well, and slowly Edwards walked into his seat. He actually didn't know what to do, but the market wouldn't wait while he made up his mind. Arguments with Harris, checking the taped phone conversations to see exactly what had been said - all that would come later. For the moment, the truth was that he was long something over fifty thousand tonnes of copper, and he was going to have to get rid of it. The problem was that the loss was probably going to cost him his job. He looked around the Ring. Commet was offering at 17, then 16, where he sold a bit to one of the smaller brokers. Commet should have been buying, if it was concerted Japanese action. It was looking as if the clerk had been right - Harris had bluffed him to get a high closing price to suit some physical pricings on the other side. Time to test the water - "15 I'll sell a hundred," he called across the Ring. There was a moment's hesitation, as the others recognised that the former big buyer was now turning seller, then pandemonium as they all started trying to sell. They recognised Edwards' problem, and they were going to try to capitalise on it. He was clearly going to have to sell, so the rest of the dealers would attempt to get in before him. Normal LME trading - see the other guy has a problem, and try and make it worse to make your own gain out of it. Stumpy leaned over, and said "Phil doesn't want to follow the Kerb. Says he's a bit tied up on the other line at the moment." Edwards nodded in acknowledgement. He had no alternative but to sell; he couldn't sit with a fifty thousand tonne position. They were all sellers now, and he joined in, offering the price lower and lower. That meant his loss was getting bigger and bigger. The chemicals were wearing off, and the adrenaline that had boosted their effect in the Ring was gone. Mechanically he sold the market down and watched his career go up in smoke.

The morning Kerb closed that day back at £975, where the first Ring had begun. Edwards got out for a loss of around thirty pounds a tonne, making about one and a half million in total. He lost his job, as expected. No-one really understood what had caused the blip, and Phil Harris certainly was not about to enlighten anybody. As always with these events, it entered into LME folklore, and the most popular story peddled by those who claimed to be in the know was that Edwards, high on his cocaine, misheard what Harris was telling him to do. Another favourite theory was that he just got confused with the numbers, for the same reason. The concrete result was the end of Myerson Brothers, whose parent company finally decided enough was enough, and sold the company for virtually nothing to a competitor. In fact, though, that day was the first real appearance of a rapidly growing power in the market.

Chapter One

October 1988

The black Mercedes swung in through the open gates. The sign announced that this was the Firth-Johnson Clinic, but gave no clue as to what was practised here. Phil Harris looked appreciatively at the opulence of the grounds, and then at the elegance of the Georgian mansion that came into view as he rounded the last bend in the drive. He drew the car up amongst the others parked at the front of the house, and then headed for the front door. The pretty receptionist smiled at him as he approached the desk.

"Good morning. Can I help?"

"Good morning. Yes, I've come to visit Mr. Jamie Edwards. He's not expecting me."

"Certainly. If you'd like to step into the waiting room, I'll fetch him. Can I say who it is?"

Harris smiled. "No, don't tell him. I'm an old friend, and I want to surprise him." The receptionist smiled back conspiratorially, and walked off towards the staircase. Harris went into the room she had indicated. If he had told her to give his name, Edwards would probably not have seen him. They had not spoken since that day in March.

He was standing looking out of the window when he heard the

door open. "Morning, Jamie," he said as he turned. Edwards was clearly taken aback.

"Phil. You're about the last person I would expect to see. You cost me my career, you bastard. What do you want?"

Harris looked at him. "I didn't cost you your career. I may have pushed it over the edge, but what caused it was the same reason you've been in here for the last three months. Since I hear you're about ready to leave here, I guess you must be clean now. Anyway, why I'm here is easy. I was over for the LME dinner and I thought I'd take the time out to take a drive in the country to visit my old buddy."

"Well, while you're here, sit down. Would you like me to arrange some coffee?"

"I've got a better idea. It's a nice day and you've got some pretty grounds here. Let's go and have a walk." Harris grinned. "That's if inmates are allowed out, of course."

"Yeah, yeah," said Edwards, "Come on, then. Let's go outside."

As they walked out through the front door, Edwards pointed to the 500SL. "New car?" he asked.

"Yeah. Part of this year's bonus. You're a Porsche fan, aren't you?"

"I sold it before I came in here. This place isn't cheap, you know, and my father only agreed to pay part of the cost. But I think it's worth it. I feel pretty good, finally. I should be leaving soon, within the next week or so."

"Yes, that's what the doctor told me when I rang at the beginning of the week."

"You rang? Why?" Edwards was genuinely puzzled. The sort of business friendship he and Harris had had normally stopped dead as soon as one of the parties was no longer of any use to the other. It revolved around going to bars, restaurants and clubs together, but most importantly, trying to make as much money out of each other as quickly as possible. Why on earth would Harris waste his time on a burnt-out, reformed junkie ex-dealer, however good he may have been in the past. Edwards had basically reconciled himself to not working in the metals' business again. The clinic had been a rehabilitation of his life, not his career.

Harris said nothing for a minute or two, as they followed the path round between the house and what had formerly been the stable block, before it had been turned into an institution.

Then he started speaking, without seemingly answering Edwards' question. "The business is changing, Jamie, and I'm not sure how much you understand that. The LME doesn't know it's got a tiger by the tail. Those old fools who run it still think they're in the 1950s, where the good old boys sit on top and the barrow-boys in the Ring do their bidding. There is money there for the taking, for the few people who understand what the base metals business really is. I don't mean the few hundred thousand a year we've all thought we're rich on. I mean there is millions of dollars for the taking. Serious, I can do anything I like in the world, millions of dollars. But you gotta look at the business in a way that those blind, stupid men who run the LME won't even begin to be able to grasp. They're so self-satisfied all they can do is look in a mirror and tell themselves how clever they are." Edwards had always known Harris had little more than contempt for the institution of the LME - it was one of the reasons he insisted on keeping his base in Munich, rather than the more logical London - but there seemed to be something more at work than he had seen before. Harris continued "On your last day at Myerson's" - Edwards winced - "you lost what? A couple of million?" He didn't wait for a reply, but continued, "We made much, much more than that. And as time goes on, we are going to do it more and more often."

"Good. But why did you have to take it out of me?"

Harris looked at him for a moment, and then continued, seemingly on a completely different tack, "How much do you know about the copper business, Jamie? I mean really know."

Edwards shrugged. "Like every other broker, I suppose. Enough to know where it's mined, where it's consumed and how to trade it."

"Every other broker knows nothing except the numbers in front of his nose. And for how to trade them most of them rely on somebody else. So-and-so's buying, so-and-so's selling, the mad Jap is borrowing - that sort of thing. They don't have an original idea in their head, most of them. They just follow like sheep, because that's how LME brokers made their money in the past. A nudge and a wink from somebody who's supposedly in the know." Another seeming change of direction - "Incidentally, what do you know about the mad Jap?"

"Yamagazi from Kanagi Corporation. He's a big, big punter. Nobody really knows if he makes any money, though. He's been trading for about nine or ten months, mostly through Union and you, and a bit through Commet. Why?"

"Jamie, that's a typical LME broker answer," said Harris. "Forget what he really does, and just focus on the LME part of it. Would it surprise you to know that he is the biggest supplier of physical copper into the Far Eastern market and looked on as a market guru by most of the Japanese, Taiwanese, Korean and south-east Asian consumers?"

Edwards shrugged. "If you tell me. All I know about him is that he throws some big volume around through those two, and is extremely difficult to get to meet. Anyway, why are you asking me about him? Is it just to show me I know nothing, or is there a point?"

"Yeah, there's a point. Listen, are you allowed out? I mean really out, like can I buy you lunch?"

Edwards grinned. "Yes, I'm allowed out. I'm effectively cured. I leave here at the beginning of next week. No drinking, though. I have an addiction prone personality. To stay clean, I have to be abstemious - from everything."

"That's good. You know I hardly ever drink, anyway."

That made them almost unique in LME terms, where at least half the lunches were exclusively liquid.

They walked back towards the front of the house. "If you want to turn the car round, I'll just go in and let my keepers know what I'm doing," said Edwards.

"Where are we going?" Harris asked, as they drove off down the drive.

"Turn right out of the gates and about two miles down the road there's a pub on the right as you come into the village. It's got a reasonable restaurant attached to it. We may as well go there."

Harris nodded. "Okay. Then I'll start to tell you a bit more of what this is about."

"Sounds good to me. This is quite a nice car, actually, isn't it?" They discussed the merits of Mercedes sports cars for the few minutes it took to reach their destination, where they were shown immediately to a table in a typical, folksy old-world pub restaurant that was almost empty. The only other occupants were right over the other side of the room. Their orders were taken quickly, and Edwards looked expectantly at Harris.

"OK," he said, "last time we spoke, you got me into serious problems and now you turn up out of the blue, and seem to want to tell me you've found the Holy Grail of metal trading. What's it all about, Phil?"

"Jamie, to understand what I'm intending to do, you need to get out of the LME broker mindset. Insularity and laziness in the market - firstly amongst the big boys who run the companies and then trickling down to the dealers - has created a big hole where illusion has taken over from reality. The illusion is that the LME is the base metal market. The reality is that it is in essence just the price setting element. If you actually stop to think, the real market is the movement of metal around the world, from mines to end consumers."

Edwards interrupted. "Not entirely. Some of the flows of metal are only justified by factors created by LME prices. Arbitrage shipments, from London to Comex, for example." Comex was the New York Commodity Exchange, which also traded a copper contract; sometimes price differentials between the two were sufficient to justify moving metal stocks from one exchange to the other.

"You're getting there, Jamie, but you're still thinking the wrong way round. Instead of picturing a situation where LME prices dictate a physical metal operation, think of one where you already know your physical commitments, and using the LME price is how you are going to make your profit."

"Phil, that means you're going to try and take on the whole market. It doesn't work. Too many people have tried it in the past, and it's cost them fortunes. I thought you knew enough about the business not to come out with crap like that. I thought you said you were going to tell me something worthwhile." Edwards' expression was contemptuous as he spoke. "Maybe you can get away with it for a short while, a week or two, but in the end, the market always wins. It has to. That's why there's a market there in the first place."

"In general terms, I don't disagree with you. However, you need to look at the specific situation right now to understand what we're able to do. And going to do."

They paused for a minute or two while the waitress served them. Then Harris spoke again. "I guess I'd better start this off at the beginning, so you can get to understand what I'm talking about."

"Always the best way, Phil," replied Edwards.

"Okay. As I said before, you've got to think about what the business really represents, not just the LME punting that sits on the top of the pile. When I asked you about Yamagazi, you gave me the standard answer about trading on the LME - the futures market. But that's less than half an answer. As I said to you, that company is rapidly becoming the major force in Far Eastern physical copper. Now you know yourself how big that market is - or you should. Taiwan and Korea import half a million tonnes a year each, Japan probably twice that plus concentrates to feed its own smelter production, Malaysia, Thailand and Indonesia are all growing at big annual rates. On top of that is the biggest potential of them all - China. At the moment, these guys have all been buying a chunk of their needs from the producers, at the average price of the year - good standard pricing terms that have been going on since the market started. The balance, though, comes from the physical traders and is bought on the spot price. But the traders decide when they want to sell, not the buyers when they want to buy. The result of that, as you can imagine, is that the buyers always end up uncertain of their supplies; add to that the natural oriental distrust of westerners, and you can bet it's not a happy relationship."

Edwards interrupted " Yeah, okay, but that's how the world's been for twenty-odd years, so it's not anything new."

"Sure. But just because something has existed in the past, doesn't mean it's always got to be that way. These guys in the Far East are getting stronger and stronger, you know. It won't be long before they're in the driving seat. Into the picture comes Yamagazi-san, representative of Kanagi Corporation, one of the biggest and strongest of the Japanese trading groups. He tells them a different story. He tells them 'Come to me with your copper needs. I'm your friend. I won't exploit you like the western traders. I'll supply you with metal when you want it, not dump it on you when I want to sell, and then tell you it's so tight when you want to buy that I screw you for higher and higher premiums on top of the spot price. I'll take your long-term stocking and stock financing needs off your hands, because I'll always be able to supply what you want. Ignore the westerners, they don't understand our needs.' Bit by bit, he's getting the oriental market eating out of his hand."

Edwards again interrupted "Phil, if he's effectively going to finance the Far East's stock of copper, it's going to cost him money. You know that as well as I do. There's no magic formula that's different for Yamagazi than for anybody else."

"I've only given you stage one so far, Jamie. Eat your lunch before it gets cold. We'll do stage two and the clever bits in a minute or two. Meantime, what are your career plans?" Harris grinned as he waited for the answer.

A grim expression came over Edwards' face. "I don't know, frankly. I've been an LME trader since I left school at eighteen. I'm now thirty-two. That's fourteen years, and it's the only business I know. *I* can tell anybody I've cleaned up my act after three months in this bloody clinic, but who's going to believe me? I've caused too many people problems in the past, even though I've made good money for them as well. And you really screwed me up six months ago. I don't really think I'm going to get another job in the business. So I don't know where I'm going, but I still need money from somewhere. I'm not set up for life yet. You owe me one. What do you suggest?"

Harris held up his hands. "Okay, okay. I wasn't very kind to you. I do have something in mind, but we'll get to that in due course. Incidentally, did you know Terry Prichard's retired?"

"Yeah. He rang me and said he was going. I rather think he was retired, more than he chose to go himself. It's a pity. He was one of the few genuinely decent honest people in the market. I don't think he got on with McKee" - that was the head of the company which had absorbed Myerson's - "or the sort of business they do."

"Are you surprised at anyone not getting on with McKee? The guy's so arrogant. Assumes because he runs a big broker and is on the LME Board he knows more than the rest of the world. He's heading for a fall, I tell you."

Small talk and gossip about market personalities occupied them while they ate. Then, as the coffee was served, Harris began again.

"I'm leaving MacDonald and Thompson. Keep it to yourself, but I resigned this morning. They're still trying to persuade me to stay, so it's not public knowledge yet. And before you ask, yes this is connected with what we are talking about."

Although his face showed nothing, Edwards felt a flood of disappointment. The way Harris had been talking to him, he had allowed himself to believe that maybe the American had been going to recruit him for M and T. If he was leaving that wasn't going to happen.

"Okay, Jamie, as you rightly pointed out a few minutes ago, anyone who is going to look after the stock financing of copper is going to incur a cost. What we're going to do is manipulate things to make that cost bearable. Let me give you an example. That last day of your career" - he grinned again as he said it - "I told you I made a lot more money than you lost. I'll tell you how, and then you'll begin to see how you fit into all this. Yamagazi had told me early that morning that he had some big pricings" - that meant that as he had made sales of physical copper at the price to be determined on that day's official Ring trading, he had to buy to ensure he was hedged - "maybe around five hundred lots. Talking to all the brokers, you included, had made me fairly sure there were no major sellers around, so I was comfortable that I would be able to push the price up if I wanted. I also knew a little bit about your state of mind. I knew you were getting desperate to get back some of your recent losses, and your buddy Ferret had told me Prichard had had another go at you that morning, so I thought you might be suggestible to do something I needed done. So I had five hundred lots to buy. I know how aggressive a dealer you can be and I was pretty sure you'd take the bait if I implied much more than reality. So I made up an arbitrary target closing price I had to have, gave you a big order and let you go. At the same time I was listening to your clerk on the Ring, my boys had three or four of the other brokers on. They put in sufficient selling to cover whatever I bought through you. When you went crazy - or your old chemical friend took over - we just kept selling it to you. We finished the Ring very, very short. Add to that the five hundred we booked out to Yamagazi on the close, and what we sold in the Kerb, see where the market went in the next few days, and you can work it out. We made a hell of a lot of money from that trade."

"So you're telling me my stunning performance was all orchestrated - manipulated - by you?"

"Yup. That's it, Jamie. That's what I'm telling you. The Ring, the pricing, can be manipulated to suit the underlying reality, providing circumstances are right."

"But what about Yamagazi? He can't have been happy to pay such a high price."

"Yamagazi is - ah - helping us to ensure that the circumstances are right more often than not. Don't worry about him. You'll learn about that later."

So you're paying off Yamagazi, thought Edwards. A Japanese taking money from a westerner rather than following the tradition of loyalty to the honour of the firm? That was a bit of a first. But how do they think they can sustain it for more than the very short term? Surely somebody would spot what they were doing if they tried it more than a couple of times?

Harris spoke again. "I shall be moving to the UK very soon. We're starting a new company, which will mainly be concerned with placing Kanagi Corp's LME business. We think it's going to be rather successful. And that's where you come in, Jamie. I want you to come on board and work with me."

"Well, you've told me how you took advantage of a particular situation, how you exploited my weakness, but you haven't made me see how you've got the basis of an ongoing business. What you did that day was really no more than a punt, with the odds stacked a little way in your favour. That's not necessarily always going to be the case."

Harris signalled towards the waitress to bring the bill. His voice was harder as he looked straight into Edwards' face - "That's the deal, Jamie. You want to work for me, fine. I'll tell you the rest. You don't, and that's the end of the discussion. I've told you nothing confidential so far." He signed the credit card slip for the girl. "Come on. I'll take you back to your kennel, and you can think about it. But remember what you said before - you're not too likely to get another job in the business with your record."

Which you helped to arrange, you bastard, thought Edwards.

They were both silent on the short journey back to the clinic, occupied with their own thoughts. As the car drew up outside the door, Harris said "I'll just drop you and go. I need to be back in London for a meeting this evening. The offer's there, Jamie. It's up to you. We've got the ability to take this market apart, and make serious money. You know my home number. Think about it and let me know what you want to do."

"Thanks for the lunch, Phil. Yeah, I'll give you a call in a couple of days and see where we go from there."

He stood watching for a moment or two, as the Mercedes rolled off down the drive.

The rooms in the clinic were not as luxurious as the public areas suggested. A single bed, a wardrobe and an armchair were the only furnishings, and the bathroom off the room was basic rather than comfortable. Not really surprising, since the object of the place was to get its patients ready to face the world again as quickly as possible, not to encourage them to linger. Edwards sat alone that evening, thinking over what Harris had told him. It was all very well for the American to have said he had passed on nothing that was confidential, but Edwards had been around long enough to read between the lines that there was something, if not illegal, then at the very least questionable, about what he was proposing to do. It had been clear from the conversation that Yamagazi was colluding to make money out of his employers, but it would certainly not be the first time that had happened on the LME. Neither would that alone be sufficient to persuade Harris to give up his comfortable, well-paid existence at MacDonald and Thompson. He was no fool, and Edwards could not envisage him risking his career for a one shot rip-off of a Japanese corporation. He smiled inwardly at that thought: he was no fool himself, and yet he'd sacrificed his career for something far more ephemeral - his old addiction. And that was really the point. Forget the morals of it, as Harris had implied with his parting words, his offer was there, others were unlikely to be forthcoming. He'd probably slipped too far for anything fully legitimate to be possible. He actually had no real alternative, he had to make that call to Harris very soon and throw in his lot with them. But he would really have preferred to know exactly who "they" were and what they were really trying to do. Ah well, the doctors supervising his drying out kept using the phrase "one day at a time". Maybe that was how he had to look at his career, as well.

Chapter Two

Harris's meeting that evening was with a firm of lawyers in the City. Although still nominally working for MacDonald and Thompson, he had in fact been spending a lot of his time recently on other matters. Today they had finally acquired a shelf company to be the vehicle for the trading he intended to do. John Roberts was the partner who had been acting for Harris, and they sat together in his comfortable modern office in a small street just off London Wall. Roberts' assistant was also in the room with them.

"Everything's in order, Phil," said Roberts, "we just need to confirm what you're doing about the re-capitalisation of the company. That's the one point that's still outstanding. Of course, the company legally exists without it, but it's only worth the hundred pounds you paid for it. I guess you won't be able to do much business on that basis."

"Indeed not. But as we're setting it up as an I/B not a contracting party, we don't actually need that much." Harris pulled an envelope out of his pocket. "Meantime, if your boys could take care of this, it should be enough to give us a degree of credibility." He handed the envelope to Roberts, who opened it and saw a draft for $100,000 drawn on an obscure Liechtenstein private bank. He passed it to his sidekick.

"It's none of my business, but I'm intrigued by that issue of credibility," remarked Roberts. "Isn't there some kind of stigma attached to the I/B status, some kind of feeling that everything is not quite kosher?"

"Well, traditionally the Introducing Broker has been regarded as a bit suspect, a guy nobody really wants to employ, but who does have a few contacts who want to keep putting business through him, normally because he's an old buddy. So he works in a broker's office, for no salary and takes half the commission he generates. The reason it's always a bit suspect is that you wonder if he's happy with half the commission, or if he's trying to steal an extra buck out of the executions he gives. But things have changed, and the LME now has a full clearing system, and I think that creates a better opportunity for someone like me."

Roberts' assistant, Nick Gooding, spoke " I've been doing some work for a client on the LIFFE" - financial futures - "market, which has involved looking at the position of the brokers versus the clearing. But the system there is different from the LME, isn't it?"

"Yeah, what we operate under is an interesting hybrid. The contract between the client and the broker is a principal to principal one, but the other side of it, the broker/broker deal that hedges it, is matched between brokers through the London Clearing House. At that point, the LCH takes over the deal, and calls the broker to pay margin on it to protect itself. Then, if one broker goes bust, you don't have the risk of a domino effect taking them all down, because the Clearing House always has enough in margin to cover the value of all the contracts it's holding. I'm not particularly familiar with LIFFE, but I believe there, both sides of the deal are immediately passed over to the clearing, so the end client actually has a contract directly with them, and the broker drops out."

Gooding nodded. "That's right," he said, "the broker purely executes the trade, and the end result is that the only money changing hands between client and broker is the commission. So brokers don't need anything in the way of capital to support holding open forward positions. What do you intend to do? Have a clearing account with one broker, and arrange to be able to trade with any of the others and give the deals immediately to your clearer to hold?"

"Yeah. That way I get to be able to trade wherever I get the best price, but I only have to have one financial relationship. But most trades will be in the names of my clients; the arrangement will be the same, though. And now, if you gentlemen will excuse me, I have a dinner appointment with the guy I hope is going to be my clearing broker."

The two lawyers saw Harris out, and then wandered back into Roberts' room. "You know, Nick," he said, "something tells me we're going to see a lot more of him. A friend of mine is quite senior at MacDonald and Thompson, and he tells me that guy has made *at least* a million dollars a year since he started there seven years ago. He's not giving that up lightly. I can't see yet what he's doing, but it smells as if it's on the edge of the law. And that means he's going to need legal help at some point. Ah well, the fees keep coming in. It's the best profession in the world, Nick." He looked at his watch: 6:45. "Come on, I'll buy you a beer downstairs, then we can call it a day early, for a change. I'd anticipated that meeting being a bit longer."

Mack McKee was a larger than life character, in two ways. Six foot six tall, broad to match and with a stooping gait, he was nicknamed "Jumbo" on the LME floor - but mostly out of his hearing. He also had a loud personality, and liked to party, so he was well known in bars, clubs and restaurants across London. The brashness hid an acute mind, though. He ran an LME broker called Commet, owned by a sprawling conglomerate, Mining and Metal Commercialisations, S.A., which was based in Luxembourg. They owned base metal mining properties worldwide, and smelting and refining plants in Europe. Traditionally, they had always been strong in supplying German industry with its metallic raw material needs, and the broking arm in London had originally been set up to enable those same customers to hedge through them as well. McKee was shrewd, though, and when he had taken over as Managing Director of Commet he had committed himself to diversification away from Europe, looking especially for growth in the Far East. The effect had been to propel Commet to near the top of the first division of brokers, and McKee, with his aggressive personality, to a position of power in the Market. Given Harris's connections with the Far East as well, it was inevitable that the two should have bumped into each other again and again as competitors for oriental customers. They had a healthy respect for each other's abilities and had spent many evenings together in various haunts in Tokyo and Hong Kong. McKee had an extraordinary ability to pick up market gossip, and had already got wind of Harris's resignation from MacDonald and Thompson. He assumed the American had suggested dinner that evening to propose joining Commet, a prospect guaranteed to appeal to his ego. However, he wasn't going to offer, he was going to wait for Harris to ask.

They met in a restaurant just off Knightsbridge, the latest chic. It was typical of how McKee spent Commet's money that he was able to get a booking at short notice, when others had to wait weeks. It was reflected again in the recognition and welcome he got from the maitre d'. Harris had arrived first, and watched the big man revelling in the attention and the looks he got from the other diners. Social climbing in Britain was something he had never been able to get to grips with, but it always amused him to see how easy it was to seem important. And flattery was probably going to be the way to get what he wanted out of the evening. McKee eventually reached the table.

"Phil, how are you, my friend? Good to see you. Sorry I'm a bit late, but we had some big business to finish up at the office."

Harris grinned to himself. One of McKee's foibles was that he always, but always, had to try and make you think his company was consistently busy, always outdoing everyone else in how much business they were doing. In point of fact, Harris had spoken to his boys at M and T, who had told him it had been a quiet day.

"I'm fine, Mack. Glad you could make it this evening. I've been out of touch today. Did the market do much?"

"Prices didn't actually move much, but we had a big day in turnover. It looks like it's going to be another record month. But I'm led to believe that it may be a bit more than 'out of touch'. I've been hearing rumours about you all day."

The American cursed inwardly. He had arranged this meeting as soon after resigning as he could, in the hope that the news had not already reached McKee. Ah, well. Nothing to do about it now.

"Yeah, I guess the rumours you heard are true. I just quit M and T. I've been there in Munich for seven years, made a few bucks, so I thought I might take the chance to see if I could do a few things a bit differently. I haven't really had the time to begin to enjoy the freedom yet, though, what with having been over here all week. But Mack, it's not really official yet, so how did you get to hear?"

"You know me. I like to keep my finger on the pulse. We're a strong company, everybody tells us things. One of the guys in Luxembourg heard it from a banking contact. I was surprised, though. You're the backbone of that operation. What are they going to do? Replace you? Or try and carry on with Klaus?" Klaus Fischer was Harris's deputy in Munich.

"I don't know, Mack. I quit. It's up to them now. But I guess it's Klaus' big chance, if he wants to take it."

The waiter approached to take their drinks orders. " A large gin and tonic, and what will you have, Phil?"

"Just an orange juice, for the moment, thanks." The waiter walked away.

"Have you been in Tokyo lately, Mack? We haven't had an evening there for a long time. When was it last? Late January in that club in Roppongi, wasn't it?"

"Yeah, that was a good one. I've been there since, actually. Early August. It was bloody hot. I was hiring people, in fact. You know

I've now got six people over there on brokerage, as well as the three Luxembourg have trying to increase the physical business. In fact, just between you and me, I'm working on getting my hands on that Far Eastern physical operation. Those guys in Luxembourg haven't got a clue." If McKee ever said 'just between you and me' it meant he was trying to tell as many people as possible. It was part of the act - the things he really wanted confidential, he kept strictly to himself. Still, he'd probably make a better job of that business than those Luxembourg had there at present. McKee went on, "You and I are the only ones who really understand the importance of the Far East, Phil. You know that, don't you." The drinks had come while they were talking, and now the waiter was back to take their food order. "Phil, I know the guys here well. There's a couple of things they do really well, not on the normal menu. Are you happy to let me order for you? I can guarantee you'll like it."

Typical again. "Sure," said Harris. "I trust your judgement, as ever." McKee gave the order, making sure the waiter understood exactly what he wanted.

"So, you've quit M and T, what do you have in mind? Have you made enough to retire, or are you looking at getting in to something else? Somehow I don't see you sitting on your backside at home."

"After seven years in Munich, I don't know where home is any more, as a good Californian boy. No, I have a couple of things in mind, a few ideas I'd like to have a shot at. There are some things we may be able to do together, possibly. You know we've talked about getting together before - this might be a good time."

"Well, as I told you, I've expanded my Tokyo office, but ideally I'd like a white boy in charge. The Japanese are very good, but for kind of corporate things, it helps if the overseas offices are run by people of the same culture. If you want to go and stay in Tokyo for three or four years, then we may be able to work something out there."

Harris thought he'd play along, try and see how much he could get out of McKee about what Commet were doing in Japan. He trusted - almost - his buddy Yamagazi, but it would be interesting to see if he had let slip any of their intentions. Yamagazi was a regular drinking partner of Commet's main man in Japan. Perhaps he had said something he shouldn't at some dubious late bar in the Ginza. "Well, I've gotta say Tokyo wouldn't be my favourite city to live in, but there's no doubt the business is interesting. I'd be happier based in Hong Kong, you know, ready for the jump off into China. That's going to be the big one. Japan's already overbroked."

The first course arrived, breaking the conversation. When they were served, McKee said "I agree in principal it's been overbroked, but the game has changed. You're no longer at M and T, so your business is up for grabs. You bring that across to us, and that makes us the biggest. Klaus may be able to keep the European stuff, but unless they replace you quickly with someone who knows the Japs, they'll lose them. Take your pal, Yamagazi, for example. He does some business with us - you know that - but he does a lot more with you. That alone would justify me taking you on."

"Yamagazi's a good corporate customer. Kanagi and M and T have a relationship that goes back years. I wouldn't assume their business would follow an individual."

That set off bells in McKee's head. He was much smarter than even Harris realised, and he *knew* it was a personal friendship between Harris and Yamagazi that underscored the business. Why would Harris try to play it down, when he could so obviously use it to leverage himself into a big money position with Commet? McKee didn't believe for one instant that Harris was intending anything other than to get straight back into a bigger job than before. He knew the American was just as mercenary as he was himself. Therefore, there had to be a game being played here. It could be a long evening, but he wanted to get to the bottom of it.

"Don't give me business school crap about corporate customers. Yamagazi always wants your view before he trades."

"Believe what you like, Mack. I certainly wouldn't like to take a job on the assumption that I could bring Kanagi's hedging with me. I wouldn't feel comfortable."

"I'm not sure how much 'comfortable' has to do with it. We all have to live, and we can only do that by selling what we have that's valuable to someone else. You're going to be inundated with people making you the same suggestion I just have, and you know you're better off with me than any of the others."

"If I just wanted to carry on being a broker, I don't think I would have quit M and T. They've been good to me, over the years, and they appreciate I've done a good job for them. They had no metals business when I started, and now they're comfortably the biggest non-Ring trader. But if, having left them anyway, I did want to move elsewhere, then I agree, I would be best off with you. You know you and I have pretty similar ideas about where the LME's going, and what's wrong with it. And, more importantly, how it should be moving forward."

"Which it isn't doing at the moment, and won't until some of those old farts on the LME Board get their brains in gear." The Board of the LME was elected from amongst the directors of member firms, and had the responsibility of ensuring the market remained efficient, properly regulated and, most importantly, that it kept serving its members' interests. It tended to be an extremely conservative body, as most of its members were of the older generation, who had time to spend away from their own businesses. McKee had recently been elected, but was already finding it irksome that he had - publicly - to appear to support policies he privately despaired of. "They persist in behaving as though nothing ever changes. Anyway, what do you think of the wine?" With McKee, it was futile for Harris to protest that he hardly drank. Over the years, he'd become inured to waking with a hangover after their evenings together.

"Yeah, it's good," he said. He looked at the bottle. "Tignanello. Tuscan, isn't it?" He may not drink much of it, but he wasn't going to be out wine-snobbed by the big man. "But I think there are some opportunities available in the market right now. The Far East is set to surge, and - being a Californian, I can give you the surfing cliché without embarrassment - you gotta be damn sure you catch this wave; I have the feeling it'll be the big one. If you look at the growth rates across the region, and just see the number of joint ventures the Japanese are putting in to Indonesia, Malaysia, Thailand, together with export-led demand from Taiwan and Korea, you must see regional demand is going to boom."

"Well, you know me. I prefer to rely on personal reports from our people on the ground rather than a load of statistics, but I've got to say I'm getting the same message. But I also get the feeling that Kanagi is really going for it. Our physical copper guys tell me they are getting more and more aggressive on their terms to the consumers. They seem to be making a real play to dominate that trade. That's another reason you should join us. If we can't get the physical business, then at least we'd get the bulk of the hedging."

Harris smiled. "Maybe," he said, but I've got a better idea, and it's going to be good for us both. I may as well come clean to you, Mack. The reason I left M and T was because I could see the chance of setting up my own company, so that I'd have full control over what I'm doing. I've enjoyed being at M and T, but in the end I'm not an investment banker, I'm a metal trader, and some of the constraints of being a bank have been an irritant. You know that: how many times have we seen that, as a metal trading group, you've had the flexibility to do things that have been impossible for me. Think of some of the Chinese stuff you do, that I can't get permission to look at. It's not a criticism of the bank, just a recognition of what the rules are. But now I've got an opportunity to do it a different way, and I would be stupid to ignore it."

"Mmmh. What do you have in mind? I guess you're thinking of some sort of I/B deal." McKee's mind was racing. He could now see just where this conversation was likely to be heading. Did he want to take the credit risk of Harris' business, in return for just a share of the commission? Or, knowing as he now did that there was a readjustment of relationships going on in Japan, would he be better to make a play for the business directly, and see if he could squeeze Harris out? He'd see first of all how much he could draw out of Harris, and then think about his move. A perfect situation for McKee: those that knew him well knew he had a remarkable ability to appear to agree to something, while nevertheless always leaving himself with a way out, a way to deny tomorrow what you felt he had unequivocally agreed to today.

"Yeah, I'm looking basically at an I/B arrangement, but slightly different from the conventional one. Strangely enough, since you know how critical I've been of the LME Board's tinkering with the rules, there is an anomaly which helps me, something which isn't allowed on any other exchange in the world, as far as I know. Look, we both know that the real money in this game is not made from commission from clients, whatever we may say publicly. Our profit comes from trading margins, and from being able to benefit from knowing clients' intentions in the market. A normal I/B just repeats the broker's quote to his customer, takes half the commission and that's the end of it. The broker/dealer is the one who benefits from his bid/offer spread, and from the subsequent positional trading. On most markets in the world, that's it. I/B means half the commission, end of story. The only other benefit is in reduced overheads, because you don't have to run and pay for a full office. Now, the rules of the LME as they stand give me an extra advantage. I can actually trade as a market-maker in my own right to my clients, which gives me the potential profits of the bid/offer spread, and the ability to run them as my own positions. I can then, not necessarily immediately I have traded, pass to my clearing broker the client's position - for his account - and my position for my account." Harris grinned. "Broadly," he said, "it gives me the licence to rip my customers off." He knew this would appeal to McKee, who, although he managed an extremely well-run company, loved to give the world the impression he was a pirate. "And I can trade with any broker I choose, when I want to hedge my customer trades. The other brokers will love it. They won't have to do the difficult bit, trading with awkward Japanese, argumentative Koreans, devious Chinese and the rest. All they will have to do is quote good old Phil Harris, who they all know. I'll guarantee to give them big volume so they look like big boys. I'll only pay them a minimal commission, but they won't care. They'll be able to sit in the Ring and look important. And if anybody raises the prospect of really doing the business themselves, instead of letting me get in the middle, you know as well as I do that they won't go for it. They'll always take the easy way out." He paused for a moment. Then, "So that puts me in the driving seat. You know how much effort I've spent cultivating some real strong relationships with customers. I think the time is now right for me to profit from that. I'd like to make you my clearing broker. I know how you work well enough to be confident that you understand the business I do, so we shouldn't run into too many disputes over customer creditworthiness, which may be the case if I went to one of the banks - it's part of the reason for some frustrations at M and T."

McKee looked at him. "It's interesting, Phil," he said, "but before I agree anything, I have to talk to my colleagues. We are, after all, competitors, however friendly, and we have to think about how a greater degree of co-operation would suit us both. But I like the concept."

Harris cursed inwardly. This was the answer he didn't want. McKee made all the decisions at Commet himself, and talking about conferring with colleagues was so much bullshit. It meant he liked the idea, but wanted a bit of time to see if he could find a way of making more money out of the situation than just the clearing fee. The reason for seeing him on his own, out of the office, had been to get a decision, not prevarication. A helpful clearing broker was a prerequisite of what he wanted to do, and despite his confident talk, he knew this was potentially the most difficult question to resolve. Well, if McKee was not going to decide this evening, there was no point in trying to convince him, by giving him any more information that he might use for his own purposes. "OK, Mack. That's given you something to think about. Why don't you talk to your boys and we can get together again in a week or so. I shall be back and forth between here and Munich anyway, I've got to find somewhere to live in London."

"Oh, I didn't realise you were intending to live here. Where are you looking?"

"I haven't decided yet. I guess a short-term rent to start with, while I make up my mind what I want."

"I've just bought a new place in Chelsea. It's the only place to be. You can drive to the City in twenty minutes, you're convenient for restaurants, theatres, shopping, everything." And McKee spent the rest of the evening lecturing the American on the London property market. Not for the first time, Harris thought that if it weren't for his larger than life character, his enthusiasm in talking, the big man could be a real bore, with his determination to know more than anyone else on any subject that came up. His sheer effervescence always swept you along, though.

They finished dinner around 11:30, and went their separate ways, Harris to Brown's Hotel, and McKee back to Chelsea. They had drunk three bottles of the heavy red wine, and a fair few calvados'. Harris knew he would feel horrible next morning, but, as ever, McKee's huge frame seemed to absorb the alcohol with no effect at all. As soon as he got home, he went straight into his study and picked up the phone. It was just before 8am in Tokyo, early for a man who had been awake until after the New York close last evening, 7pm London time, 3am in Japan. But McKee had no qualms about ringing the head of his Tokyo office; he paid his people well, so he expected them at his beck and call. The contents of the phone call would have disturbed Harris, because McKee instructed his man to get hold of Yamagazi and pressure him for information, and to see what sort of a deal Commet could propose to secure the lion's share of Kanagi's hedging. He had virtually decided not to work with the American, but to try and squeeze him out. He wouldn't discuss it with his colleagues, he would tell them - when he was ready - what he was going to do. But the excuse had bought him some time, he hoped, time to out-manoeuvre Harris.

Chapter Three

Jamie Edwards was back in his house in London. It was almost a week since his lunch with Harris, and he knew he had to make his decision. He was hesitant, and yet as he had rationalised to himself, there was really no alternative. His mind tracked through his career, as he mused about how he had ended up here. He had been an average pupil at school, and his choice of going directly to the City rather than to university had been a rational one, even if generating a touch of disappointment in his parents. But he had done well, he'd made a good dealer and was earning a lot of money by his mid twenties. Always close to the edge, though, first with increasingly frequent drink binges and then, during a six-month stint for his company in New York, he had developed the addiction. It had been a relatively open secret amongst his peers, and he was by no means unique in his use of the stimulant. He had been unable to control it, though, unlike most of the others, and bit by bit employers began to tread warily when it came to Jamie Edwards. Quite a few had tried to rein him in, looking at the good side and assuming they could handle the bad, but each in turn had had to give up the struggle. And now? He was, for the first time, confident that the problems were behind him, but nobody else would believe that. They had all heard it too often before. So all roads led back to Phil Harris, who looked like being the only person likely to pay for his services. Well, okay, perhaps it was dubious, but Harris wasn't so stupid as to get himself involved in anything really illegal. Just loading the odds a little in his favour, that was all. He reached his arm out for the telephone.

Harris was working at the desk in his apartment in Munich when the phone rang. "Phil? Hi, it's Jamie. Look, umm, I'll join you. When can we get together to talk about the details?"

"Hey, that's good news. I'll be in London in two days time. Let's meet on Friday evening. I'll be staying at Brown's, as usual, so why don't you come there at about six thirty. I've got to spend the afternoon with property agents, looking for somewhere to live."

"Okay, I'll look forward to it."

Harris smiled as he put the phone down. Things were moving in the right direction, although there was still the unsolved issue of McKee and the potential of Commet as a clearing broker. But having Edwards on board may help with that as well since he knew the brokers from being one of them. Harris was confident that between the two of them they would be able to work it out.

Brown's hotel in Mayfair is old-style, traditional and very discreet. Harris had picked up the habit of using it a few years back, when he tired of the sameness of the corporate hotels. The bar is dark, panelled, quiet and seemingly left over from the Edwardian era. On that Friday evening, Jamie Edwards walked in and saw Harris sitting at a table in the corner, leafing through the day's Evening Standard. "Good evening, Phil," Edwards greeted him.

"Oh, hi Jamie. You're right on time. Why don't you take a seat? Do you want a drink?"

"Er, yeah. Is it possible to have a coffee in here?"

"I should think so." Harris beckoned the hovering waiter over, and ordered coffee for both of them. "So. You've decided to throw in your lot with me."

"As you made fairly clear when we met last, and as I realise, I probably have no alternative, with my record. But I'd really like to know a bit more about what you're trying to do."

"All in good time. Anyway, you shouldn't look at this as a last resort, because it's actually a real good opportunity I'm putting in front of you. Think about where we got to at that last lunch. I showed you how I made a lot of money on a one-shot chance. That was really just flexing the muscles. The real focus is on the inter-action of the LME futures market and physical copper movements. I told you part of the story, the approach Yamagazi was making to the consumers in the Far East about how he can be relied upon to supply when and where necessary; quite correctly, you pointed out the financing cost of always being long, always holding enough stock to deliver. The simple way around that is to provoke a backwardation. Look, Jamie, before we go further into this, I think you should look at the contract I've prepared for you. Just give me a couple of minutes and I'll go upstairs and fetch it."

He left Edwards sitting there, musing over his last statement. In normal circumstances, in any market, the nearby commodity is cheaper than a further forward date. This is called a contango, and is simply understood because if you buy the spot commodity and hold on to it, then clearly you are incurring an interest cost on the money you use to buy it and an expense in warehousing and insuring it. So if you buy one month forward, for example, then you would expect the price to be higher than spot by those extra costs. That's what Edwards had meant when he had said that financing stock for immediate delivery would cost Yamagazi something. However, in exceptional circumstances, the nearby price can be higher than the forward price. This state of a market is known as a backwardation. In this case, the holder of the nearby commodity can always make a profit, by selling spot and buying the (cheaper) forward. In Edwards' experience, backwardations were normally short-lived, created either by real events - a strike at a mine, for example, causing a shortage and therefore an increase in nearby prices - or provoked by a trader who was prepared to risk the investment of trying to corner a market. This had to be carefully managed, and was normally based on some particular knowledge of an impending shortage for some reason, which could be leveraged to make a profit. As with any market manipulation, though, there was always the risk of getting it wrong, with potentially disastrous results. Did Harris think he could do better than those who had tried in the past? And if so, then why? And the same question as before: if this were to be just a one-shot rip-off of Kanagi, then why had Harris left M and T and why was he talking as though this were something different? Well, I'm about to find out, thought Edwards, as Harris reappeared and sat down, a brown A4 envelope in his hand.

"Jamie, I'm gonna want you to sign this, but I'd like you to take it away and read it seriously. One question, though. Have you genuinely decided you're going to join us, all the terms in here being acceptable?"

"Yes. I can't pretend I'm totally happy with the lack of information I've got, but in the end I've got to trust you. I'm ready to join - well, I don't even know the name of the company yet."

"Yeah, I thought a bit about that. In the end, I've kept it simple. Chelsea Metals, on the basis that your buddy and mine, Mack McKee, tells me Chelsea is the only place to live." Edwards smiled as Harris continued, "I'm going to lay it out for you now, on the basis that I trust you to sign that contract. You've given me your word, and if we are to work together, that had better be enough for me."

"You're a strange character," said Edwards. "Suspicious enough last time, and yet now you're ready to tell me your plans just on my word."

"Jamie, I mean it. If we're to work together, then we have to trust each other. Loyalty is a two-way street." As he said it, Harris' eyes bored straight into Edwards'. "Don't forget that, or we'll fall out in a big way." Edwards saw a cold intensity in the American he had not experienced before. "In that contract, you'll find you can say anything to me, but if you breathe a word of what we're doing to anyone outside, I'll have your balls." He paused to let it sink in.

Then, "Okay. You've probably guessed by now that we're gonna be working pretty closely with Yamagazi. His business will be the basis of what we do. He has managed to achieve two things, one of them his relationships with Asian consumers, as I told you before. The other thing he's done is to win the confidence of the Japanese smelter pool, the JSP. Now the JSP is an interesting animal, because it's a cartel where there shouldn't be a cartel. But anyway, it exists, to look after the interests of the Japanese copper producers. The names of those companies are all so-and so Mining Ltd, but in reality they haven't been miners for a few hundred years, since their domestic reserves ran out. These days, they're purely custom smelters, who import concentrates and smelt and refine them into cathodes, for sale to cable makers, fabricators, auto companies and so on. The absolute price level of copper, therefore, is almost immaterial to them. Their risk is if prices move between them buying the concentrate and selling the cathode. Effectively, it's a spread risk." He grinned at Edwards. "I'm not trying to teach you to suck eggs, Jamie," he said, but I want you to understand right from the beginning where we are."

Edwards nodded. "Okay," he said, "it's pretty simple stuff so far, but I guess we'll get to the serious bit eventually."

"Yeah. Anyway, Yamagazi has managed to make an agreement with them to manage a hedging programme for them to protect that spread risk. Nothing to do with physical sales, just around a million tonnes a year of hedging to play with. Obviously, since the cartel shouldn't be there in the first place, this agreement is strictly, strictly confidential. The reason they've done it is that they don't trust the LME brokers. Yamagazi has been working on building up that distrust for a while, and add that to the fact that Kanagi is one of the main trading houses and a pillar of Japan Inc and you can see how he's managed to manoeuvre them."

It was said very glibly, but Edwards knew that if it were true - and given Harris's comments about trust between colleagues, he had to assume that at least part of it was - then this would be a major change in the way things were done. Until now, as far as he was aware, the smelters in Japan had not embraced the use of the

LME with the same degree of enthusiasm as the trading houses. They had been very hesitant about dipping their toes in, as Harris had said, reluctant to trust the western brokers. That was a big chunk of business Yamagazi had managed to secure. This was getting closer to the reason Harris would have given up the security of M and T.

"Next," Harris continued, "there are the Chinese. As you know, China is both importer and exporter of all forms of copper, because their internal systems aren't sophisticated enough to match domestic buyers and sellers. Kanagi has for a long time been the foremost Japanese trader in China, and our boy latched onto those connections a while back. Add to all that the south-east Asian business I already indicated to you, and you can see that it's a big piece of the world's copper this guy is controlling."

"Sure it's big business, Phil, but I still don't see where we're going to make the kind of money you've been talking about."

The bar was beginning to fill up with a mixture of hotel guests who looked as if they'd come in from sightseeing and smart, well-dressed people who were obviously meeting for pre-dinner drinks.

"I found a house this afternoon. I've still got the key, the real estate broker doesn't want it back until tomorrow morning. Do you want to come and see it? It's getting a bit crowded in here."

"Sure. Why not?"

"Okay, just let me grab the bill" - Harris signalled to the waiter - "and we'll take a cab ride down there." They walked out through the country house hall into Dover Street, where they waited a moment or two while the doorman whistled up a cab for them. It was dark, gloomy and drizzling, with the lights reflecting off the wet pavement slabs. Edwards grimaced. "You're a Californian, what on earth persuades you to come and live in this filthy climate, instead of sticking with the sun?"

"Money, Jamie. I don't like the cold and wet any more than you do. When we're through with all this, there'll be enough money to go and live in whatever sun you want. Two or three more years should be all I need." The black cab drew up, and they got in.

"Where to, mate?"

"Onslow Gardens."

"Wow," said Edwards, " that's a pretty smart address. You're obviously richer than I thought."

"No, but I think property in central London long-term is going to be a good investment, so why not take advantage of where prices are right now? Anyway, it's actually quite small, as you'll see in a minute."

Not for the first time, Edwards reflected that in the end almost every conversation he had ever had with the American was about money - making it, losing it, keeping it.

They were stuck in the traffic round Hyde Park Corner. "I tell you this is one thing it'll take me a long time to get used to in London. It's worse than Tokyo, these days."

"You just have to get used to the fact that it takes longer and longer to get anywhere. It's not going to get any better until they spend some money making the Tube usable. But, you know, you get into the office early enough so you're before most people, and you're OK."

Harris looked at him. "That for sure. We've gotta be there when the Jap wants to trade, and that means early, early mornings. He's heavily on our side, but we need to be competitive for him." He paused for a moment. "Or at any rate, we have to be there when the others aren't, so whatever our price is, *is* the competitive one." The cab turned into Onslow Gardens, and Harris indicated the house to the driver. "This is the one," he said, as they drew up outside. As they got out and paid the cab, he said to Edwards, who was looking appreciatively at the property, "It's actually not a house, it's what you call in this country a maisonette, so it's just two floors, not really that big, but it's all nicely finished and with some good furniture it could be good. I've been buying some antique pieces in Munich for the last couple of years; some of them will fit better in a place like this than they do in the flat over there. Anyway, come and have a look round." Inside the house, Edwards had to agree - it wasn't very big, but the rooms were beautifully proportioned and decorated. The big windows giving - presumably - on to a communal garden at the back suggested a lightness and airiness in the daytime.

"Yeah, it's nice, Phil. Are you going to buy it? What happened to the idea of renting until you were more settled in London?"

"Well, I like this, and as I said, I may as well take advantage of prices now. I'm going to make them a bid tomorrow, and if we get it sorted out quickly, then I can ship my things over and get settled before we actually start trading."

"What about Annette?" - Harris' on/off long-term German girlfriend - "what does she think of moving to London?"

"Playing it a bit cool, at the moment. But she'll come round, she knows where she's best off. If not, that's life, Jamie, you know that."

Edwards snorted. "Tell me about it." He had been married for a couple of years, but the drink, drugs and partying with the boys had destroyed it. Harris grinned. "Ros would probably like the clean-living man you've become since the clinic."

"I don't think she would ever like anything about me again, Phil. But as you say, that's life. Anyway, more important things. You were about to tell me how Yamagazi's increasing importance in the physical copper market is going to make you and me rich."

"Yeah." A pause. "Look, you clearly must have picked up by now that I have a bit of a deal going with him. They way it'll work is that he'll pick up a share of the profits of Chelsea Metals. He will provide us with enough volume to move the market around, and what we bring to the table is knowledge and experience enough to use that volume to manipulate the market to suit us all. As I said before, we're going to want to get it into a backwardation, so we make money out of the way Kanagi Corp will always be long nearby."

"I can see that would be interesting, but you still haven't explained how you're going to finance the cost of creating and then holding that backwardation. That's the bit that always causes backwardations to collapse after a pretty short time - look at the history of it. And yet you seem to want to have something semi-permanent. I don't understand how we're going to keep it going."

"Alright, you can see two thirds of it, right? Yamagazi has the volume, we have the market experience to use it." Edwards nodded. "Well, the third leg of the stool is Kanagi Corp themselves. They've done something very silly, something unforgivable. They have put Yamagazi in sole charge of copper business - he not only trades it, he has a free hand to oversee the settlement of his trades and, most importantly, to arrange the financing of his trading. He is in a position - and this is all documented in Kanagi - to borrow money from banks to finance the corporation's copper trading activities. So what will happen? In broad terms, he will buy copper at forward prices, sell at spot prices - in other words, keep his word to the physical customers by always having metal available for them. To make that work, he needs a back. We create that for him on the LME, using his volume to provoke it - remember the combination of his own traded tonnage and the smelters. To do that, he's gonna have to pay money to the market to keep it going, as you rightly say. That money comes from the banks, and you name me a single major bank that won't love to lend money to one of the strongest of the Japanese trading houses. And there will always be enough copper to use as security for the loans. So the banks will assume their money is being used to finance the physical trades, not for a market manipulation. And our profit comes because little old Chelsea Metals will be there trading for it's own account, all the while knowing exactly where the market is moving to, because we're the ones moving it. It's a house of cards, Jamie, but we can sustain it long enough to reap the rewards."

Edwards was impressed. The American had managed to complete the circle, filling the gap that most market manipulators stumbled at - having enough ready money nearby to keep the game going long enough to take the profits when they were available further forward. One little doubt niggled at his mind, though. "Who's the one doing something illegal, here, Phil?"

Harris shrugged. "Not us. Immoral, probably, but not illegal; let's face it, Jamie, in this business we stopped worrying about that years ago. I guess its Yamagazi, because he's technically defrauding Kanagi. But that's his problem; he likes the idea, so he must be happy with it."

"Fair enough. I guess we can't lose, as long as we can keep hold of the market."

"That's right. That's why I was talking to McKee last week. We need a friendly clearing broker to make sure we can put the right trades in the right account. I thought he'd be the most amenable, but I'm not convinced how keen he was."

Edwards just stared at him. "Are you mad? The last thing we need is to get him involved. If he gets wind of something going on, he'll just keep shaking at it like a dog with a bone until he gets to the bottom of it. We need someone stupid."

"I know, Jamie. I was working on the old Nixon principle, that it's better to have people inside the tent pissing out than the opposite. I thought if he were making money anyway, he might just accept it."

"No, no, no. That's not him. Yeah, he'd like the money, but he wouldn't be able to leave it at that. He has to feel he knows what's going on, all the time. He just can't leave things alone. Look, Phil, I know you've been in the business a long time and that you know people, but you don't know them like I do, from seeing them on the market floor every day, from lunching with them, drinking with them all the time. We need somebody stupid and greedy, and I know who."

"You're in this for market knowledge, as well as your trading ability, so that's fine. You tell me, and we'll have a serious look at it. Who do you have in mind?"

"Captain Mainwaring," said Edwards. It was Harris's turn to stare.

"Who the hell is Captain Mainwaring?"

"I forget sometimes that you haven't had a proper English upbringing. Captain Mainwaring is a character in a TV show called Dad's Army. It's about the Home Guard in world war two; that's a kind of local militia made up of people too old and doddery to be in the real army. They have to guard things in case there's an invasion. Mainwaring is the bank manager who is in charge of the platoon, and he's a short, fat, bald man who is pompous and bumbling. Nevertheless, he thinks he's absolutely it in soldiering, even though he's clueless. Anyway, there's a guy who looks just like him and shares his pomposity at BancSud Commodities. You know, it was a scuzzy little commission house that was bought about two years ago by Banc du Sud, from Switzerland." Harris nodded. "Well," continued Edwards, "they've never done much in metals, but apparently they've decided to beef it up. I know they've been looking to hire a few people recently. They would suit our purposes much better than Commet, because we'd be more important to them. They don't have the sort of breadth of business that Commet do, so they would be more anxious to please us. Look, I've had enough of standing around in an empty house, can't we go somewhere else?"

Harris nodded. "Sure. Let's go and have some dinner. You may be right about BancSud. What concerns me a little is that I may already have whetted McKee's appetite. I may have made a mistake by telling him as much as I did."

Edwards shrugged his shoulders. "Can't be helped. We're going to get noticed soon enough anyway."

They would have been rather less sanguine about it had they been able to eavesdrop on a late evening meeting happening across the other side of town in Commet's boardroom. McKee liked to have a quarterly strategy meeting with his three most trusted lieutenants, Rory Davis, head of trading in London, Stu Benson, head of New York and Matsuda, the senior man in Tokyo. " The last item I want to discuss," he said as the meeting drew towards it's close, "is what's going on with Phil Harris and Kanagi Corp? I had dinner with Harris a week or so ago, and I'm sure he's brewing something. He's setting himself up independently, and when I mentioned Kanagi he was very offish about it. But we all know Yamagazi doesn't wipe his arse without discussing it with Harris first, so what are they hatching? Matsu, did you find anything out since I mentioned it to you?"

Matsuda was a smooth, very well-dressed Japanese of about 35, who had given up the kudos of working for a major Japanese corporation for the much greater financial benefits offered by a foreign company. Like McKee himself, his strength lay in his ability to build relationships, and to draw information from a huge network of contacts. "So sorry, Mack-san," he said. "Not much information to report. However, we have been developing our relationship with one junior trader in the aluminium department at Kanagi, and he reports Yamagazi-san is becoming stronger and stronger in Corporation. He has a new title, not just General Manager, but also Head of Copper Trading Worldwide. As you know, it is very unusual for a Japanese company to use such a title. It makes us believe he has very much more power. Also, our colleagues at Commet physical section in Tokyo report more and more difficult to compete with terms offered to physical customers by Kanagi. It's almost like they're trying to buy market share."

"Actually, we've heard some comments in the States about things happening in Japan," put in Benson. "The concentrates sales guys are telling us the Japanese smelters seem to be getting a lot smarter about the terms they'll buy on. One of my buddies says it's like they've just discovered how the LME works."

"Not good for their profitability, then, Stu, I suppose," said Davis.

"Absolutely not. They're getting a touch pissed off about it."

"Rory," said McKee, "is there anything going on on the Exchange that might give us a clue?"

"Not really, that I can see. I mean, we know there's been some consistent Japanese interest on the buying side, but you can put that down to slightly more buoyant markets than we might have been expecting. But it's only a week or so since he resigned, so I wouldn't really expect to hear any real rumours. But he asked you if we'd do his clearing, didn't he?"

"He did, but we're not going to. It's not our sort of business. Stu, I'm interested in what you say about the smelters. When you get back to New York, get out and schmooze a bit with those concentrates traders. See what else they've got to say. And Matsu, when you get back, go round the smelters again. If they're learning more about LME, this may be the time to get in there. Offer them some LME pricing formulas, see if they're really interested. Rory, make sure he has some competitive numbers for them. Let's find out if Harris and Yamagazi are trying to bushwhack them."

McKee picked up his papers and put the Mont Blanc pen back in his pocket. "Come on. We've had another good month, let's go to Annabel's and celebrate."

Chapter Four

Banc du Sud occupied a prestigious building on Bishopsgate. The security guards in the marbled reception issued Harris and Edwards passes to the fourth floor, listed on the directory board as "BancSud Commodities Ltd". Edwards had spoken to them in general terms about what he and Harris wanted, and they had a meeting arranged with the chairman, Ronald Waverley, who, he had already warned Harris, was of a totally different style from McKee; he was a general commodity broker, not a metal trader. "Don't talk to him about the real business," Edwards had said, "he'll pretend, but he doesn't really understand it. He's going to be interested in how much clearing fee we'll pay, what our financial status is and - most importantly - how many lots of business we may do. It's not general knowledge, but I happen to know that when the Swiss bought his company, they were suckered into a deal whereby Waverley gets a fixed amount per lot of business, as part of his bonus, taken out before profit and loss calculations. Volume is what he wants more than anything else. They're quite big in soft commodities, they're trying to grow in financial futures, and the LME is the bit they don't really have a handle on. If we can offer them what amounts to almost a ready-made business, they're going to go for it. The biggest hurdle will be our balance sheet, because they won't be keen to give credit to a company of our size, and we need it to be able to trade on our own account." Harris had an answer for that one, but he had seen no need to disclose it to Edwards before the meeting. Why tell anybody anything before you have to, was his watchword, despite his comments to his partner about mutual trust.

The hallway they came to out of the lift was a sharp contrast to the plushness below. Shabby carpet tiles and scratched wooden doors, through which the sign indicated them to the reception. The girl at the desk, though, smiled pleasantly enough at them and asked them to take a seat for a moment while she told Waverley's secretary they had arrived. They sat in silence, until a slim middle-aged woman came through the double doors and asked them to follow her. She showed them into a large, airy boardroom, like the area outside in need of decoration, and told them Waverley would be with them very shortly. Again they sat in silence, until the door opened and Ronald Waverley came in. The Captain Mainwaring reference had been completely lost on Harris, but to Edwards the likeness was uncanny, emphasised by the pomposity of the greeting "Gentlemen, welcome to BancSud Commodities." Edwards made the introductions, Waverley served them all coffee from the side, and they sat themselves at the board table.

"I understand you are in the process of increasing your activities on the LME," began Harris, "and as we are right now establishing our company, Chelsea Metals, as an I/B specialising in Japanese and Far Eastern business, Jamie suggested to me that we should come and see you and talk about where we may be able to co-operate."

"Certainly," replied Waverley. "I'll give you a bit of background about us first, and then maybe we can look at specifics. This company was founded just over a hundred years ago as Sime and Co., and went through a number of ownerships until my partner and I bought it around fifteen years ago. Its strength has always been in soft commodities - cocoa, sugar, coffee and so on - and we carried that emphasis on. My partner decided to retire a couple of years ago, and at the same time we got an offer for the company from Banc du Sud. That got my partner out with his share, and I stayed on as chairman, with the bank as a hundred percent shareholder. We are still a separate company, though, not a division of the bank. One of Banc du Sud's strengths is their mining project finance section, and they see us as a vehicle to increase their metal trading exposure through our membership of the LME. They want to be able to offer hedging facilities as part of the mine finance package, so they are very keen for us to grow our LME business, which has historically been a pretty small part of our activities. They are therefore extremely supportive in building customer relationships." He beamed at them, with his round face and glasses. "As you know, Jamie, we've just hired another two dealers to strengthen our metals team, and we're keen to develop more business. Obviously, we'd like to do end-customer business, but our marketing tends to be concentrated more in Europe and North America, so to the extent that you are Far East oriented, it may be that there's a good fit there."

"Yeah, our business will be very much representing Japanese interests firstly, and we then expect growth into China. We may have something to do also for Taiwan and Korea but I guess that's most likely to come via the Japanese, at least to start with."

"Well, it would seem that we may have the possibility of a deal. From the conversation I had on the phone with Jamie, I understand you're looking for a clearing arrangement, in the names of specific customers and in your own name as well. We have quite a lot of experience as clearing brokers on other markets, and I don't see any reason why our staff shouldn't be able to handle what you want as well. Subject, of course, to the customers meeting our requirements of financial strength."

"I understand that. As far as the Japanese are concerned, they will all be major corporations, so I guess that won't be a problem." Waverley nodded at him, and Harris continued, "For our own account, Chelsea Metals is at the moment only capitalised at $100,000, although that will increase. Initially, I would suggest that we should deposit margin with you to cover our exposure. It would be cash or some acceptable securities." Edwards looked surprised. The margin requirements could be big money; one day he'd find out what Harris really had behind him.

"That's fine," said Waverley, smirking, "we're always ready to hold your money. Obviously we would need to look at the Japanese companies individually in terms of credit lines, but I can't envisage any serious problems if they're the big corporates you describe. Gentlemen, I think this is all going to fit together very well."

They haggled back and forth a bit concerning the commissions to be paid to BancSud for clearing, but Harris and Edwards left the meeting well satisfied with their progress. In the cab afterwards, Harris said "You're absolutely right, Jamie. This is the sort of guy we need. McKee was all over me, trying to find out what we're doing; Waverley doesn't seem to care, it's like he just sees his company as a functionary. I think we'll be able to do almost anything we want, as long as we pay him his clearing fee."

"I told you, Phil, volume is more important to him than anything else, and we will be his biggest client. He'll fall over himself to keep us sweet. What we might also do is put some trading through them as well. I know the guys he's been hiring; some of them aren't bad. He's paying big money to attract them, you know. I think the bank has given him a kick up the arse and told him to do something with his LME membership. They've been Ring dealers for quite a few years now, but they've never been more than a bit player. My guess is that our timing is perfect for them, 'cos it's going to help them get their profile up. And that'll make us very popular with them."

"I think we're nearly there, Jamie. We've got work to do on getting credit agreed with BancSud for the initial clients, which will be Kanagi, obviously, and the Japanese smelters. That won't be too difficult and I guess BancSud will process things fairly promptly. But I'll keep on top of that, anyway. What you need to do is to get together with some of the brokers and make sure we'll get liquidity from them. We've got a couple more weeks in

November, then December, Christmas, New Year and stuff. We should be ready to trade in early January, so that's what we're gearing up for. I heard from the agents this morning that we can get the office space I wanted - the place off Sloane Square, I see no point in paying City rents - you'd better come along and see it. We've also got to hire a couple of junior dealers. You know the boys on the Floor; have a think about which of the younger generation could be taught to handle what we want." Edwards nodded. "For the back office people, there are a couple of guys at M and T who are quite keen to follow me. You know their back office administration was always in London, not Munich, so it's a pretty easy move for them and I trust them to do the job properly. One thing I haven't really stressed to you is how important it's going to be to make sure our records are accurate. At some time, some regulator will inevitably look at us, and we've gotta be seen to be clean. That means tapes on all the phones, and it means our records have got to be spotless. You make sure when you choose your assistant dealers they understand I want no seat-of-the-pants stuff, with administration to follow. I want systems right before any trade is done. And I'm going to remind you again, confidentiality is essential. We don't need things leaking out about our operations. So the ability to keep their mouths shut is a serious consideration in hiring anybody. We don't want just the normal LME hacks who tell their buddies everything they're doing."

"Yeah, I can think of a couple of the boys who might be OK. One of them has just passed his dealing test and the other one is still a clerk. I think they'll both be prepared to move away from Floor trading, and as they're not that experienced, then they won't be set in their ways so I can train them how I want. You know one of them - Stumpy, the clerk who used to give you the run at Myerson's. He's already pretty much used to my way of working. I was speaking to him a few weeks ago, and he was telling me he hasn't really settled in at Commet since they took over Myerson's, so I'm pretty sure he's ready to move. The other one's just started sitting in the Ring trading lead, but he doesn't really seem cut out for it. He'll be better trading from the office. I'll get on to them this afternoon and set up some meetings. Any particular time you want to see them?"

"I'm easy. Whenever suits. To be frank, I'm more concerned with getting the infrastructure in place, getting the phones connected, the computers in, all that kind of stuff. You choose who you want. I mean, I'll see them, but I don't need to interview them or anything. I'll leave all that to you - you've got to work with them. I'm going to have to go to Japan before we open the doors, as well, just to massage our boy's ego. You've never met him, have you?"

"No. I did a tour round some of the Japanese customers a couple of years ago, but I didn't see him. I met some other guys from Kanagi, but we didn't get anywhere with them. It must have been just about the time when he was promoted to run the copper book. Since then I've seen him at one or two conferences, but I've never spoken to him."

"It might be an idea if you came to Japan with me. You need to meet him, but more importantly he needs to get comfortable with the idea of dealing with you as well as me. He's a strange character - very egotistical, but at the same time very reserved with people he doesn't know. He knows his interests and ours are very similar, but he'll still insist on having the upper hand in the broker/client relationship. But for the money we'll make, we can humour him as much as he wants."

The cab was caught in the traffic snarl-up around Aldwych. "Jamie, I've got to go to M and T to finalise a last couple of things about my leaving. Their office is just across the way there. Why don't you take the cab on and I'll get out here. Think about your sidekicks, OK? I'll talk to Yamagazi tonight, and try and fix up a trip out there. I'll call you tomorrow." And he stepped out of the stationary cab and crossed through the traffic. Edwards redirected the driver to his address in Maida Vale.

The telephone shrilled its insistent ring, and blearily Edwards looked at the clock. Three a.m. He picked up the phone. "Yeah?"

"Jamie, it's me," came Harris's voice. "I've just been talking to Yamagazi. He's leaving for Hong Kong this evening, Tokyo time, and he's going to be there for a few days. His suggestion is that we meet him there rather than Tokyo. There'll be a flight at around midday we can take. I'll confirm later. By the way, you weren't asleep, were you?"

"Of course I was. It's three o'clock in the bloody morning."

"Welcome to the twenty-four hour world. This is how it's gonna be, kiddo." And the phone went dead.

Chapter Five

The approach into Kai Tak airport is one of the most spectacular of all, not principally for the splendour of the hills and mountains marching north-westwards into the unknown of China, but more because of the intimacy of peering into people's apartments as the aeroplane takes a tight approach line across Kowloon to avoid Chinese airspace. Edwards was sitting in a window seat on the upstairs deck of the 747, and his stomach lurched as the pilot made the final, skidding turn to line up with the runway, the plane's wheels seemingly inches above the rooftops.

"Amazing, isn't it?" said Harris from the next seat. "No matter how many times you come here, you always want to grab something to hang on to at that last turn. My rule is always fly Cathay into Hong Kong. Their pilots have had more practice at landing here than anyone else."

The wheels bumped onto the runway, and they were thrown forward against their seat belts as the brakes came on and the engines wailed in reverse thrust. "This runway was never built for 747s. But if the Brits and the Chinese can sort out their differences, there'll be a new airport here by the time it goes back, in '97."

Disembarkation and customs and immigration formalities were swift, and they walked out of the airport to the waiting car.

"Where we're staying, the Island Shangri-La, doesn't have the snob appeal of a couple of the older-established hotels, but I've got us on the top floor, and the harbour view from there is awesome." Harris seemed to Edwards to be more relaxed than in London, less driven. Commenting on a view was something he would not have expected from the American, unless he was talking about how he could buy it.

"So, what's the form with the Jap?"

"Jamie, one thing. I'm sure you know this really, but you gotta be careful. Never, and I mean never, refer to any of them as Japs. That shortening to them is a real insult. You have to call them Japanese."

"Yeah, I know." Edwards grinned. "Careless words cost lives, right. Anyway, where are we seeing him?"

"He'll be at the Kanagi office this afternoon" - it was then mid-morning - "so I'll call him there and fix up somewhere for this evening. It's possible he may want to party. One of the reasons he comes here is he holds himself in such tight control in Tokyo he likes to get away from time to time."

For once, the traffic was relatively light and they arrived at the hotel in good time. After checking in, Harris said "I'm going to relax for a bit, I never really sleep properly on flights. I'll give you a shout when I've got hold of Yamagazi, and we know what we're doing later on."

When he got into his room, Edwards had to agree that the view was something else. He didn't know that the bright, clear day was the exception not the rule, and that usually there was a haze obscuring the distance. But he was able to look down over the harbour, to see the boats and ferries scurrying about, and the bigger ships sitting at anchor. And all around him, the high-rises sprouting from tiny pocket handkerchiefs of flat land hacked into the steep-sloping rock of the island. An aeroplane caught his eye, curving over Kowloon and then smoke spurted from the tyres as they touched the runway. The approach looked as hazardous from the ground as it had felt from the air. He stretched out on the bed; he didn't sleep too well on aircraft, either.

The phone jangled. It was Harris. "We're meeting him for dinner at the Chinese restaurant at the top of the Mandarin Oriental. It's s'posed to be one of the best in Hong Kong. Then he's got some new club in Wan Chai he wants to go to. I think it's some sort of sleazy table-dancing place. Anyway, I'll see you in the bar up here at around eight, and we can walk down there. It's not far. Oh, and he's quite formal. You better wear a tie."

Edwards was intrigued as they took the short walk down to the Mandarin, right on the Harbour side, across the road from the Star Ferry terminal. He was finally going to meet this Japanese who was developing such an influence on the world's copper market. It was also rare, he believed, to come across a Japanese who was so clearly corrupt, putting himself ahead of Japan Inc. But maybe not, mused Edwards. Who knew how he had managed to persuade the smelters to go along with his plans? Perhaps they were all taking kickbacks, and the impression of probity was just another way of fooling the gullible westerners. Anyway, he was looking forward to seeing Yamagazi.

The restaurant was a modern chic representation of traditional Chinese decor - black, highly-buffed lacquered walls, bamboo screens with abstract designs and stainless steel low-hanging lamps, formed to look like lanterns. As they were shown to their table, Edwards saw a nondescript oriental - he wasn't familiar enough to distinguish Chinese from Japanese, or Korean or whatever - sitting waiting. He had slightly greying hair and glasses, and a cigarette in his hand. He smiled as he rose to greet them, and Edwards could see the fashionable European cut of his jacket, and the Hermes tie. "Phil-san, so good to see you again," he said shaking hands with Harris.

"Likewise, Hiro," answered Harris. "I'd like you to meet a friend of mine, who will be working with me at Chelsea Metals. This is Jamie Edwards. Jamie, Yamagazi-san, Head of Copper Trading at Kanagi Corporation, and I hope to become one of our best customers."

"I don't think one of the best, Phil-san," smiled the Japanese, "I think definitely *the* best. So, Mr. Edwards, Phil has told me much about you. It is a pleasure to meet you at last." Yamagazi fished in his jacket pocket, and then proffered his business card, held, with Japanese courtesy, in both hands.

Edwards reciprocated, and replied "It is a great pleasure for me to. I have heard a lot about you, not only from Phil, but also from many other contacts in the market. Your reputation as a physical copper trader is getting stronger all the time. And of course we have all heard rumours of your hedging activities on the LME."

Yamagazi looked at Edwards' card. "So, Trading Director. You'll be the one who will make me the prices I need. I hope my friend here has explained how important it will be for you to be competitive so that I can place my business with you."

"Yes indeed. I think the more we can help each other, the better it will be for all of us."

"Come, let's sit down," said the Japanese. "Phil, I know you are an expert in Chinese food, but I came here a little early and I have taken the liberty of ordering a meal I think you will find interesting. This is one of the best restaurants in Hong Kong, and they have a wonderful menu." Edwards noticed something he would get used to in the future - as Yamagazi began to relax with people, his English became more fluent and idiomatic.

Harris laughed. "Hiro, compared with you, I'm no expert. I'm more like a beginner. I'm sure what you have ordered will be excellent."

"Also, as we have some serious things to discuss, we will just have Chinese tea with our meal. Time for some drinking later, right? I think you will like the club I have chosen. The girls are beautiful, including some Russians." Yamagazi signalled the waiters to begin serving them. "Now, Phil, I assume we can speak quite freely in front of Mr. Edwards?"

"Yeah, absolutely. Jamie is an integral part of our operation, and he will be responsible for the making of prices for Kanagi to trade. The proprietary trading, the position taking for Chelsea, will obviously be a matter of policy decided by the three of us together. But you know Jamie's a very experienced LME trader, and, I have to say, more intelligent than most of them."

"Good. Now, Jamie - if I may call you Jamie?" Edwards nodded. "The potential of our business is enormous. I have managed to put together for the JSP a hedge plan which protects them, but also gives me huge power in the market, because of the volume I therefore have to trade. Clearly, it is in my interest to place this business through Chelsea, but I also have people watching audit trails in Kanagi. Therefore it is important to be able to demonstrate that trades we do together make economic sense for the Corporation, even though we know that may not always be the case." Edwards' face showed nothing, but his mind was racing. He was staggered at such an open admission of fraud by the Japanese. Yamagazi continued, "I am different from any other trader you will meet at a Japanese house. I can go into my boss tomorrow and threaten to resign, and he will not allow me to. Why? Because I am the only person within Kanagi who truly understands the copper position. Without me, they have no idea where they are. This gives me immense power, but I have to be careful to use that power sensibly, to prolong its life, if you like." He paused while the waiters took away the first course and brought the next. "We shall need to work very closely together, but you must understand sometimes I shall need a great deal of flexibility in answer to some requests I shall have. I understand from Phil that positions will all be cleared by BancSud. This is a company we do not know in Japan. I hope you are confident they will be able to do what we need."

Harris interrupted. "Hiro, at first as you know I thought we should use a well-known name. But Jamie introduced me to the chairman of BancSud, and I believe he is exactly what we need. He's greedy, and he doesn't really understand our business. To me, that means we're gonna be able to dress things up and blind him with science."

"Yes, from our side it is acceptable. But don't forget that we will also need to trade on behalf of the smelters, and that they must therefore be satisfied with the financial status of their counterparty. The accounts will be in their names."

"Yamagazi-san," said Edwards, "that should not be a problem. BancSud has one of the highest capital bases of all the brokers, and it is also a one hundred percent subsidiary of Banc du Sud, which is itself one of the largest banks in Europe. I appreciate they are not well-known in Japan, but I do not believe that it will be a problem to introduce their name. After all, the truth is we are not using them for their professionalism - in fact, we almost hope that's lacking - but for the size of their balance sheet and their LME membership."

"Yes. I think it will be possible, but it will depend on the strong personal reputation I have with the smelters. You see," he looked at Edwards, "they trust *me* and *my* professionalism."

Edwards was beginning to understand what Harris had meant when he had referred to Yamagazi's ego. Napoleon complex, he thought, the guy can't be more than five foot seven.

"I will need to visit my friends at the smelters to give them confidence in this BancSud. Phil, maybe you should come with me in order to explain all details to them." Harris groaned inwardly. He'd done that tour before, and it was just an excuse for Yamagazi to demonstrate he had a pet westerner. "But something else, Phil, something maybe of significance. You know Matsuda, from Commet, is one of my very good friends in Tokyo." Harris nodded. "Well, the smelter people have told me that he has become very active in approaching them for business, and when I asked him what was the reason, he told me McKee-san believed the time was right for smelters to look again at the possibilities offered by LME hedging. Right at the time we have made an agreement with them, I find this a strange coincidence. Do you think Commet know what we are planning?"

Edwards looked across at Harris and raised his eyebrows.

Harris shook his head almost imperceptibly, which was missed by Yamagazi, who was just being served with another course.

"I doubt it, Hiro. As Jamie will tell you, McKee is like a jack-in-the-box, he's always worrying away at some new idea. My guess is Commet Tokyo hasn't been performing too well recently, and Matsuda's just been given a kick up the arse and told to justify that big salary of his. You just concentrate on keeping your boys sweet. I'll come round them all with you, in fact I've got with me the necessary account-opening forms and legal documentation to give you their authority to trade on their behalf. If we can get all that finalised with them, then that keeps us moving forward. Shall I come back to Tokyo with you now, tomorrow or whatever, or a separate trip?"

"If you can wait until the day after tomorrow, then that will be good. I have one or two other things to do here, and also that will give me time to set up meetings with smelters' General Managers, who will have the right authority to sign our paperwork. Now, Jamie, as I said, I have to be careful to ensure the audit trail of my trading looks good. Therefore, I would be foolish to trade exclusively with one counterparty. I shall set up accounts, or in fact in some cases continue to use the accounts I already have in place, with several other brokers. This will enable me to spread my trading out." He grinned. "But of course, my friend, as an interested party in the future of Chelsea Metals, I shall be able to ensure that we are always well-placed in the market." Again, Edwards was astounded by how blatant it was. "It will also have the added advantage that you will be able to place some of our own business through my accounts elsewhere, to help disguise what we are doing. I shall maintain the relationship with Matsuda-san at Commet, and with Union. We shall have to see if Klaus is able to replace Phil at M and T. As the business grows, we shall need to bring in more counterparties. I shall be grateful for your advice on that subject."

"Of course," replied Edwards. "I shall give it some thought and maybe we can discuss it in a few weeks."

Yamagazi nodded sagely. "Good. I think we shall be able to work together most satisfactorily. So, let's enjoy the rest of the evening."

As he had promised, the food was excellent, each course chosen to complement the others. Edwards discovered Yamagazi was a man of catholic interests, able to converse about a wide range of subjects, from Japan's growing interest in the game of rugby, to the origins of modern Japanese verse, to the potential political effect of Japanese investment on the Chinese government. He was clearly not the stereotypical Japanese businessman, with few concerns outside corporate promotion. Until it came to the table-dancing club, that is, when he behaved like all his compatriots that Edwards had met.

Wan Chai is not the most salubrious area of Hong Kong, but the club was already packed when they walked in at around ten thirty. There didn't seem to be any spare tables, but a quiet word from Yamagazi to the manager saw them miraculously found a table directly in front of the stage. A bottle of vintage Krug appeared as if by magic - together with Edwards' inevitable mineral water. Although in the past he had frequented a number of similar clubs in London, he had always been at the very least drunk when he went into them. This was the first time he had been to one since sobriety had been forced upon him, and he looked around himself with interest. The girls on the stage were dancing mechanically, fixed smiles on their faces. They were a mixture of Orientals and westerners, presumably the Russians Yamagazi had referred to. He, meanwhile, was again whispering to the manager, and a space was cleared directly next to their table. Three giggling Chinese girls came over, already wearing very little, and set to dancing while removing the remainder of their clothing inches from the faces of Edwards and his companions. Yamagazi was well down the bottle of champagne, and another was rushed to the table by a waiter. In the cold light of total sobriety, Edwards had to admit that the girls were extremely attractive, the more so as the clothes came off. But nevertheless, without the stimulant of alcohol, he found it difficult to get too involved. And so the evening progressed. Yamagazi continued to lay into the champagne, Harris joined him at a slightly more modest rate and Edwards found himself getting more and more detached from the whole affair. He could remember how he'd enjoyed himself before, how the girls had got progressively prettier and the dancing more erotic as the level in the bottles had gone down, but without drink it just wasn't happening. Anyway, he consoled himself with the thought that he at least would feel human when he woke up in the morning.

By around one thirty, Yamagazi seemed to be homing in on one particular girl, a blonde who must have been close to six foot tall. She was stunning, and her dancing was getting more and more explicit as Yamagazi paid for dance after dance in front of him, until she was left wearing nothing but a thin gold chain round her waist.

Harris leaned over and said to Edwards "Looks like our friend has fallen in love. Normal form is that he'll start negotiating to buy her out for the night pretty soon. He always likes the tall blondes. Anyway, once he's away with her, we can all go. Unless you're keen yourself, of course?"

"Phil, you know I used to be a big fan of clubs like this, but I'm still adjusting to life on mineral water. Quite frankly, if you're not getting pissed, it all seems a touch sleazy."

"Yeah, well. We've achieved the object of the exercise, anyway. Hiro likes you, and is happy with your degree of professionalism. He's gonna be quite ready to trade with you." He nodded in the direction of the Japanese, whose tongue was virtually hanging out as he watched the girl and simultaneously negotiated vigourously with the manager. "Looks as if he's about to set Chelsea Metals' expense account back a bit."

Yamagazi finished talking to the manager, and the girl slipped away. "Phil-san, I must leave," he said. "The Russian girl will be waiting for me outside. Thank you for a most pleasant evening, I shall call you tomorrow. Jamie, I have enjoyed meeting you." And he stood up and walked off, although he seemed to be having difficulty in not falling over. "Looking at the way he's struggling just to walk, she's not going to have much of a time of it," observed Edwards.

"Maybe not, but she's picking up a lotta dough. Come on, let's get the check and move on."

As they walked out of the club, Edwards asked, "So have you got another few nights the same to come in Tokyo?"

"No. I told you, he keeps himself very much in check at home. You must have picked up he's a very complex character. He just goes to a couple of drinking places most evenings, either with one of his buddies from the smelters or with Matsuda. Those two are very close. I really think I screwed up letting McKee know we were doing something. He's gonna be on Matsuda's back about it until he gets something. Anyway, Hiro understands the need to stay quiet."

"Well, I can easily do some business with Rory round there, to get their dealers on our side. I'd want to do that anyway, they're very good. And as long as Hiro really is discreet, like you say, we'll be alright."

The cab dropped them at the Star Ferry terminal, and they walked down the gangway onto the boat. It was the first chance Edwards had had to see the harbour in full night-time, with the lights from the buildings and the advertising signs blazing out over the water in a riot of light and colour.

Harris noticed him looking greedily at the view. "This is one of the best cities in the world. Stay a couple of days to have a better look at it. I've gotta go to a couple of banks with Hiro tomorrow - it's a bit delicate about financing, he won't have you there - and then off to Tokyo. But there's no immediate rush for you to get back, you may as well do some sightseeing. If you want any cameras, electricals or things like that, it's a great place to buy them." They were the only passengers on their side of the cabin. "I don't know if you've got your mind completely round this, Jamie, but everything's going like a dream. We've got pretty much everything in line now, and when we hit that market, they won't know what's happening. We're gonna make fortunes, and all because of an egotistical Japanese who thinks he's bigger and better than his company. I don't recall saying this to you before, but he brought the scheme to me, not the other way around. It's his idea."

"How long do you think we can carry it on - realistically, until somebody gets too wise to what we're doing?"

"I don't know. At some point, we won't any longer be able to complete the circle with borrowings - even Kanagi's name won't support infinite amounts. The trick is, you and I gotta be out before we reach that point."

Edwards noticed there was no mention of Yamagazi also needing to get out, but thought better of commenting.

Harris continued, "That's another area where you need to be close to the market, we have to be able to keep track of the rumours. You better believe the regulators are gonna be on our backs, so we need the brokers on our side to help fend them off through the LME Board. So you need to let them make money sometimes out of the business you give them. If they rip you off for a buck here and there on executions, let them get away with it sometimes. Always concentrate on the bigger picture, the real total profitability. That's what matters to us."

In fact, Edwards actually stayed in Hong Kong for a week after that meeting. He went to change his air ticket the following morning, and was attracted to the Cathay Pacific girl at the desk. He persuaded her to lunch with him, and the result was that she went back to his hotel with him that day. He spent the rest of the week with her. What the clinic had done for his physical rehabilitation, the Chinese girl did for his mind. There'd been no true relaxation since he left there, he'd been plunged straight back by Harris into the world where money was the only object, it's power to buy anything demonstrated by Yamagazi in the table-dancing club. His body had been cleansed of the demands of the drug, but his mind was still in the same place it had been before. The Chinese girl slowed it all down, showed him a side of life that wasn't dominated by making money. They went to Lantau, where he saw the simplicity of the Buddhist monastery, they went to one of the fishing villages - not tourist packed Tai-O, but further out-where they ate fresh-caught fish (she assured him it was caught 'a long way out', not in the filth of the polluted harbour) and lazed away the afternoon in the sunshine, watching the boats come and go from the rickety jetty. And they took the hydrofoil across to Macao, where they gambled in the casino, not the pressured gamble of rigging a market, but insignificantly, for fun, for nothing amounts of money. They laughed a lot, that evening.

And at night, she was sensational. Her fragile body, so delicate, was attuned to his desires, her fingers and lips dancing a tattoo across his body that drove him to ecstasy. Countless generations of the oriental belief that the woman can control her man by pandering to his whims gave Edwards an interlude he wouldn't forget, an insight into the spell the east exerts on so many westerners.

He'd left the girl with assurances that he'd call, that she'd come to London. He knew already on the flight back home that he wouldn't try to see her again, that she'd just been the last part of the therapy.

The week with her didn't change him or make him a better person, but it put him back into balance. It gave him back a perspective on his life that the drugs had robbed him of years before. He knew what they were doing was if not technically illegal, then at the very least questionable, but he could now look at it with a more detached eye, as if he were playing a game. It made him a tougher adversary, not a softer one. He became focused on winning the game as quickly as possible.

Chapter Six

July 1989

"Jamie. Ferret for you on line four." Stumpy the clerk called across the dealing desk to Edwards, who was on another line. He held up his hand, gesturing that he wouldn't be long, that Stumpy should keep him on. He wound up his call, and punched the button to pick up the Union Metals dealer.

"Ferret, how're you?"

"Pissed off with you, mate, to be honest."

"What's the matter? What have I done?"

"I've been selling to Rory Davis all morning to see the little shit off, and now I've got your Japanese mate buying off me as well. 'As it been you buying with Commet all along, so I'm gonna get my arse handed to me when I try and get it back?"

"I've bought some this morning, yeah."

"Why d'you do it through Commet? You don't even like the bugger."

"Come on, Ferret, you know I have to spread my business around. You had a good week from me last week, so stop moaning. I may not like Rory, but I can't ignore the fact that he's very good. Anyway, he told me he had selling - I didn't realise it was you. Anyway, if you want my advice, I'd cover it."

"Thanks a lot," said Ferret sarcastically, and hung up.

Edwards picked up another line and dialled Rory Davis' direct number at Commet. "Rory? It's me. Looks like it's working nicely. I just had Union on whingeing that you'd been buying, and now the Japanese are following up. I would guess he's pretty short by now."

"Well look, it's half past eleven now. There won't be too much ahead of the Ring. When I get in there, I'll start bidding as aggressively as I can. That should start winding them up nicely."

"OK. I'll be following the Ring with Union, so I'll make sure I put in a bit more buying to keep the pressure on. Let me know after the Ring what you've done. I'll split it fifty/fifty with you. Are you and McKee still on for lunch?"

"Yeah. We'll be with you as soon after one thirty as we can. Is Phil going to be there?"

"No. Just me this time."

"OK. I'll talk to you later."

Edwards was having the time of his life. Knowing what the biggest player was doing all the time gave him an enormous edge. He was making lots of money, mostly out of playing the brokers off, one against the other. The overall position Yamagazi needed was building nicely, and they were taking money there as well, but the big profits on that were still to come. Meanwhile, none of the brokers could fathom what was going on, and as Harris had prophesied, they were all so keen on the commission Edwards was paying them that they didn't stop to think too clearly. The only one he confided in at all, and it was to a limited extent but he did need somebody he could trust in the Ring, was Rory Davis. Harris was still edgy that McKee would bang on until he got to the bottom of it, but he was prepared to go along with Commet for the moment.

Edwards rocked backwards in his chair, and surveyed the room. It wasn't that large, dominated by a six-position dealing desk in the middle. Harris had ensured that they had the latest Reuters and other on-screen information systems, and the desks themselves were of the most modern moulded-plastic style. Throughout, from the reception area, to Harris' own private office, to the boardroom, it was obvious that no expense had been spared on furniture and fittings. On the walls were some of Harris's own collection of paintings. In addition to Harris and Edwards, they had in the end employed three dealing assistants, the two back office administrators and a secretary/receptionist. With all of them, Harris had insisted that he was happy to pay top salaries, but the quid pro quo for that was that he demanded absolute discretion about the company's business.

That morning had been a perfect example of how the scam worked. Yamagazi had rung Edwards before he left home to let him know that he would be a buyer of quite good quantities for the second Ring closing pricing; that he would start his buying towards the end of the pre-market, and continue through the Rings. Obviously, Chelsea Metals tactics that morning would therefore be to buy first thing in order to make sure that the brokers were scrambling to cover their short positions when Kanagi's buying pushed the market higher. That would then enable Edwards to sell into the higher market they had created later in the day to realise what were almost risk-free profits. So that he could disguise his involvement, he had got Commet to do most of the buying for him. As Harris had said to him at the outset, they were using Yamagazi's clout in the physical market to manipulate the futures market to their benefit. He hadn't told Rory Davis that he would be selling out later - no need to let anybody else too far in on the game. Besides, if he got his timing right, he could earn brownie points by appearing to be the brokers' friend, by selling to them as they became more and more desperate to buy back their short positions - as long as they didn't really understand how the shorts had been created in the first place.

The phone went. It was Davis again. "Jamie, have you boys got as big a long position as I think you might have?"

"Why?"

"Well, it looks like the LME Board are getting a bit twitchy about undue influence on the market by the longs. They're not going to do anything yet, but they're looking seriously at it."

"BancSud are our clearers. I'm sure if we had anything to be concerned about they would have told us."

"BancSud don't know, Jamie," said Davis. "The July Board meeting's just finished. Mack's on the Board. It's not supposed to be general knowledge, so don't spread it around, but just watch yourselves, OK?"

"Yeah, thanks, Rory, I'll bear it in mind."

Keeping on the right side of the Commet dealers was paying off, thought Edwards. There was no way McKee should ever have disclosed what went on in an LME Board meeting, even to his colleagues. But he was known for being sometimes indiscreet where it was in the interests of his company and its favoured customers. Chelsea didn't have a problem - the growing long position was in the accounts of Kanagi and the smelters. Nevertheless, Edwards knew that if questions did come to be asked, then he and Harris would have to orchestrate the answers the Japanese gave. Prior knowledge in this case could be worth a lot. He got up and walked into Harris' office.

"Phil, it looks like the LME Board are getting worried that someone with a big long position is trying to manipulate the market."

"How do you know?"

"McKee - with his normal degree of confidentiality - has just told Rory Davis what went on at today's Board meeting. Rory passed it on to me, and asked me not to spread it around."

"OK, well something like this is not unexpected. I'll mention it to the Japanese."

"I'm not sure that you need to yet. This is the LME Board we're talking about. They're not going to do anything yet, they're just thinking about it. From thought to action with them is probably months. By which time, the way Hiro's going, we'll all be sitting on a *real* long."

Harris grinned. "You're at lunch with McKee today, aren't

you?" Edwards nodded. "Well, see what else you can get out of him about how the discussion actually went. Pour a few drinks down his neck - that normally means you can get what you want out of him. You've been buying this morning, haven't you?"

"Yes. Hiro rang me at about four thirty this morning to let me know it would be a good day. He's just started buying himself now. Union were moaning; they seem to have got caught short - some of the others as well, I should think."

"Mmm. Try and get out of it within today, take your profits. Just in case they decide to look further right away, better not be seen to be long."

"Yeah, my intention was to start selling into Kanagi's buying in the second Ring, and let the boys lose the rest of it this afternoon while I'm out with McKee and Davis. We should clear quite a lot of money on it."

"Sounds good. You're the man who does the trading, so I'll leave it to you. I've gotta go out in a couple of minutes. You remember I told you I'd been approached directly - not through Hiro - to do some business for the Chinese state metals agency?" Edwards nodded. "Well, one of their guys is in London this week, and they want me to go and see him. It's somewhere over in Paddington they have an office. It's not that far, is it?"

"No, you'll be quite quick in a cab. That lot do some good business. There's a couple of the brokers who make a bit of a fuss of looking after them. I'll be interested to know how you get on."

"Well, obviously it depends how Kanagi are placed in China. You know it's always been my idea to do some of the more speculative Chinese business direct, but I'd thought we'd be handling the state-run stuff through Hiro. I guess I'll just play this by ear for the moment, and see what comes out of it. One thing for sure, though, we're not going to fall out with our friend about how we handle it."

Edwards smiled. "Yes, that would be just a touch counter-productive, given how everything is going. Anyway, I'll see if Rory and Mack suggest there's anything serious with the LME and we'll talk about it later." He walked out, and back to his seat just in time to hear the beginning of the copper Ring commentary coming across the speaker system built into the dealing desk.

It went to plan for the rest of the morning. Edwards heard over the commentary how Rory Davis aggressively bid the market up in the first Ring, without needing to buy very much. The others, who had been caught during the morning, were the ones who ended up buying. And then in the second Ring, with Yamagazi - as agreed with Edwards - putting his pricing purchases through two of his other brokers, Edwards was in a perfect position to begin selling out his longs through Ferret at Union, into the strong buying that he knew was going to be there. The realised profits were ticking up. He instructed his assistants on how he wanted the balance of his position liquidated during the afternoon, confident that the market would hold up, working in his favour.

In the cab on their way over to Chelsea, McKee and Davis were arguing about the fact that Davis had passed on the warning about the LME Board to Edwards.

"You've got to understand, Rory, that you can't go spreading confidential Board information all around the place. It potentially makes me look very bad, if it ever comes back that it was me who started it."

"Well then, why did you pass it on to us in the office in the first place?"

"Look, you've been running your book long, so I obviously want to make sure you're aware of what's under consideration. But a quiet word to you should stay precisely that. I don't want Jamie Edwards shouting his mouth off."

"The reason I've been running long is because I'm picking up the vibes from what Jamie Edwards is doing. I'm making a lot of money out of trading with him at the moment, and it's pretty low risk because I'm building a good relationship with him. My responsibility is to make money for the company, and this is the best piece of new business we've seen this year. It wouldn't be so important if the a/e's were coming up with lots of new clients all the time, but they're not. I'm building this business up, and you shouldn't let your conscience get in the way of it. Anyway, let's face it, you would have told Harris if I hadn't told Jamie, you know that."

McKee grinned. He relied on Davis' trading more than he liked to admit. Commet had a big customer business, but the real profitability came from their proprietary trading, and Davis was the man who managed the corporate positions. "Yeah, I probably would have done. But the fact remains that if I want to be indiscreet with information I have, then it's up to me. We're not going to have a row about this, but in future be careful."

"OK. We both know it's really in our interest that Chelsea should be warned, and they have been. Let's leave it at that and go on from there."

They both felt they had won the argument, so they were both happy.

"You know," McKee spoke again after a few moments of silence, "I would still love to know what Harris is up to."

Davis considered for a moment, then said, "Matsu hasn't been able to get anything out of the Japanese. I spoke to him about it only this morning. Our direct Japanese business has hardly changed, but that must be where Chelsea's getting the volume from. Kanagi still trade with us, just the same as always, and I think that's true of their other brokers. And we've offered the smelters any number of pricing formulas that should make sense for them, but they don't want to know. They just keep saying, 'ah, very interesting, we must go away and study', in true Japanese style, and then forget about it. I can't believe that's where the new interest is coming from. I'm not sure how much Jamie Edwards really knows; before, when he was pissed or high half the time, I always thought he was a waste of space. But now he seems to have got hold of something, and he's very controlled about what he's doing. Obviously, Harris is there in the background, but I wouldn't push it too hard, you know. We're doing well out of it for the moment, so why not just carry on and bide our time until we can find out more."

"You're probably right, but it irritates the hell out of me not to know. Still, as you say, it looks like it'll help us to a good year. But I don't want our boys getting complacent." And in truth, he found it more than irritating. His whole persona was built on being able to present himself as knowing more than others about the market, but this time he was in the dark.

They arrived at Chelsea's office and were shown directly into the dealing room, where Edwards and the junior dealers were tidying up their morning Kerb trading. It was the first time they had been there, and they looked around appreciatively as Edwards welcomed them.

"This is a nice office, Jamie," said McKee.

"Yeah, we're pleased with it. There's no need for us to be in the City, and this is very convenient for Phil, and quite convenient for me - better than the City for me, anyway. And it's Phil's money, so I guess he can have what he wants. The other half of the floor is empty at the moment as well, and we're thinking of taking an option on it in case we need to expand."

"Business must be good, then," put in Davis.

"It is. Things are happening much faster than I expected. We're actually running way ahead of our notional budget - although one of the advantages of being a small private company is that we don't really have to concern ourselves unduly with things like budgets." He grinned at them. "But anyway, we're making some good money at the moment. Look, we're not going anywhere special. Just an Italian round the corner. But we use it quite a bit, so they treat us well and it will be pretty quiet at this time. Shall we go straight down there? There isn't anything you want to see here for any reason, is there?"

Davis shook his head. "No, I don't think so. Why don't we go on?" As they walked out through the reception area, he pointed at two of the pictures on the wall - bright, forcefully colourful abstracts. "I like those. Are they some of Phil's?"

"Yes, he's got a fair collection, actually. Some more to my liking than others. Those two are by an artist called Sama, he's a Cambodian or Thai or something like that who lives down in the South of France. Phil's quite a fan. I know he's got two or three in his house as well. He thinks they're going to go up in value - well, you know what he's like: everything he buys has got to be an investment, right?"

Davis nodded. "He's right. You've got to make your money work. It's no good letting it just sit there."

"Like your cars, I suppose," put in McKee sarcastically. Davis was renowned on the LME for his love of exotic sports cars, which he never kept for more than six months or so, always finding one that he liked better.

"That's a different matter," he said, smiling. "They're my release from all the shit I get working for you." They were all laughing as they got into the lift.

As is the way of the business, they spent a lot of their meeting joking and gossiping about the market. In the back of their minds, Edwards waited to see if McKee raised the subject of the LME's concerns, and McKee waited to see if Edwards showed any sign of alarm, or if he even referred to it. In the end, Edwards cracked first, and said:

"Mack, I understand from Rory that the LME may be looking at the build-up of some long positions, and the effect that might have on the market as a whole. Do you think they're serious, or is it just sabre-rattling?"

"First of all, I have to say that this is confidential, and is the sort of thing we would only discuss internally, or with responsible counter-parties like you, who we think should be informed about what's going on." Davis smiled to himself - by now he was used to

McKee's ability to turn things around to make himself look good. That wasn't quite the gist of the earlier discussion.

McKee continued, "I don't think it's a big issue yet. You know how the Board have been criticised in the past, when they haven't said anything and just let the market be squeezed. Well, this time they're trying to pre-empt potential complaints by giving a general warning. There will be a note sent out to all clearing members telling them to keep an eye on what their clients are doing." If they were going to publicise it anyway, thought Davis, why make such a fuss about mentioning it? "I assume BancSud will tell you if they think you've got anything to worry about. But don't tell them you already know. I wouldn't want it thought that information was leaking out of Board meetings." Yeah, thought Davis, because he'd be the obvious suspect if leaks did become known - his reputation would guarantee that.

"Sure, that's understood, Mack. Anything you tell me or Phil is kept strictly between us. We appreciate your openness, we've got no intention of jeopardising that. But in this case, I don't think we have any concerns. We're certainly not holding a big position. Sure, we've been running our position from the long side, but I've mostly been taking profits as the market's been rising. But some of our clients, who also clear through our arrangement with BancSud, are quite long, so I guess we'll have to talk to them about it. But mostly, their long positions are necessary because of the way they run their physical trading. There isn't really anything they can do about it, if they want to keep their price risk hedged."

"This would be Kanagi and the other Japanese, would it, Jamie?" McKee thought he could see an opportunity to get some more out of Edwards, who grinned at him.

"Mack, you know we've always been pretty open about the fact that most of our business is from the Far East, but you can't expect me to list the names for you. Yes, some of these people may be Japanese." He paused. Then, "they may be Korean, they may be Chinese - want me to go on? Mind you, they may even be Europeans. Phil had quite a strong following in Germany and

Switzerland when he was down in Munich. Incidentally, do you ever talk to Klaus Fischer? D'you know how he's getting on at M and T now?"

"From what we know from our European clients, they're still pretty active," said Davis. "You know we don't trade with them ourselves, but I guess they've kept most of their European client base. The market believes that you guys are pretty much exclusively active in the Far East."

"Mmm, maybe," said Edwards, neutrally, determined not to give away any more than he wanted to. "Look, I'm very pleased with the way the relationship between us is developing. Obviously, BancSud are our clearers, and we have to rely on them for a lot, but we all know you're much more keyed into what's going on in the market. For example, although we haven't got a problem over this stuff about longs from the Board, it's the kind of information we would like to know. I know you can't reveal things which are really confidential" - unless it suits, thought Davis - "but I would be very grateful if you could keep me as well informed as you can. It will help us a lot in looking after our clients. We're doing some good business together, and I think we should be able to keep that going."

There was the veiled threat, thought McKee. Give me the information I want, or I'll stop pushing business your way. Not a bad trade-off, all things considered, provided Rory Davis could keep making the profits.

"I don't think that's a problem," he said. "You're in pretty constant touch with Rory, and he knows what's going to be of interest to you. I suggest you two keep that contact, and it should be to all of our benefits. You know I talk to Phil once or twice a week when we're both in the country, as well." He paused. "What do you think the market's going to do, Jamie? You seem well plugged into it - what's your opinion?"

"I think there's a very strong chance it's heading higher. We've been facing low copper prices in historic terms for quite a few years, but now there appears to be a genuine pick-up in physical demand. Since, during the low price years, there hasn't been a great deal of investment going into developing new production, there's likely to be a squeeze on availability. That will push prices more towards what we would reckon to be a fair price for copper - which would be higher than now. When I said our clients were long because of the demands of their physical business, that's what I mean. They're concerned about future availability, so they're making certain that they're always long, so that they have metal available to deliver to their customers. The next point is that you've got to look at the technical chart picture. I've been speaking recently to a couple of investment fund managers, and from the point of view of the price charts, they are very bullish for the copper market. They're looking at bigger potential gains in copper than in the rest of the commodity markets. So again, that creates more potential buying, helping to push the price higher." As he spoke, Edwards reflected to himself that in the past, McKee had never given his opinions the time of day - he'd always regarded Edwards as a wastrel, a talented dealer, but without the ability to make the most of his talent. Not such a bad judgement, in fact; but now he had a lot of business to do, the big man seemed to be listening intently. Maybe it was all pretence, though.

But his answer suggested he had been paying attention. "I don't disagree with your general analysis, but I think what you're forgetting is the potential the producers - the copper mining companies - have to make hedging sales if the price continues upwards. That selling could certainly put a stop to a price rise."

"Yes, but remember they've been suffering from low prices for quite a few years now, so they're going to be keen to let the price rise, to get as much benefit as they can. They know the business is cyclical, so when the going is good, they want to take full advantage."

McKee smiled, a touch patronisingly. "In my experience, Jamie, producers never take full advantage. If they see, say, a ten percent improvement on last year's price levels, they jump in and sell all they can to take advantage. And they're like sheep: if one starts, they'll all follow. The only way you're going to see them wait is if they become convinced that someone is really getting hold of this market, is going to squeeze it and get the price up that way. If they think that's on the cards, then they'll wait. But just talking about stronger economic fundamentals" - he shook his head disparagingly - "that won't stop the big sellers. Not today or tomorrow, but quite soon, if it keeps going up like the last few months, they'll sell. Don't forget our group's got mining interests - we know how producers think. On the other hand, if you are looking at a serious operation to squeeze the market, then get us involved; we can be very helpful in orchestrating things."

Edwards smiled and shook his head. "Mack, Mack, we're just brokers and small-time proprietary traders. We don't have the power to be market manipulators. We just like to be able to give our clients meaningful advice."

Like hell, thought McKee. Harris isn't interested in anything small-time. Neither is he stupid enough not to have thought about producer selling. It was time to have a chat with the managers of the mining side of Commet's parent company and get their view.

The afternoon drifted on. McKee sank a lot of calvados and smoked his way through more than one of his trademark fat Monte Cristo cigars, but the conversation became more general and McKee more strident as the alcohol took effect. Edwards gave up trying to extract any more information from him, and just sat back and listened as he and Davis reminisced highly entertainingly about a ski holiday they had shared that last New Year.

It was close to six o'clock when they finally left the restaurant, McKee to go directly home, Davis and Edwards back to their respective offices. As he ambled the few hundred yards back, Edwards reflected that it had not been a complete waste of time. True, he hadn't really got a feel for how serious the LME Board were in their putative investigation of long positions, but he had got a tacit agreement to keep him informed of future decisions taken at Board meetings. He had also got an indication of McKee's thinking on the market - and if Commet were thinking the price rise must be capped quite soon, then that could be very important.

He mused that it might be time to start concentrating more on building up the backwardation, rather than working largely on the outright price as they had been doing up until now. That was something he needed to talk to Harris about, and to Yamagazi as well.

But he was beginning to feel like a puppetmaster; in the past, he'd been one of the boys, he would have been drinking with McKee and Davis, not just watching them, trying to direct them to give him the information he wanted. And in the office, it was the same. There was a detachment about what he was doing, and he was recently enough on the other side of the fence for it still to feel strange. Maybe this was how life always was for Harris, who seemed to be made for the role of conductor. No question, Edwards also enjoyed the new feeling of power, but he was still settling in to it.

When he got back to his office, Harris had already left. There were some small trades to be done in New York, but Edwards also called it a day at about seven. Another satisfactory day.

Chapter Seven

Harris was in the office early the next morning, already waiting when Edwards walked in at about seven, just ahead of the first of the clerks, who had the early morning duty that week.

"Jamie, do you want to come through here for a moment?" They went into the security of Harris's private office.

"I've been talking to Hiro this morning," Harris began, "and we're probably in a position to start cranking things up a bit more. We seem to be doing pretty well up till now just piggybacking on what Kanagi are doing, but it's time to start being a bit more aggressive. First of all, though, we need to be sure we're clear on this LME Board stuff. Did McKee have anything interesting to say about that yesterday?"

"Not really. His view seems to be that it's just the LME wanting to be seen to be aware of what's going on - so they don't come in for criticism for being out of touch with the market. He thinks if we have anything to be careful about, then BancSud should inform us. I was half expecting to find a message from them waiting for me when I got back yesterday, but there wasn't anything. I'll check tactfully with them later on this morning. But I think we can safely assume we're OK at the moment. On the other hand, as you know, the cash positions start getting quite chunky over the next few months as all the stuff we've bought becomes prompt." Cash positions were the way spot (prompt) metal was described. The purchases they had made had all been forward, but as time wound on, those forward dates would become prompt, and that was the point where, if they wanted to keep hold of what they had bought, they would have to pay for it, and ownership would actually transfer to them; ownership of as much cash as possible is always a prerequisite in squeezing a market, because if you own it all, then you set the price at which it trades and the others have to come to you to cover their requirements. "I guess that's when they may start getting agitated with us, because then it'll become a lot more obvious. That's assuming we are going to take delivery and finance bigger and bigger amounts of the LME stocks."

"Yeah, we are. But leave that for a moment. What we have to concentrate on is deflecting any investigations of our cash holdings as they build up. The smelter positions are straightforward - they reflect a genuine hedge of their spread exposures, so we don't have any concerns there. Our account as Chelsea reflects a lot of in and out trading, but the net position is relatively small." Edwards nodded in confirmation. "So, the one where we may have to do some explaining is the Kanagi account itself, which will start to get very long, not only of open futures positions, but also of the spot material that it will be holding. D'you think we can cover it?"

"Yes. We've always known we were going to have to watch this, and we've always had the same answer in mind - Kanagi need to be long of LME to cover their physical delivery commitments to customers. I've made a point of emphasising that when it seemed appropriate to the brokers, and I don't see any problems sticking with it."

"OK," said Harris, "I think you're right. But what we have to watch is that even though in one sense it's true, any serious investigation of Kanagi will at least question whether it makes economic sense for them to be trading as they are."

"Yeah, but that's where Hiro's position comes in. He is head of copper in all senses. You remember what he said in Hong Kong –

'I'm the only one who understands Kanagi's copper trading' - he's got to be able to keep that up. We can't really help him there."

"No, we can't. But what we can help with is in giving a good picture; making the presentation look right. What we need to do is to get the authorities at the LME on our side, and we do that by flattery. You know what they're like: make them feel important, and they're not gonna want to question what we're doing."

"Yeah, I'd go along with that. What do you have in mind?"

"Well, I think what we're gonna look at is the idea of getting Hiro over here, and hosting a little dinner for him and a selected group of the Board members. We can get Hiro to make a bit of a speech, outlining how the LME is so important to him, how he wouldn't be able to do his business without it and how he's widening use and understanding of the Market in the Far East. We can make it pointed enough for them to see that their interests are best served by letting him carry on."

"That's true, but there is a downside, of course."

"What?"

"If he lays it on too thick, then what's going to happen is that they will all want a slice of the action, and they'll all be pestering him to start trading with them."

Harris nodded his agreement. "Yes, but in the end that's gonna happen anyway. You know how his profile is increasing. Since we can't keep him under wraps, then in a way it works to our advantage; the better known he becomes, the more all the brokers chase him, then the more he becomes an accepted part of the furniture and the less likely they are to question what he's doing. And, when he makes his speech to them, we make sure he refers to his close relationships with his friends at Chelsea, and his clearer, BancSud. In fact, rather than make it exclusively Board members, we need to have Waverley there as well. Tie him in more and more with what we're doing."

"Have you asked Hiro if he wants to do it? Make a speech, I mean."

"No, not yet." Harris smiled. "But he'll do what he's told. He'll listen to our advice on how to manage the relationship with the LME. That's what we're good at. Anyway, all he has to do is repeat what we tell him to say. He doesn't have to think it up for himself. Leave him to me. You have a word with Waverley, and sound out some of the Board members. Sometime after the summer holidays - mid September, I would think. And best that McKee isn't one of the ones invited."

"That's easy enough. We just promise him a private meeting with Hiro the following day, or something. And then unfortunately, he'll be called back to Japan urgently, and we'll have to cancel."

Harris smiled again. "That's good, Jamie. You're learning."

"There's something else we need to talk about, and to talk to Hiro about." Harris raised his eyebrows, as Edwards continued, "Up to now, we've been concentrating simply on pushing the price up. Since we now start getting long of nearby material, we are actually going to need to get the cash price moving up more, rather than focussing our efforts on the three months. One of the things McKee said yesterday was that they're getting the feeling round at Commet that it won't be long before the producers start thinking about selling into this price rise. Now, that won't suit us, and the best way of stopping them doing it would be to start winding up a backwardation."

"Yeah, that's normally a good deterrent to producer forward hedge selling, because they don't want to pay the back when they come to buy back the cash to close out their hedges. But don't forget that the producers are also aware of Hiro's activities - he's a big customer, particularly of the South Americans. So they've actually got the feeling that there may be more to come. McKee's falling into that old trap of not looking beyond the LME market. He's not thinking that Hiro is also playing the physical market. I suspect when he speaks to his own Group companies, he may be a bit less bearish. But you have got a valid point. We do need to start looking to build a back. If we wait until we get Hiro over here talking to the LME, then we can soften them up - get him to talk about how he needs nearby material, describe his physical operation, that sort of thing. So again, we try to get them on our side, make them feel that a big trader like Hiro really cares what they think - that way they're less likely to look too far into what's going on."

"OK," said Edwards, "I think that's fair enough. I'll set up Waverley and a few others for a little pep-talk from our friend. But I will talk to the compliance guys at BancSud, just to make sure they don't think yesterday's notice concerns us."

"OK. It may be a quiet day today. Hiro told me he's out with Matsuda this evening, and hasn't got anything special to do. Just make sure his boys are kept in touch this morning, and they'll probably call it a day at the end of the morning Kerb. Look, I guess I'd better give you the rundown of how I got on with the Chinese yesterday."

"Yes, but before that you better give me a clue as to how we're going to pay for the cash metal we'll be taking up. I mean, I know technically it's Kanagi who're doing it, but I assume we're privy to how he intends to cover it."

"We are. You remember in Hong Kong I said he and I had some banks to visit?" Edwards nodded. "Well, that was for discussions about financing. In theory, it's not too difficult - where we need money to pay for actual metal we're taking up, then obviously any bank will lend it to us because they can have title to the metal warrants as collateral. So, when it comes to it, then we simply instruct BancSud to release the warrants to the bank in question against their payment. The daylight exposure gap between paying the Clearing House and receiving from the bank will be covered by BancSud. They have no risk there, because they will have an irrevocable agreement to pay from the bank against receipt of the warrants. A pretty standard financing arrangement."

"Standard, yes, but not normally for the sort of amounts we're going to need in the end. Why don't we just use BancSud - the parent, I mean - as the bank we need? Keep it all in the family, as it were."

"We thought about that, but it wouldn't be a good idea. We don't really want one group to get to see too many different aspects of what's happening - they might start trying to put things together, which isn't what we need. No, the bank who were most helpful was the good old Union Bank of New York, the guys who own Union Metals. We saw the Hong Kong branch, not head office in New York, to help keep up the illusion that this is a Far Eastern deal, not a London market scam. They were very positive, and Hiro got confirmation of the facility from them about a month ago. He will need to come over to see BancSud with us to confirm to them that we will have the necessary authorities to them to swap warrants for money for the account of Kanagi. We may need to bring other banks in going forward, but for now we'll be using Union."

Edwards was curious anyway about the size of the deal they had, and this looked like an opportunity to delve a bit more. "What size facility are they giving?"

Harris looked at him for a moment. "Please don't take this the wrong way," he said, "but right now I think all you need to know is that it's enough. I realise that sounds harsh, but trust me that it's for the best that that's kept strictly very secret."

"Come on, Phil, I'm working hard for you here. You can't just shut me out of things because you obviously think I'm going to blab them to all and sundry. That's not fair."

The harsh look Edwards had only rarely seen was in Harris' eyes, and his voice was flat: "Fairness has nothing to do with it," he said. "I find the ammunition, your job is to fire the bullets. That's the way it is, because that's the way I want it. You're doing a good job, Jamie, keep it that way. And I'm not suggesting you're about to open your mouth to everybody. I'm just telling you that it's in nobody's interest that you necessarily know the details of how much money is going into this thing."

"OK. But I'm not very happy about it. I can recall you talking to me about trust between colleagues."

Harris spoke in a hard voice. "Drop it, Jamie. This isn't gonna get us anywhere. It's not a question of trust, it's just a question of what is necessary. Leave it alone, it really doesn't affect you."

"All right." Edwards shrugged his shoulders, turned and walked out of the room. As he sat down at his desk, he felt hurt; but in reality, he thought, it didn't actually make any difference. Harris was right when he said there was no need for him to know. It was just that he had been feeling himself to be a partner, and now he realised he was just an employee. Fair enough, that's the way the world was.

Behind the door, Harris stared across the room. He knew his reaction to Edwards' question had been harsh, but he was determined to keep all the players in what he regarded as *his* game neatly each in their own box. The only way he was going to be able at the end to close the circle and get himself out at the right moment was by being the only one who knew the whole story. He was beginning to develop a pretty clear idea of how long the game could last, and his route out was mapped in his mind. It wasn't time to take it yet, though, the big bucks had still to be made. But it was time to put another stage in motion. He picked up the phone, and dialled Ronald Waverley's direct number at BancSud.

"Ronald, good morning. It's Phil Harris, from Chelsea Metals. I hope I'm not too early for you."

"Not at all, Phil, I always need to be in early. We're getting quite busy, what with your activities boosting our LME side, and the financial futures markets are really taking off just now."

"Yes, I've seen the press reports of booming volumes on the LIFFE floor. You're getting some of that action, are you?"

"We certainly are. As you know, it's a new activity for us, so it was budgeted to show a loss this first year, but the way things are going, I wouldn't be surprised to see them break even by the year end. That would be a big result."

Harris didn't say it, but in his book looking at break even as a success was pathetic. His view was that broker/trader entities had to make money, otherwise there was no point in continuing with them. Still, what did he care, as long as BancSud gave him what he wanted?

"That's good to hear, Ronald. I hope you continue to make progress. Meantime, there's an idea I have that I think may attract you. I wonder if I could come over and see you in the next few days?"

"Well, I am quite tied up, because I'm off to South America with a delegation of bankers at the week-end. Does it need a meeting? Isn't it something we could discuss on the phone?"

Harris wasn't about to give the reason, but although his private line had no tape on it, he was not prepared to risk whether or not Waverley's did. "No, it's got to be face to face."

"Alright, Phil, I think I can reschedule something tomorrow morning. Could you make ten?"

"Sure, no problem."

"Just you, or will Jamie be with you?"

"Just me. We're so busy at the moment I can't let Jamie away from the dealing desk."

"Yes, we've seen the cleared volumes are increasing pretty rapidly. The business seems to be developing well. Looks to be profitable for both of us, I trust."

Harris mentioned the meeting they were intending to set up to introduce Yamagazi to, as he put it, "some of the more influential figures in the LME business" and confirmed Waverley's interest in being there. He then wound up the phone call and hung up. Waverley had said nothing about LME investigations into position size, although of course that was not conclusive; the concern might be expressed by his compliance department, to whom Edwards would be speaking later on. But it looked as if they were in the clear. The rest of the morning he spent with John Roberts, the lawyer, talking about the ownership structure of Chelsea Metals. He had some ideas about how that could be used to further his advantage.

Edwards meanwhile was able to confirm that the LME had not

made any comment to BancSud to lead them in turn to question the positions in the various accounts controlled by Chelsea. It looked as though what McKee had said to them was true - it was just general sabre-rattling, and there was nothing specific in their sights.

The next morning, Harris didn't go first to his own office, preferring to make his early morning calls to Japan from home. He explained to Yamagazi the idea they had in mind to bring him more into the fold of the LME, in order to defuse potential criticisms of their activities. As expected, the Japanese was not particularly keen, but Harris was insistent, and eventually secured a grudging agreement to the plan. He was very clear that the text of a short speech would be prepared by himself and Edwards, and that Yamagazi would only have to deliver it. In the end, what tipped the balance, as Harris had expected, was an appeal to Yamagazi's ego – 'they'll be keen to hear from one of the most significant figures in the business.' Edwards may have felt he was a puppetmaster manipulating the floor traders, but Harris was truly conducting the orchestra - and he was the composer as well.

He drove across town in the German-registered black Mercedes SL he was still using, and parked in a basement NCP just along the road from BancSud's office. He went through the security procedures, and was allowed into the lift which took him up to the fourth floor. The receptionist recognised him by now, and he was shown immediately into Waverley's office, and greeted warmly by the man. "Phil, it's a pleasure to see you again. What brings you over to the City?"

"There are a few things I wanted to talk over with you, and as I said on the phone, it's easier done face to face. I hope I haven't upset your schedule too much."

"No, not at all. I've re-arranged a couple of meetings to make sure we have enough time. This trip to South America is proving quite time-consuming in its preparation."

"Why are you going? Commodities business, or some of your banking responsibilities?"

"The latter." Waverley preened himself. "The Bank of England regards us as one of the most significant European banks in the City, and because of my breadth of experience our Board tends to use me as our representative on some official matters. This one is a deputation of City-based institutions, which is visiting several South American countries to try to develop some stronger links. We shall be seeing generally the Ministry of Finance and the Central Bank of the various countries we visit. I find these official visits quite stimulating, in that one meets some very powerful people in the political world."

Harris didn't say it, but personally he thought it a waste of time. His view was that business contact was intended to make money, first for the company but then, more importantly, to flow through to himself. Political involvement was about as exciting to him as watching paint dry. What he did say was, "Yes, I guess you've traditionally had quite an interest in South America, haven't you. It must be useful for the delegation to have the benefit of your experience."

"Well, one tries to be of some assistance to the less knowlege-able of the party, and certainly the name BancSud is very highly respected in South America. If our local office can arrange it, I'm intending to stay on for a few days in Chile, to visit one or two of the copper producers, to see if we can't expand our metals business down there."

"It's certainly worth trying, Ronald, but I gotta say it's a pretty overbroked market. Most people have been down there for quite a few years. You'll have seen from the clearing that we've done a few deals for the largest miner. That's come about because Kanagi are big with them in physical copper and we've had to do some physical/LME swaps for them."

Waverley held up his hand. "We're not trying to muscle in on your business, Phil. You know we wouldn't do that. But..."

Harris interrupted immediately. "No problem. We always

regard the Far East as our protected area with you, but apart from that we've got no difficulty with being competitors, or joint venturers or anything else. We've both got our businesses to run. But I have got some new things for you." He reached down and extracted some papers from his briefcase. "I had a meeting recently with some representatives of the Chinese state metals trading concern. As you know, they have some dealings on the LME through a couple of the brokers." Waverley nodded. Harris continued "Again through the good offices of our friends at Kanagi, they have expressed an interest in a relationship with a strong bank, with us as their broking intermediary. Frankly, they're concerned that their existing brokers are potentially too great a credit risk, and they would rather be exposed to a bank. At the same time, they've been convinced that they need our expertise on the LME trading side. So what we need to think about is how *you* will regard *them* in terms of credit. I've got some information here" - he passed a thin brochure across the desk - "but I have to admit it's pretty slim. They don't like telling too much to the capitalist world."

"Mmm." Waverley looked at him. "In fact, we did some business with the Chinese state a few years ago. We did some of the hedging of grain purchases from Australia. Their performance was very good, but I have to say that it was before we were taken over by BancSud. I don't know what their attitude to Chinese risk will be. From our point of view here at Commodities, we would be rather keen, but you know from what we've done so far that I have to get approval from the bank's credit committee to grant customer credit lines. Do you have any thoughts on what sort of size facility we would be talking about?"

Harris shook his head. "That's one of the problems with them. When I tried to get them to answer that question to me, they wouldn't. They just nodded and smiled and told me to make them a proposal. On the back of my experience in China, but it's mostly with speculators not the official organisations, and from what

Kanagi have said, I would think we need to give them a facility of around ten million."

"That's a lot," said Waverley. "I will need to be very persuasive to get that through. But on the other hand, the relationship we have with you has been good so far, so that works in our favour."

Harris was pleased to note the use of we and our: that meant he had Waverley on side for this one. He forbore to mention that M and T had never really been prepared to do business with the Chinese government, but Europeans were more likely to be flexible about dealing with the red peril than true-blue US investment banks. Waverley continued: "Leave all the financial information you've got with me, and I'll get our credit boys working on it. It'll take longer than the Japanese facilities did, because I'm going to have to explain and justify in person what we want to the credit committee. There's no way they'll just nod this one through."

"Sure, that's fine," said Harris. "I'll also get Jamie to call your credit guy and give him an idea of volume and therefore clearing fees you can expect. He can get that estimate from Kanagi."

"That's good. It always helps if we can show them projected profit figures."

"Appeal to the greed factor, right?" Harris grinned. "OK, there's another matter I wanted to raise with you. This is slightly more delicate." Waverley raised his eyebrows questioningly as Harris went on: "As I guess you realise, we've had a very successful start to our trading. The accountants tell me that in the first six months, Jan through June, we've made a profit of around thirty million dollars." Waverley's face showed nothing, but it took years for his plodding company to make anything like that. "You know our finances pretty well - your guys looked at us hard before we set the deal up, so you know our issued capital is $100,000, in 100,000 one dollar shares. Obviously, I have to distribute a part of that profit as bonus to the staff" - he grinned - "including me, but it will still leave us with a healthy net worth. Also, as you know, our business is increasing, so I guess I expect to see progress

continuing in the same way. We've got a bunch of happy shareholders."

"Who are the shareholders, Phil?"

"Incorporated in Liechtenstein, share certificates bearer
documents - I can't tell you."

"If you're thinking of asking for an unsecured credit line in
your own company name, even with what you've just told me, it
will be difficult. You know the bank's credit committee insisted on
full collateralisation when we started - that's why we hold the
deeds to your house, apart from the cash margin you have with us.
They were very twitchy when you moved the company offshore in
the first place. Obviously, the fact that you've increased the value
so much will impress them, but I suspect they will want to see at
least a full year of similarly successful trading before they're happy
to reconsider the situation."

"Please don't take this as a threat, Ronald, because that's not
how it's meant, but McKee at Commet will give me a credit line
any time I ask." Not necessarily true, but Waverley wasn't about to
ask McKee, so the bluff was safe. "But look, we have a good relationship with BancSud, and on our side we're very pleased with
the efficiency of your boys on the clearing. We haven't used you
for that much execution of business, but I know Jamie is keen to
broaden his scope in terms of counter-parties, so we could work
on that. The deeds to my house don't really matter that much
right now, but I can't pretend we don't have better things to do
with cash, so I'd be keen to see if there is some way we could
structure things to allow you to release some of that back to us."

"We at Commodities would not have a problem looking for
something. But whatever we come up with, it's got to be
something I can sell to the bankers. I need something to work
with. The problem is that they tend to take as fine a toothcomb to
the short-term credit lines our clients want as they do to a long-
term, multi-million dollar loan; that makes the hoops you have to
go through tough. Knowing who the shareholders are would

undoubtedly help, if only because it would give me something to show them."

Keep working at it, Harris thought to himself, he's taking the bait.

"Shareholders I can't do, Ronald," he said, " I really can't. But let me ask you a question. What do you wanna get out of this business?"

Waverley looked at him in surprise. "Profit, of course. Profit for the company which eventually feeds down to become bonuses for me. Just like you, and everybody else in the business."

"Right, so we've got a potential trade-off. If I can show you a way of substantially increasing the profitability of the account, then maybe you have a chance of persuading the bankers to look again at the risk profile. And so far, I think we must have exceeded your expectations when we started, so the track record is good, even if it's still a bit short."

"That's certainly true. Yours has been a very good account for us. So what are you proposing that you think is going to impress the bank sufficiently to modify further their credit policies?"

"Go back to what I said earlier. We've got one hundred thousand shares, representing a net worth of, let's say after the distribution I mentioned, maybe $20 million. By the year-end, I expect that figure to be more like $50 million, and climbing. Clearly, for the shareholders, it's a great performance. What I have in mind is a deal to give you part of that equity, so you can participate directly in the growth. In return, of course, you will give us some unsecured credit."

Waverley nodded his round bald head. Harris could almost see his mind turning, as he contemplated the impact it would have on his personal earnings. "How do you envisage the deal working, Phil?"

"Well, what I'd like to do is sell you an option for you to buy, say, thirty thousand new shares at par value - a dollar each. The option would be declarable at the year end, so you get to see if I'm right about our value then before you have to decide. I would charge you a premium for the option of $100,000, but we can defer payment of that until declaration, so you're not actually parting with any cash until the end of the year. In return, although the link between the two is purely verbal, you grant us the unsecured credit lines I want."

Waverley doodled on the pad in front of him while he thought furiously. The trade Harris was proposing was massively in the favour of BancSud. If the net worth of the company at the year end was $50 million, then with the new thirty thousand shares, there would be a total of 130,000, valuing them each at around $380; BancSud's thirty thousand, therefore, would be worth about eleven and a half million dollars, for which they would have paid the par value of thirty thousand dollars, plus the option premium of one hundred thousand. And in return, he was going to have to convince his credit committee to advance credit lines to Chelsea Metals, effectively secured on the future growth of the company, and make sure they approved some Chinese credits. An unconventional approach, but one that had quite a strong appeal. But why was Harris prepared effectively to give away 23% of the company? "That's a good deal, Phil," he said.

Grinning, Harris replied: "Actually, in pure commercial terms, it's too good, but my shareholders are looking at the long term. They've seen the relationship with you guys develop, and they want to make sure it continues to flourish. Sure, we could just go on using you as clearers, constantly screw you down on costs by threatening to go elsewhere, and create resentment. This way, we can make the two companies move forward together. Much better. But one thing you have to watch is whether your regulators will like the idea of a regulated broker owning a stake in one of its clients. I'm not sure on that one."

"That's easy. We can hold the stake in Chelsea in an offshore sister company. The regulator need never know."

Harris' expression didn't change, but inwardly he was exultant. The oh-so-correct and proper Ronald Waverley could be persuaded to abandon his principles and do something totally against the regulations for the promise of eleven million dollars. Jamie had been absolutely right when he described the man as greedy. Harris had what he wanted.

"OK, that's up to you. Do we have a deal?"

"I will recommend to the credit committee that we should give unsecured facilities to Chelsea. I am reasonably confident that I can persuade them. Can we leave it at that, and I will come back to you within, say, a week?"

Harris noted there was no mention of whether he would detail the option to them. "That's fine. I'll leave it in your hands, and look forward to a positive reply."

They finished the meeting with the normal niceties, and Harris was soon back in his car, in a traffic jam down the Embankment. He was pleased with himself. He'd achieved his purpose, and Waverley didn't even realise what it was. Unsecured credit lines were no big deal - sure, they'd use the facility, but more important was tying Waverley and BancSud into them. When it all exploded - as Harris knew it must, one day - the more people who were implicated, the better, because that was one way to cover his tracks. And regardless of the 23% of the company BancSud would own, the original shareholders still had absolute control and the ability to distribute profits when and how they liked. It had been a satisfactory morning.

Chapter Eight

That afternoon, though, things started not so well. As he walked back into the office, he could already hear Edwards and the junior dealers shouting into their phones. He glanced at his watch, as he went through into the dealing room - just after twelve thirty, so they were just into the second copper Ring. He sat down next to Edwards, who grimaced at him, and gestured at the screen. The copper price was down around thirty pounds from where it had started the morning. He listened to the commentary, and to the orders Edwards was giving to the others to relay to the Floor. He assumed Yamagazi was on the other end of Edwards' line. They seemed to be buying, but the market was being pushed lower by selling from several brokers named across the speaker by the floor clerk. The commentary got louder and more excited as the close approached, and finally on the bell, the price was down again, despite Edwards having given some big buying orders for the close. He wound up his conversation with Yamagazi, and then turned to Harris. "That was interesting, Phil." He smiled. "But don't worry. It wasn't *too* expensive for us. Hiro gave me the nod this morning that he was going to be buying, so I started going long in the normal way. But the price didn't move up, so I held off for a bit and just watched it. As soon as I stopped buying, it began to come off, and the selling seemed to be coming from Commet. Now Rory's not going to tell me who he's trading for, but he did hint that it was their own position or Group interests, not outside clients. So anyway, during the Rings, I managed to book out what I had bought back to Hiro, taking a loss obviously, and he was still quite a big buyer over what I had to sell him. Then you saw the close - we were still buying for him, but basically we were seen off. The biggest seller again was Commet. I wonder if this is related to what McKee was saying to me yesterday, about producer selling."

Harris shrugged. "Could be. What does Hiro think? Is he particularly concerned?"

"Doesn't really seem to be. He's going home now, he said, and didn't leave any orders with us. He was surprisingly calm, considering this is the first time everything hasn't gone as he wanted. But he wants a conference call with you and me tomorrow morning. I guess that's to talk about the next step we need to take, as we were discussing yesterday."

"Sounds good to me. But how are we left with a dropping price? What's gonna be the effect if it keeps going down for a bit? Does it cost us much?"

Edwards screwed up his face and nodded his head from side to side. "Not too bad, in fact, as long as it doesn't really collapse. Obviously we're long, but as I just said, we got out of today's purchases not too badly; that was the highest price stuff, so what we're left with is the long we've been building up longer-term. That's not too big a position, so we're OK. Kanagi won't be looking so clever, though, if it keeps going down. I have a strong suspicion that when we get the fax allotting today's trades, we may find quite a lot of it is for the smelters."

"Not our problem, Jamie. How he sorts himself out with his buddies is up to him. More important for us is when he's gonna get the market moving again, so we can think about whether we should keep the long position or let it go for the moment. I'd certainly play it cool this afternoon."

"Yeah, I'll have a quiet word with Rory during the lunch break, and see if I can pick up any pointers about how much he has to sell. And why they're selling - if he'll tell me."

Over in the City, Davis and McKee were arguing over the phone link between the LME Floor and the office. "We don't need to sell any more," Davis said. "It's crazy to take a position of that size just on your feeling. It could cost us serious money, and then I've got to go and make it back again."

"Rory, how much have you sold so far?"

"Eight hundred lots for Luxembourg and four hundred for us."

"Right. And what did the market do? It went down, and we've got to keep the pressure on to push it down further. Chelsea and their mates have forced it too high, and it's ready for a reaction. We need to provoke that."

"Mack, you're talking rubbish." Davis had never bothered to watch his words to McKee, although the latter was his boss. "It went down because Edwards stopped buying when he saw that we were keeping on selling. He's just waiting for us to finish and then he'll start again, and we'll be forced to cover as he pushes the price back up again. Keep on selling, and you'll cost us a fortune. We don't need to take this kind of punt."

"Bullshit. The guys in Luxembourg are not selling for a punt. They're selling because they agree with me that this market is overdone, and as a producer it makes sense for them to put some hedge sales on. We're going along with them. Look, I've got to go out now, and I won't be back this afternoon. I've just been speaking to Luxembourg and they want to sell the same again this afternoon, and I want to sell the same again for us. I don't want you taking it on to your book - I want it actually sold out into the market, OK? That's an instruction."

Davis slammed the phone down at his end without saying any more.

He was still fuming when he got back to the office at about quarter to two. He punched a direct line button. "Stu," he called, "can you pick this up, please?"

"Yeah, sure. Morning Rory," came the reply from Benson as he picked up the handset in Commet's New York office, "How're you today?"

"Pissed of with Mack. He's still convinced the market's going down. He's sold this morning, and he's forcing me to do the same again this afternoon. We could lose a lot of money at this. He just refuses to believe that Chelsea are getting this market by the balls; he's still wittering on about fundamentals. For Christ's sake, he's squeezed enough markets in his time to recognize the signs."

The American laughed. "That's for sure. But I agree with you. When I speak to the producers over here, they're not looking for the price to run out of steam just yet. Mind you," he added, "with their cost of production, they gotta be optimistic. But seriously, I don't expect to see US producers ready to sell just now. Not until they get a stronger signal than one day's move."

"And that one day's move was us. I was by far the biggest seller this morning. All right, I put some of it through a couple of friends to disguise it, but nobody else came in with me for any size. I don't think this is the time to be taking the market on without any help."

"Yeah, I think you're right. Shall I give Mack a call, see if I can persuade him it's not a good idea?"

"You can try. He's out at the moment. You could try the mobile, I don't actually know where he's gone."

"All right. I'll see if I can get him. I'll let you know how I get on." Benson hung up.

Davis spent the next ten or fifteen minutes checking through his card and the morning's trades with his clerks, as the latter input them into the trade matching system. As usual, the few minor discrepancies they found were easy to resolve, leaving him free to sit at his desk and eat the sandwich he had brought in with him. He'd barely started it, when the phone went for him. It was Edwards, anxious to try and find out the strength of Commet's position. The conversation was guarded on both sides, with Davis reluctant to confirm that what he had been selling was for Commet themselves and their Group companies, and Edwards not prepared to say at all whether he would be back pushing the price up again. The short-term prospects for the world's price of copper

- after all, a basic raw material of the industrial society - were dependent on the ability of two moderately-educated young men to see through each others' bluff. On balance, Edwards got more out of the discussion; over the last few months, Davis had been fairly forthcoming about what he was doing. The fact that he was so reluctant to commit himself now made Edwards believe the business was in-house, that it was largely speculative and Davis had a position of his own to protect, rather than having been working for clients.

Half an hour later, Edwards was sitting in Harris' office making the same point. "I don't think they've really got anything behind the selling. I think they're just testing to see what we do. Don't forget what McKee said when I saw them a few days ago - he thinks the market is over-valued, and that the producers should be selling into the rally. My feeling is that he's trying to force that picture."

"So do you think there's more to come? Or will they sit back now and wait for the rest of the market to react?"

Edwards paused for a moment, considering his answer. "McKee's an aggressive guy. I wouldn't normally expect him to do anything by half measures. I think they'll have more to do, probably this afternoon."

"Yeah, I guess you're right. So, Hiro's gone home without leaving you any orders, right?"

"Yes, but I'll call him and let him know what's happening, if we're right and Commet keep selling."

"No, I don't think you need to. I think we just sit on our hands this afternoon and let good old Mack push the market down, if he wants to. Give him a bit of encouragement. Maybe we even sell a bit ourselves - that should make him more confident."

"And then when he's nice and short, we start buying again and force him to cover it back."

"Mmm. I think for the moment we've got more money

available than he has, so we can hang on longer if things go against us. There's no sign of anybody else getting in on the act, is there?"

Edwards shook his head. "No, overall the market's been pretty quiet. If you take out what we've been doing for the last six months, the rest of them are really just marking time. I think that's what McKee's seen - all the buying's coming from us, so he's only got one opponent. He's trying to build up a head of steam to get a bandwagon rolling on the downside. They must have sold somewhere over a thousand lots this morning, so they're pretty serious about it. But you're right - what we want to do is give them a bit more rope to hang themselves with. I'll do nothing at all this afternoon, and see how much they're really prepared to sell. Then let's talk to Hiro tomorrow morning, and see how he wants to play it."

"One thing he'll tell us is that he's got the Chinese on side. That meeting I had with them was clearly just tying up the loose ends. I've got Waverley working on credit facilities for them, because they would rather trade their LME with us themselves than carry on putting it through Kanagi." He laughed. "It's not that they don't trust each other, let's just say they've got a healthy respect for each other's dishonesty. They want to spread their exposure."

"Is Waverley going to do it? It's not exactly a prime credit risk for his bank."

"No, it's not. But they've had some experience with China in the past, which worked out OK for them, so that helps. Anyway, Waverley is going to do what we want for the moment. I have an understanding with him."

Edwards raised his eyebrows questioningly, but didn't say anything. Again, he had the uncomfortable feeling he wasn't being told the whole story. This time he decided not to query it.

Stu Benson, meanwhile, had had an unsatisfactory conversation with McKee on the latter's mobile while he sat at a noisy lunch with some of his cronies from the LME. The worst possible environment to try to persuade the big man to change his mind - he sat there, a trademark Monte Cristo clamped between his teeth, loudly demonstrating to his pals how he kept a tight control over his employees and company. In the end, Benson hung up and called Davis back, just as the dealer got back to the floor for the afternoon session. "No dice, Rory," he said. "He just doesn't care what you or I think, he's totally convinced he's right. I guess you just got to go ahead and sell what he wants."

"Yeah. I had Chelsea on over lunch, sniffing around, trying to get me to tell how much more we were going to sell. I'll be surprised if I don't get Jamie Edwards asking to follow the Rings with us this afternoon."

In the event, he was surprised. Edwards didn't pick up a phone himself all afternoon, leaving his junior dealers to monitor what was going on, while he sat and played computer games at his terminal. The result was that Davis had it pretty much his own way, with nobody taking him on. By the time McKee got back to the office from his lunch at around six, Davis was already there. He had sold the balance of McKee's orders, and the price was down another twenty-five pounds. On the sales made that day in total, Commet and their parent company were both showing a healthy profit. Davis knew he was in for an I-told-you-so conversation with his boss, and didn't relish the prospect. He actually left the office pretty immediately, pleading that he had to get home to spend a bit of time with his two year old daughter, who was beginning to forget what Daddy looked like. That left the others to take the full force of McKee's bonhomie, rampaging round the office with yet another Monte Cristo in his mouth. It was a no smoking building, but he was the boss and he was on top of his business, so who dared comment? Benson suffered for his lack of belief earlier in the day, getting an earful down the line from London. Shortly after seven, McKee collected a gang of clerks and back office staff and carted them all off to the west end for an evening's drinking and karaoke in some of his favourite haunts.

They were a perfect audience to hear how much cleverer than the rest of the market their boss was.

Edwards and Harris were in the office well before seven the next morning, with their call from Yamagazi linked through on to a squawk-box in Harris's room. The Japanese voice came through the airwaves with a metallic tone and a delay caused by the connections. "Phil-san, Jamie-san, good morning. So sorry to bring you into your office so early, but we need to have some discussions."

Harris answered. "Don't worry, Hiro. Where are you calling from?"

"I am in the office of one friend of mine, a real estate broker."

Edwards grinned at Harris, and said into the microphone, "Hi, Hiro, this is Jamie. Just to confirm, this line also is not taped, so you can feel comfortable to say anything." He briefly pressed the mute button, and said to Harris "I assume that was the purpose of your question."

Harris nodded; "Hiro, I guess you saw there was a bit of action yesterday afternoon, with Commet continuing the selling they had started in the morning. We estimate they sold over two thousand lots during the whole day. We're not sure yet whether they will have any more follow-through today. D'you have a view as to what they may be doing?"

"As yet I have not really considered their move. I have a chance to meet my friend Matsuda-san this evening, so maybe he will give me some clues. But we should not be too concerned; indeed, this maybe will work in our favour. We have been buying and buying, but as yet we had not met any resistance. Now we know that there is a big short position in the market, we will have a chance to push prices up so that they are forced to cover. That will do some of our work for us. When planning a campaign, it is always better to have an enemy in view." Edwards pushed the mute button again. "As Confucius might have said," he remarked with a laugh. Releasing the button, he continued, "Hiro, I agree with you. Phil and I spoke of this yesterday and our view is that it is best to let Commet have things their own way for a short while, and then come back when they've got no volume left to resist us with. But I think there were some other matters you wanted to discuss this morning?"

"Yes. First of all, I find that I shall be able to attend your dinner meeting with some senior LME figures. I agree with Phil that it would be appropriate to ensure that we take the opportunity to explain a little more about our business. That may be helpful in the future if we are asked any difficult questions. So please make arrangements, and tell me the date. I think also that as you wish me to make a small speech, maybe you could write down some ideas for me and we can then discuss. You will need to make sure my English is correct."

"Yeah, OK," from Harris. "We've got a couple of possible dates in mid September that look good for most people. Jamie will put together an outline of the kind of things we think you need to say to them to head them off from looking too closely at what's going on. We'll get something faxed across in the next few days, then you can tell us if you think it's in line with your ideas." He looked over at Edwards, who nodded his agreement with that schedule.

"Very good, Phil. This should be easy enough. Now, we have a more important matter to consider. As you know, we have until now been focussing our effort on the three months price. This has been quite successful, even though our friends at Commet have had a small short-term success, as we have been discussing. Now, in order to continue to push the market higher, and to increase the pressure on Commet to cover their short position when we see the time is right, we need to begin to put some effort into forcing the market into backwardation. You know we have enough funds through our credit lines at Union to finance the metal we will need to take up, so we have only to decide our timing." Edwards had pricked up his ears at the mention of the Union lines; maybe this time he would find out how much money they had to play with.

"Yeah, Hiro, I think we need to delay," said Harris. "Not for long, but I just think we would be better to let Commet have their way a little longer. The way Jamie put it yesterday afternoon was - give them enough rope and let them hang themselves. This is a saying we have in English. I guess you can understand the meaning."

Yamagazi chortled down the phone. "Yes, Phil-san. I may be just an oriental, but I can understand the concept. I agree also that this is the policy we should follow. But there is still the question of whether we should in fact act too much before we have had our meeting with the LME. This is our critical point, and we must get it right, without giving opportunities for questions to be raised before we have made all our preparations. If we begin to really squeeze the market before we have cleared the path we may have problems."

Harris answered. "I agree with that, but what we're really talking about is how we justify what we're doing."

There was a touch of impatience in Yamagazi's voice as he answered: "Phil, we discussed this many times, many months ago. The story has always been the same. I need to be long of cash copper, and I need to hold copper warrants because I have commitments to deliver to my physical customers. The LME has always called itself the market of last resort - I am just using it as that. We have the smelters' accounts so that we can hold part of the long position there, so we can say we alone are not responsible for the backwardation which will come. What is important is that we make it clear that the smelter business I place with the market I do just as an intermediary. That I do not control their position. *We* know the truth is different, but nobody else must know."

"OK, so we're saying that as far as your position is concerned, it will be established in order for you to have secure supplies to deliver to your customers. As far as the smelters go, their natural hedge position is to be long, and their holdings of cash will be established to protect themselves from the backwardation which by then will be there," Harris agreed.

"Exactly. So we come back to timing. We must first establish a backwardation with our position, and we can then switch our emphasis to the smelter accounts."

Edwards' face showed nothing as he listened to Yamagazi, but he finally understood the full picture. The implication of what the Japanese had just said was clear - by the time they had finished, the smelters were going to be left holding the baby. They were intending to transfer the whole position to the smelters, no doubt using Chelsea as the broking intermediary, where the profit would stick. Nicely held in Liechtenstein, where the shareholders had to be Harris and Yamagazi. This was not, as he'd feared to begin with, just an exercise in front-running Kanagi for the sort of money they'd taken so far, it had the potential to be the biggest market scam of all. The only limiting factors on the profit were going to be regulatory interference or the exhaustion of the nearby bank financing lines. There was also the potential to wreck the copper market for years to come.

Harris was speaking. "And in your view, we should wait until we have gained some more respectability with the LME. I'm happy with that. Jamie, what do you say?"

Edwards cleared his mind. "Yeah. I think there are in fact two things. One is to get Hiro really in with the LME, because if the others sniff the chance of big business, they're going to go along with us. The other factor is the position Commet have now taken. And there again, I would like to get them into a position where they feel secure, before we start fighting them. So I agree, we just mark time for the moment, and come back with a bang later in September."

"Good," said Yamagazi, "So we agree on strategy. I have one more point. Jamie, we must also begin to consider the chart patterns. Sometimes it will be most helpful to us if we can push technical traders to act in a particular way. Their influence is becoming more important, no?"

"Yeah, definitely. A few years ago, nobody in the copper business took any notice of historic price charts. Now, with more investment-style money coming into the market, more and more traders are using them, so it makes sense to watch what's going on. Whether we could manipulate them - which is what you're saying - I rather doubt."

"Ah so. Maybe we think about it."

And the discussion finished.

So through the rest of that summer of 1989, the market was quiet. Summer holiday shutdowns amongst copper consumers reduced demand in the normal seasonal way, and that had the effect of letting the price drift lower. Commet took some fair profits on part of their short position, but the bulk of it remained open, as McKee became more and more convinced that the market was due a big downside break. Yamagazi kept things ticking over through Chelsea with the genuine pricing business he had to do for his physical book, but Edwards took only a few small proprietary positions. There were those in the market who told each other that Chelsea was a busted flush, that all the business in the first half of the year had been punting, and that they'd always known Jamie Edwards would screw up again. Phil Harris disappeared from the scene for the whole of August, claiming that it was the first holiday he'd had for years, and knowing that once they got the game going again in autumn, he was not going to be able to take another one for some time. While he was away, he spoke a couple of times with Waverley, and the outstanding questions of credit lines, Chinese customers and share options were all resolved to his satisfaction. As he lounged around the Cote d'Azur, he felt justified in congratulating himself on the edifice he had constructed.

Chapter Nine

September 1989

Jamie Edwards had spent most of August exchanging faxes with Yamagazi of a stream of drafts of the speech the latter was to make to the assembled luminaries of the LME. He was beginning to understand what Harris had meant when he had talked about the size of Yamagazi's ego. They seemed to be coming from two totally different directions. Yamagazi's attempts in principle were used to demonstrate what an honour it was for the LME that he and Kanagi Corporation should deign to use the LME for their business. Edwards, on the other hand, was trying to suggest that it was only the flexibility of the LME as a hedging market which enabled Kanagi to operate such a large and successful copper book. They had had endless discussions on the phone, and each time Edwards thought he had got across his point, that they were trying to get the audience on their side, not patronise them, Yamagazi came back with another unsatisfactory draft. Edwards knew he couldn't give up, because they needed the meeting to go their way. Letting Yamagazi loose as he wanted to be would torpedo the whole thing. In the end, Edwards knew he was going to have to insist, on the grounds that it should be written by a native speaker, for consumption by an exclusively British audience. His trump card was going to be not letting the Japanese see the final version until the same evening he had to make the speech. The only thing the exercise had going for it in Edwards' eyes was that it kept him occupied while they were mainly out of the market.

Harris walked into the office half way through a sunny morning in the first week of September. He was looking tanned, relaxed, every inch the successful businessman. "Morning, guys," he said as he went into the dealing room. "Have you missed me?"

The junior dealers and clerks grinned, and Edwards replied "Yeah, you can sort your bloody Japanese friend out. He's been driving me absolutely nuts for the last three weeks. But I'll get through to him."

"Come through into the other room and give me a run-down of what's been going on. I've got a few things to tell you that'll make you smile, as well."

They went through to Harris' office. "OK, first I'll give you the good news. I've been in touch with Waverley, and he's got approval from his credit guys for the line we wanted for the Chinese state agency." While he listened, Edwards was again struck by the American's intensity; most people had something to say about their holiday when they came back. Harris was straight into business, as if he'd never been away. "That's good for us, because they're another group Hiro has control over, like the Japanese smelters. Gives us somewhere else to spread the position. Now, I also managed to persuade him to get them to give us a line in our own right. That means we're not going to have to put up as much cash margin. It also gives them a vested interest in our well-being, when we start to owe them money. Even if everything goes a hundred percent to plan, at least it means we won't be stuck paying initial margins."

Edwards looked impressed. "How did you get him to agree to that? I mean, I guess the Chinese you can understand, it is after all a part of the government, but us? I'm not sure *I'd* give us an unsecured credit line, so what's he doing?"

"Jamie, I told you before I went away that I had an understanding with Waverley. He knows it makes sense to help us. You shouldn't underestimate my powers of persuasion." There was a slightly uncomfortable pause. Yet again, Edwards had that disturbing feeling that he was only privy to part of the story, and Harris saw no reason to discuss a private arrangement between Waverley and the shareholders of Chelsea with anyone else.

Harris broke the silence. "Anyway, what's with Hiro? What's he done to annoy you?"

"I'm having a lot of difficulty making him see sense over the speech he's going to have to make in ten days time. He seems to think it's a commercial for Kanagi and an opportunity to show how clever he is. I think it's his chance to flatter them into letting us do what we want. We're getting closer, but it's taking up much more time than it need."

"Yeah, I thought it would be like that. It's one of the reasons I went away and stayed out of contact. I told you he had an ego - you're seeing it first hand. Show me what you've got, and I guess I'll just have to tell him to accept it."

"OK, I'll get the papers in a sec. Meantime, I guess if you've been talking to Waverley, you're pretty much au fait with what's been going on on the market?"

Harris just stared at him. "Jamie, you were the one who told me about Waverley, you've known him for much longer than me. The guy doesn't bother his important head about such mundane things as prices. I could speak to him half a dozen times a day, and he wouldn't have a clue if copper had gone up, down or sideways." His voice was scornful. Then he continued, "No, we just sorted out those few things, and that was it. No discussion of the market. But I guess it's been pretty quiet, hasn't it? On the other hand, I hope you've made a fortune while I've been away."

Edwards grinned. "Naturally. I've made so much that the only reason I'm here today is to hand in my resignation before I go off to enjoy my new wealth. No, but seriously, it's been a typical dull summer. McKee's been going round banging the drum trying to get some support together for a bear raid, but I don't think he's had much luck so far. Rory told me at the end of last week that Mack's off on a trip round some of their producer friends, trying to get them round to his view. That'll keep him out of circulation for the next couple of weeks, which will probably suit us rather well. Incidentally, Hiro's anticipating getting here next weekend. Wants to play golf on Sunday, so I accepted on your behalf."

Harris groaned. "He's crap. It'll take five and a half hours to go round at his pace. When I was first cultivating him, at M and T, I used to force myself to play with him, and it's a nightmare. I've avoided it for the last three or four years, so thanks a lot, pal."

"Don't worry. I'm roped in to, and I thought we'd take one of the boys from BancSud, to make up the four. I haven't booked anywhere yet. I wanted to know what he was like first. Now I know, I'll fix somewhere not too difficult."

Harris shook his head. "Uh-uh. It has to be a prestige course, so he can go back and tell his buddies all about it - or all about the good shots, anyway, so that's normally a short conversation. Mind you, I haven't played much recently, so I shouldn't say too much. I had one round while I was away, and it was not a good score."

"Yeah? I'm playing quite well at the moment. Anyway, are you happy to have a BancSud guy there, or do you want it just confidential, between the three of us?"

Harris thought for a moment, then: "No, that's OK. The idea of this trip for him is to give him more exposure to market people, so let's do the whole thing. There's gonna be plenty of time for all the confidential discussions we need. Now, has anything happened here that I should know about?"

"No, not really. We've kept everything pretty tight, just let the market do what it wants. I told you what McKee's still saying, but apart from that, nobody's really showing any interest. We had a good little play on nickel for a couple of days. One of my pals at Union tipped us the wink that they had something big to do for a producer, and we got on the end of it. Made about seventy-five grand in two days, which isn't bad, considering I've actually never traded nickel before. It kept us busy for a bit."

Harris raised his eyebrows. "Fair enough. But we will be getting very busy again on the copper now, so if you've got anything open in any of the other metals, you better close it out now. You gotta be able to concentrate full time on what we're really here for. So do you think Commet have built up a big enough short yet?"

"Big enough for us to panic them?" Edwards asked. Harris nodded. "Well," Edwards continued, "I'm not sure that they've done enough yet. You know Mack and Rory are not stupid, and with the market quiet they've been ready to wait, rather than try and force it. I think the key to how much further they go will be how much support Mack can pick up now. Summer shutdowns are over, everybody's back from their holidays and raring to go, all they're looking for is a lead to the direction. Mack's going to give them that lead, and the timing could work out perfectly for us. My thinking is this. We don't offer any resistance to short selling for the rest of this month, not even regular pricing business. We can take all that in, so it really looks like we've run out of ammo. By the end of the month, we've squared the LME Board round to our way of thinking through Hiro, so we're then in the ideal position to really push the market. It also happens that Commet's financial year-end is September, so if we let them have their own way, they'll be reporting valuation profits on their short in this year's figures, and they'll fight like hell not to begin the new financial year with an immediate loss. We can really squeeze them, provided you're sure you're right when you say we've got more money than them." Harris nodded again. "OK, so we can really get them on the run, so that when they finally admit defeat and cover, the market will really explode, and then if we just keep on, we'll have it absolutely in the palm of our hand. The timing could not be better. By the end of the year, we could be in complete control of the market."

"Which gives us next year to exploit it, and take our money." Harris hesitated a moment, then went on, "That's for your ears only; Hiro thinks we can keep it up for years." Again Edwards had that uncomfortable feeling that they were all just pawns in Harris's game. And Harris's game was clearly designed to benefit Harris, first, last and possibly exclusively.

Mack McKee was in New York. Concorde and a limo from JFK had got him to the Pierre, just opposite Central Park, in time for a quick shower and freshen up before heading the few blocks down to Commet's office on Fifth Avenue. Stu Benson was waiting for him as he stepped out of the lift; McKee could never visit this office without pausing to look at the view down across Manhattan, with the tip of the island, the Statue of Liberty and the twin towers visible on a clear day in the distance. Today was not a clear day. Everything disappeared in a muggy haze before the eye had seen more than halfway downtown. Hopefully that wasn't an omen. They needed a clear sight of the target, for what he had in mind. Rory Davis had been slightly disingenuous when he had told Edwards that McKee was off on a trip visiting copper producers. That was the less significant part of his journey. The real purpose was a very few meetings with a small, secretive group of investors, whose presence was only just beginning to be appreciated by the mainstream players in the financial markets. These have come to be known as hedge-fund investors, in fact a complete misnomer. Far from being hedgers, which implies a balancing of the risk of a portfolio, their method of operation was to take massive unhedged positions, huge one-way bets on the direction of a financial asset, and then to try to bully the market in their favour. They had big money available to support their plays. Base metals had never been one of their instruments, but, ever-innovative, McKee believed he could see a potential advantage for himself.

Benson led him through to a meeting room, where he'd arranged sandwiches and beers for lunch. "While you've been living it up around the world with your mining company buddies, I've been working away down here getting these guys interested enough to talk. You know we've been in discussions with one or two hedge-funds for a year or so now, and in fact we've even done some small trades with one of them, just so they can see how the LME would work for them. Where we're at now is that there is a growing acceptance that base metals in general and the LME in particular are a class of assets acceptable to most funds for inclusion in their universe of potential investments." McKee idly speculated how few of the barrow-boys on the floor of the Exchange would have been able to put that sentence together. Benson continued. "That's a real important point. These guys are big speculators, but they'll only play where they believe the market is properly regulated and transparent." He looked hard at his boss. "Point one for you to bear in mind - they don't want to hear about manipulating markets, even if you believe that is going on. That's the biggest turn-off of all for them. *We* know you think Chelsea Metals is a big scam - but that's not the way you present it to them. We give it to them that prices have moved out of line with fundamentals because of a change in approach by some Japanese players. I've got all the charts and figures to demonstrate the price history, and that's what we concentrate on."

"When do we actually see these guys?"

"OK, you're not gonna love this, but it's the way it's got to be. Tomorrow morning we have a small seminar here, with representatives of five major funds. You've got to explain the LME to them, and you've then got to sell to them the idea that now is a good opportunity for an aggressive investment. You talk about fundamentals, then I'm gonna say something about the technical, chart picture. Then, over the following two days, we've got individual meetings with each of them, so we can talk about specifics with them."

McKee wasn't going to say it, but he was impressed. Fund managers are notoriously brusque and offhand with brokers, whom they generally regard as a barely tolerable necessity in the markets. Benson had done seriously well to get them to agree to give up so much time.

The American continued. "You know how these guys are. They are really putting themselves out this time, because they are intrigued by a new market for them. But for us, this is going to be a one-shot chance to get them involved. We're gonna go through our presentation real carefully this afternoon, so we get it absolutely right tomorrow." He grinned. "I want to make sure you're word perfect. You know these funds are something I've been working on for some time, and that I believe they are the future for the market. I don't want to screw it up by you going off half-cocked."

So they spent the afternoon rehearsing the pitch they were going to make the following morning. Benson knew he had to tone down his boss; the fund managers they would be meeting were largely US business school graduates, and McKee's normal piratical, swashbuckling approach was the wrong one. The audience was more accustomed to an analytical, quantitative way of looking at investment - something Benson was more comfortable with than McKee. McKee would be more effective in the subsequent private meetings, where he would be more able to describe the particular investment opportunity he saw right now, and hopefully use the power of his personality to convince the investors. They worked hard at getting their approach right, and some of McKee's detractors - those who didn't really know him - would have been surprised by the application he was prepared to show when he thought it was in his interest. Benson began to lose his doubts over the timing, swept on by McKee's enthusiasm and fundamental knowledge of the copper market. He had shared Davis's view, that Chelsea still had the whip hand; listening to McKee, he began to wonder. Finally, they were happy with what they had.

Later on that evening, McKee pleaded tiredness at the end of dinner, and returned to the Pierre around ten thirty. Frankly, Benson was happy to head off across the Hudson River to his home in New Jersey; he had been fearing McKee was going to insist on an evening's drinking and clubbing. The truth was, though, that McKee was actually nervous about the following day's presentation. He was comfortable with anybody in the industry, but he knew that he could be out of his depth with the fund managers in the morning. He was a big character in the closed world of LME trading, used to getting his way by having the loudest voice and a bullying manner. Now he was going to be a small fish in a very big pool. He would need to try to keep the discussion as narrowly focused on what he knew as possible, and leave the wider areas to Benson. Never mind, this was potentially the big money-earner for Commet this year, so he had to get it right. That meant going to bed early and waking up without a hangover. Not his normal practice on a business trip, but necessary this time.

Promptly at ten o'clock the following morning, the representatives of five of the biggest speculative investors in the United States were shown into the meeting room where McKee and Benson were waiting for them. They stood up to welcome them, and Benson made the introductions. Then he continued, "Gentlemen, I appreciate you are all very busy men and we are grateful that you have taken the time to come and see us this morning. I don't want to waste any time on frivolities, so what I am going to do is ask Mack first of all to give you an overview of the way the LME works, and an appreciation of the current fundamentals of the copper market in particular. Then I shall talk a little about the technical factors currently acting on the price. After that, we'll be at your disposition to try and answer any questions you may have. So, Mack, if you're ready, I'll hand over to you now."

McKee was good. He knew his subject, and the slight stiltedness that nerves caused to his delivery initially soon wore off as he relaxed into his talk. As he and Benson had agreed the previous day, he didn't talk about market manipulations, or about squeezing other people's positions. He talked instead about the origins of the LME in the last century, and about the method of price discovery of a commodity through an open outcry market. He lead them through the way the ability to hedge was central to the way copper was traded worldwide, and he outlined the impact that options had had on the futures market over the preceding ten years or so. As he approached the last part of his address, Benson could see in the faces of the audience that they were interested in what McKee was saying.

"So, gentlemen, before I hand over to Stu, I just want to make one last point. I have outlined the structure and the function of the LME market to you. However, I have to emphasise that I do not believe this market is one in which you should be constant investors. Much of the time, you will find the liquidity of the market, the amount that is available to trade without distorting the price, is too limited for the amounts you need to invest. What I would prefer to recommend is that you keep it in mind for the special situations which will suit you, when they occur. Stu is going to say a few words about the current technical picture, but I would just say that it is my belief that we are approaching a time when there is a lot of money available to take from the market. This is based on my reading of the real situation in the copper market. We are going to meet you all individually over the next couple of days, and I feel it would be more appropriate to examine this one-to-one, because it will help if you can be a little forthcoming about your investment strategies, which you may prefer not to do in front of your competitors. Stu, perhaps you would like to continue."

Benson struggled for a moment to conceal his surprise. He had been expecting McKee to continue as they had planned the day before, and outline his view of the current situation. However, he had to admit it was a master-stroke on the part of the big man, because now he had the fund managers hanging on. No longer was he trying to sell them something, now they believed he had something they wanted. And they had a day or so to ponder it. So Benson got to his feet, and made his technical presentation, knowing all the while that he'd been upstaged by his boss.

At the end of it, and after they'd seen the fund managers out of the office, as they walked back into the meeting room, McKee said "I'm sorry if that caught you a little off guard, but it suddenly seemed to me better to keep some ammunition back. They're all on the hook now, so when we hit them with a definite proposal tomorrow or the day after, they're going to be keen. Anyway, I kept off the subject of manipulation and double dealings, as you asked."

"Yeah, I was a bit surprised. But they seemed interested, so I guess we've achieved the first part of the exercise. Let's hope we can convert them into real business."

Chapter Ten

In the event, the next two days were not in fact as successful as they had hoped. McKee found it bizarre, but the hedge fund managers, whose business revolved around the taking of massive risk positions in currencies, securities, bonds and the like, were in fact very conservative people when it came to their range of possible investments. While they were interested in the LME, and keen to track it for a while to see how it performed, it was difficult to encourage them to take the plunge and trade. They traipsed from one meeting to the next, with McKee beginning to show signs of irritation at the same questions again and again, questions he thought he had covered at the original presentation. Benson had to use all the diplomacy he possessed to stop his boss just walking out and giving the whole thing up. They sat down to lunch on the second day after a particularly slow meeting with the biggest of all the funds. "I don't understand these guys, Stu," said McKee, "They're supposed to be big punters, but it's almost as if they're frightened of something new."

"In a sense they are, Mack. Don't forget that if we take a punt on something, what we're risking is our own company's money. If it goes wrong, sure, we have a bad year, but that's it. For these guys, they're playing with other people's money, and they have to make big returns. But, they can't afford to underperform their competitors, otherwise they lose their investors and they go out of business. So that creates a herd mentality. They daren't risk something new, unless the others are doing it too, in case it loses money. You know, we've been working at this in the New York office for a long time now, and eventually we are going to get there. But it's tough. I sometimes think that you in London believe I'm making excuses, when I say we're getting there, but still not yet. Eventually, all this will pay off, but it looks like it may not be in time for this market move."

McKee sighed. "Yes, you're probably right. It's just frustrating because this move is going to be a big money-maker, and I'd like the funds' cash on my side. OK, who have we got left this afternoon?"

"Leopard-Star Associates. Smallest of the ones we've been talking to, run by a guy called Jason Serck. He's quite a young guy, started a fund called Leopard down in Richmond, Virginia, about four years ago, then moved up to New York and merged it with Star Associates. That was one of the original hedge funds, but it got a bit left behind by some of the more aggressive competition coming out of the arbitrage business. Serck moved in and geed it up, the old partners of Star sold out most of their equity to him, so now he pretty much runs it on his own. I don't really know him. I've met him maybe three times. He specialises in currency markets, and he's beginning to get quite a following. Definitely one of the up-and-coming boys in the fund management world. He didn't come to our presentation, he sent his main sidekick instead - he's the one I mostly speak to. I don't want to get too excited, but I think it's a good sign he's taking the time to see us himself. Before the meeting two days ago, it was going to be the sidekick we were seeing today, but they called early this morning to say we would be seeing the man himself as well. That could be encouraging." He paused, then added, "Or maybe he's just bored and wants to wind us up. He's got a reputation for being a bit of a hard bastard."

McKee grinned. "Give me that anytime, rather than these wet, oh-so-polite boys we've been seeing. I can give as good as I get."

Leopard-Star's offices were like Gordon Gekko crossed with Ivan Boesky. A smart reception led to an overcrowded, overheated dealing room through which they walked to reach Jason Serck's own office. This was vast, with a full height window giving a panorama of Fifth Avenue leading up towards the Park. Serck himself sat behind a huge glass and chrome desk, with a bank of news-service monitors at his side. He didn't rise to greet them as he spoke down the phone that was clamped to his ear, but gestured them into the armchairs in front of his desk. McKee and Benson sat in silence as Serck finished up on the phone and turned to them.

"Gentlemen," he said, with the Southern drawl of his native Virginia, "it's a pleasure to meet you. Thank you for coming in to see Leopard-Star Associates. I understand you have been meeting with some of our larger and more renowned competitors. That makes me all the more appreciative that you come to see our little operation." He took the business cards they passed him. "OK, Mr. McKee, I've met Stu here once or twice, and I know he's been speaking from time to time with my assistant, who will be joining us just as soon as he's finished a couple of things, but perhaps you could just give me a brief summary of what you have in mind. I understand you've got a proposal you would like to put to us."

McKee started in on his spiel, beginning with his explanation of the LME and what it did. Serck let him continue for a couple of minutes, then interrupted. "Mr. McKee - Mack, if I may - I mean no disrespect, but I run this company in a most profession-al way. We have been researching the LME for a while. We know how it works, we know who uses it and we are intrigued by it. You don't need to explain all this to me. You said at the meeting two days ago, where my assistant was, that you believe that there is a particular money-making opportunity on that market right now. Please talk to me about that. I would like to see if it coincides with my view of the current situation."

McKee looked at him thoughtfully. He was weighing up how frank to be. Finally he decided. "OK," he said, "Let me tell you what I think is happening. Demand for copper should be increasing. This is what the indicators have been telling us for around eighteen months now, and yet hard economic statistics don't bear out what the forecasts have been saying. In practice, there's really been no significant movement in demand. In those circumstances, one would expect the LME price to be pretty static. But it hasn't been. OK, through the last two months, mid-summer, it hasn't really moved, but for the first half of the year we saw some big price increases, and some very aggressive buying. Now that buying is coming from one source only - Kanagi Corporation of Japan, and some of it's associates. The principal one of these is a small company, registered in Liechtenstein, by the name of Chelsea Metals. Chelsea is run - and probably owned - by an American, a guy I've known for a long time, by the name of Phil Harris. He is one of the smartest traders in the business, and he suddenly upped and left MacDonald and Thompson about a year ago to set up Chelsea from nowhere. One of his closest allies in the business is the head of copper trading at Kanagi; those two have been close for many years, and I'm sure that relationship is the key to what is happening right now. You are probably aware that my company's parent, in Luxembourg, is a significant player in the mining industry and, through that, is pretty much keyed in to what's happening in the physical copper market." Serck nodded. "They, and others of our contacts in that business, have also noted that Kanagi is becoming increasingly aggressive in their attempts to control the Far Eastern copper market; they're going for it in a big way, and effectively we believe they are buying market share through an agreement with the Japanese Smelter Pool. So the strategy they're following has two interlocking pieces: one, to push up the LME price, and two, to dominate the physical market in the Far East. They link together because the only way they can profit from their physical contracts is by ensuring the LME price keeps going up, and the only way to have the ammunition to push the LME up is by having the physical sales to support it. They are currently in the building phase of the operation, and that means they have to be watching both sides, and that leaves them vulnerable to an attack." McKee paused for a moment, as the door opened and Serck's assistant came in. Then he continued. "Look, I'm laying out the whole game to you here, including some things which may be confidential in one way or another. I'm going to have to trust you to keep it that way." He looked directly at Serck, the full force of his personality concentrated in his eyes.

Serck nodded again. "Yeah, I appreciate that. You have my word we will not do anything that will jeopardise your position, based on anything you tell us."

McKee kept silent for a moment longer, then he spoke again. "Very well. I have spent the last week or so visiting some of the major copper mining companies, and I have to admit we will not get any support from them. While they don't like the way Kanagi is muscling them out of the Far East, they do like the way the price is being pushed up. They accept the logic of my argument, but they're not about to rock the boat while prices are still headed upwards. They'll give away some market share to keep on the bandwagon, and not have their shareholders screaming at them for inadequate performance, for once. Equally, though, once the price starts falling, and they think the game's over, they will jump on it and make forward sales like there's no tomorrow. But someone else has got to start the ball rolling. Which brings us to you - and other hedge funds like you."

Serck grinned. "Not others like us, Mack. We all talk to each other, and I know your meetings yesterday and earlier today have not gone how you wanted. The other fund managers you saw all told you they were interested and that the LME was a market for them in the future, not yet. But I guess your problem is that you perceive the opportunity now, and yet your own company - successful though it is - does not have the funds to mount the operation you want single-handed. You want an ally, with money, right?" McKee nodded. "And you thought that as hedge funds have the reputation of being big punters, this would be the place to come. Maybe. First, a little more background. You're not the first LME broker to come and see us. Most of those with US parents or a strong presence here have been in. Frankly, they're not too impressive. They just talk vaguely about moving markets creating opportunities, and they rub their hands at the commission they think we're gonna pay them. Commet has two things going for it; first, Stu here has done a good job in trying to keep us informed, without ever talking down to us. Right, Ed?" to his assistant, who nodded and said "Yeah, we've always had a good respect for what he tells us. It could develop into a good relationship." Serck continued "Second, and more important, you have a reputation for being prepared to put your own money on the line. Your company trades in it's own markets. I will never work with partners who don't take the risk along with me, and that's what the other LME brokers haven't understood. I would also say that your analysis of the market is very much the same as ours - but I'm not convinced by your timing." He held up his hand as McKee started to interrupt. "Let me finish. We're not as isolated as people believe us to be. We don't just sit in front of screens and computers all day, trading on technicals. I've built this company mostly on foreign exchange and interest rate trading. Sure, we look at the technicals, as you can see." He gestured towards the bank of screens. "But I spend most of my time talking to the real players in the market - understanding fundamentals, getting a hold of the sentiment at any given time. My record proves I'm good at it. Since I've gotten interested in the LME market, I'm working in the same way. That's why we're happy to talk to Stu. But we also talk to a lot of miners, smelters and consumers of metals. All these guys you've just been visiting - I guess I talk to them all at least once every couple of weeks. They're happy to have that dialogue, because they'd rather be in the loop than outside it; we're not yet fully active in metals, but they've seen what we can do in currencies. We move markets, Mack. You better believe we have that power. And the LME is a smaller market than dollar/mark or dollar/sterling." Again McKee tried to interrupt, and again Serck waved him away.

Benson reflected that it was the first time he had ever seen anyone keep holding the floor when his boss wanted to say something; that would make a lot of people warm to Jason Serck. The latter carried on. "What the market tells me is that you're already short what you sold back in July, and that you'd really like someone to come in right now and help you out. That one I won't go for. There's still more upside in this market before we can crash it. You're right when you say the miners won't act yet - and I think that's a good reason why we should keep holding off. We need to sell just when they're in the mood to; we have to give them the last push - but we have to sell before them. Now, as far as I'm concerned, I don't give a damn about your present short position. If I were you, I'd just close it out and take what's there. You may still see a small profit. It's up to you. But for the future, I am prepared to work with you, as long as we both understand that we are working together. I'm not just giving orders for you to execute and rip something off the top. Your money has got to be at risk, just like mine, OK?" He paused, to let McKee reply this time.

"Yes, we can work on that basis," said McKee. "But I'm curious to know who told you what my current position was."

Serck shook his head. "Uh-uh," he said, "information sources are something I hold very dear, and I don't disclose them to anyone."

"I thought you wanted to work together."

"Yeah, but you weren't gonna tell me about your existing position, either. We may work together, but that doesn't mean we're not independent. I'll always tell you what you need to know, but not necessarily where it comes from. And I expect the same from you."

For a man like McKee, used to dominating partners and non-partners alike, that was a lot to swallow. He weighed it up, and on balance the money he was sure was there to be taken won. Anyway, what he said and how he behaved didn't always have to be the same; they never had been up to now. "OK," he said, "so all we have to resolve between us is a common view of the timing of this."

Serck nodded his head. "Yeah, I guess that's right. But look, I think they're still ramping this market up. If you just look at your own analysis, they need a backwardation to finance the physical side of their operation and they don't really have that in place yet. In order to create the back, they're gonna have to be using borrowed money as well as Kanagi's own funds, and they'll be most vulnerable when they're exposed to that debt, but haven't yet begun to generate the big profits it will bring. I believe that's the moment to attack them - when they've borrowed all they can, so there isn't the space to get more money to keep the game going, and yet the forward profits are still just that: forward, not available cash. That way, when they're trying to squeeze the copper market, we actually push them into a vice, and squeeze *them* for cash. We've got good friends in the banks, Mack. They may not always like what we do to markets, but they respect us as a professional counterparty. And that means we get information, as well. Like, the size of credit lines Yamagazi and Harris have been arranging, mainly with Union, but bits and pieces around and about as well. So I believe we're gonna be able to tell when they're close to the edge. You know they've got a meeting about now with some of the LME Board and Yamagazi?"

McKee smiled. "Yes. They studiously avoided inviting me. They seem to be drawing sides in all this, and we are perceived to be the opposition. And yet, on a day-to-day basis, they still trade quite a lot with us; all given up to BancSud, of course, so we don't get to see what the overall position is."

At the mention of BancSud, Serck's assistant snorted derisively. "BancSud," he said, "that is one sleazy outfit. They're nagging away at us all the time to put business their way - not particularly metals, but regular stuff. They're offering sweeteners, kickbacks, call it what you will. Their guys here in New York just can't understand we don't do all that stuff. As Jason said, we wanna deal with people who take the risk along with us, not somebody who wants to bribe us." He grinned at Benson, "But don't worry, Stu, we also are very happy to pay for good service."

Serck was frowning at the levity. McKee was beginning to pick up how single-minded and focused the American was. Probably not too many fun evenings coming up with him. He brought the conversation back to the subject. "So what are we saying, Jason? You're going to keep up with what's going on through the banking side, and we'll keep in touch with the LME; I think we both have pretty good sources in the physical copper market."

"Yeah, I think that's how I see it too. We just gotta keep the powder dry until it's time to fire the guns." He looked at his watch. "Mack, Stu, it's been a pleasure. I've got another meeting downtown shortly, so I'm gonna have to call it a day on this now. I think we understand each other, and I'm sure it's gonna be mutually real beneficial working together."

Five minutes later, McKee and Benson found themselves outside on the pavement. McKee's face cracked into a huge grin. "Looks like we've got our pot of money to use. Let's go celebrate. Oh, and give me your mobile. We'd better call Rory and tell him to close out the rest of our short." His face darkened for a moment. "I'd like to know who's been talking about our positions, so Serck could find out. I'll have his balls if it's somebody in house."

Back in London, the following morning, Davis worked hard to cover the short position without affecting the price too much, but he worked in vain. Once Edwards became aware that Commet was in as a buyer, then he started to push the market up as well, and by the last half hour of official trading that day all the dealers sitting in the Ring were screaming their bids in a market that was running away. Edwards' prediction of what would happen when Commet covered was amply borne out. It was also the end of the previous cosy relationship between Commet and Chelsea: without fully knowing why, they all appreciated that battle lines were being drawn, and they were on opposite sides. Davis recorded a loss in his book, not enormous, but enough to wipe out the profit from July on the opening of the short position. The first attempt to break Chelsea had failed, but McKee, on Concorde back to London, was very confident he had the ammunition to succeed next time.

Chapter Eleven

Phil Harris was on top of the world. It was a few days after Commet had taken their loss, and Edwards' day trading had locked in some more good profits for Chelsea. Additionally, the value of their forward open positions had increased sharply with the rising price. The beginnings of a backwardation meant that Yamagazi was starting to use his borrowings at the banks, but there was still plenty of space available. He and Edwards were in his Mercedes driving down from their office to the Savoy, where they were to host the dinner to introduce Yamagazi to the invited LME members. "The money's rolling in, Jamie. You and I are gonna earn some fancy bonuses at the end of the year."

"What about Hiro? What does he get out of it?" asked Edwards.

Harris just looked at him, as though he thought he was mad. "I told you before, it suits him if the value of Chelsea goes up. Being in Japan and still an employee of Kanagi, it wouldn't be appropriate for him to start taking money for the moment. He's in it for the long-term, right up to the end, before he sees the real rewards."

Edwards was curious. "And he trusts you for that?"

"Sure. Why wouldn't anyone trust me? You do."

"Yeah," said Edwards, and thought, sort of, I do. Maybe.

They arrived at the Savoy, and turned into the only road in the

UK where you drive on the right. Outside the main entrance, Harris handed over his car for parking to the doorman, and they walked through the revolving doors into the famous but somewhat worn reception area. Once inside, they followed the labyrinth of corridors, past the function rooms all named after Gilbert and Sullivan operas. Their meeting was to be held in the Gondoliers' Room, which was decorated with photographs of twentieth century British Prime Ministers. They were deliberately early; Edwards was surprised how nervous Harris seemed to be, as he consulted with the staff yet again about menu, timing and seating plan. In the end, the guest list was relatively short. Apart from themselves and Yamagazi, there was Ronald Waverley, of BancSud, the Chairman of the LME Board and the market's Chief Executive, and the heads of five of the other major brokerage companies, who were also members of the LME Board. They had finally also achieved a draft speech for Yamagazi on which they could all agree, one which balanced the ego of the Japanese with the need to flatter the audience. The guests drifted in, one at a time. Finally, when they were all there, drinks in hand, Harris spoke.

"Gentlemen, first of all I'd like to welcome you on behalf of Chelsea Metals, and our good friend and colleague Hiro Yamagazi, of the Kanagi Corporation. The purpose of this evening is to give you all an opportunity to meet Yamagazi-san, who is becoming a bigger and bigger user of the LME. I would also say he is doing a lot of work in promoting the cause of the LME in the Far East with many of his suppliers and customers. What we propose for this evening is that after we have had dinner, then Yamagazi-san will say a few words formally to you, mainly regarding his expectations of how the LME is able to help him with his physical copper business, and I guess also concerning his experience in using the Market in the context of the Far East. I don't want to pre-empt anything he may want to say, so let's just carry on informally. Thankyou."

They were all somewhat confused. They'd never before

experienced one of their number presenting a major client to them, and encouraging them to get to know him. But, they were all old friends with a common background to fall back on, so they pretty quickly fell into the normal, regular conversations they'd been having for years. Harris made very sure, though, that he introduced the Japanese to the Chairman and Chief Executive. Getting them on his side was essential. At dinner, he seated Yamagazi between the Chairman and Waverley; he still felt it was of significance to him to make sure Waverley was closely identified with Kanagi and Chelsea - the old approach of dragging together as many threads as possible to create as much confusion as possible. He himself was sitting between the Managing Director of Union Metals and the LME Chief Executive. They kept a light conversation going, but all the while he was watching Yamagazi from the corner of his eye; he was pleased to see the Japanese appeared comfortably at his ease, conversing animatedly with those on both sides of him.

Eventually, they reached the coffee and liqueurs and the waiters withdrew after serving them. Harris got to his feet. "Gentlemen," he began, "as I said earlier, I'm going to ask Yamagazi-san to say a few words to you about his business and the way the LME copper contract helps him to conduct it. Before doing that, though, I guess I should give some kind of indication as to why I'm involved and why Chelsea Metals are hosting this evening, which I guess is a slightly unusual one. OK, as most of you know, I left my former company just about a year ago, in order to set up Chelsea, to specialise in handling metal hedging on behalf of Far Eastern clients. At that time my very good friend, Jamie Edwards, whom you all know, joined me as well to handle the day to day trading activities of the company. The reason I made this move is that I had become more and more aware over the preceding couple of years that there was an increasing need, particularly in Japan, for a greater use of the LME to facilitate the growing physical copper business. I realise that all of you gentlemen have an exposure to that market, to a greater or lesser extent, but I hope you won't be offended if I say that I felt a specialist approach was needed, given the differences between that market and Europe and the US." He risked irritating people here, because many of them had perfectly well-run operations in Tokyo, without the song and dance of apparent "specialisation." But the bullshit was better than the alternative, which would have been to admit that Chelsea was founded to perpetrate a major scam. "I appreciate some of you may not fully agree with my approach, but I guess the market is big enough for different styles to exist happily together. At the same time, I am sure you are all aware that Kanagi Corporation, and it's Head of Copper Trading, Hiro Yamagazi, has been strengthening it's position as the dominant physical copper trading company pretty much throughout the whole region. Hiro and I started working together a few years ago, and we've been able to benefit mutually from that relationship, which has been founded on the physical copper trade. I realise it may seem bizarre for a broker to introduce his client like this to his competitors, but I believe it will be helpful for us all if we understand the market better. In crude terms, there's plenty for everybody. I guess you already all know we work closely with our friends at BancSud, represented this evening by their chairman, Ronald Waverley. So I'm looking at co-operation, not just out and out competition." He paused. "Anyway, that's probably enough, so let me hand over to Hiro." There was a brief lull, then a short, almost embarrassed applause as the Japanese got to his feet.

"Thank you. Mr. Chairman, gentlemen of the Board, Mr. Waverley, Phil, Jamie, first please allow me to thank you for myself and on behalf of my company, the Kanagi Corporation, for inviting me to come here to meet you and to have the opportunity to talk to you about how we Japanese see the London Metal Exchange. It is a great honour for me as just a humble copper trader to make the acquaintance of such important people as you in the non-ferrous world. I suppose there have not been many people from my country before who have had this opportunity, so I thank you also on behalf of my countrymen for this privilege."

And he continued with a not particularly brief history of the resurgence of the Japanese economy and the pre-eminence of the main Japanese trading houses in supplying not only Japan but also her Asian neighbours with both raw materials and products. Harris and Edwards had deliberately written the first part of the speech to be fairly soporific, leaving the more contentious matter for the latter part of it. Yamagazi was not a very good speaker, although to be fair it was in a foreign language, and the words were not in origin his; but he carried on, unconcerned. Harris watched the guests trying to keep an interested expression on their faces, some of them just to keep their eyes open. "So, that is the background of Japanese trading houses. I would like now to be a little more specific, regarding my own copper trading. As you know, the trend in Japan has been for consumers of industrial raw materials to demand so-called just-in-time supplies from their trading partners." Harris began to observe a bit more keenly the reaction of the others, because what Yamagazi was about to say may have been dressed up to sound plausible, but was in fact simply a specious justification of market manipulation. He and Edwards had worked hard to make this part sound good, and they needed the others to swallow it. Yamagazi was continuing, "This has meant that for us, as copper traders, there has been a growing need to hold stocks of material in locations within close shipping distance of Japan itself, or of the south-east Asian plants of the Japanese manufacturers. This has been difficult for traditional merchants, who are accustomed to sell metal as yet unshipped from South America, which does not arrive with the Japanese customer for some weeks. We, however, have found that by holding LME warrants, we are able to make immediate delivery to customers from the LME registered warehouses in Singapore. We are able to hold large quantities because of the very advantageous financing terms we can secure from the banks. These are obviously confidential commercial matters, but I trust you can understand the principle." There were nods around the table, although Harris could sense the thought going through a number of minds, that the financing terms must indeed be extremely favourable. "This does mean," Yamagazi ploughed on through his script, "that we will at times be holding very large amounts of the LME stock, as a necessary precaution against deliveries we will be called upon for at short notice. This may, we believe, from time to time result in a backwardation appearing in the market. It is clearly not our intention to provoke this, but we recognise it will happen. Clearly, in normal circumstances, we shall always be able to offer any excess stocks we are holding to alleviate the situation." That phrase, "in normal circumstances", was the important one, Harris reflected. In reality, their intention was never to accept that circumstances were normal, and therefore to continue to play with the backwardation as they liked. He looked carefully around the table, and was reassured to see that the heads were still nodding, and nobody seemed disturbed by what they had just heard. He was acutely aware how wise it had been to exclude McKee from this meeting, because Harris was clear that he would have seen through the obfuscation Yamagazi had given them. But he already knew McKee was the only one of the LME Board who thought seriously about what was happening. Yamagazi chuntered on, but Harris ignored most of the rest of it. He was happy that the difficult bit had been slipped across satisfactorily; his confidence was boosted further when Yamagazi gave a few minutes for questions. Almost without exception, it was clear that the questioners had only one thought in their minds, and that was how could they persuade this Japanese who had been presented on a plate to them to give them some commission business. The questions were all phrased in such a way as to demonstrate how superior each company was to its competitors. Harris caught Edwards' eye across the table and grinned at him. Things were still going their way; the greed of the brokers was making sure they didn't listen too carefully to the underlying meaning of what they were being told. As the Japanese finally sat down at the end of his presentation, the mood around the table was of relaxed well-being.

After an exchange of looks between the Chairman of the Board and the Chief Executive, the former got to his feet. "On behalf of the guests here" - he looked round the table to see there was no dissent to his speaking unilaterally on their behalf - "I would like to thank you, Phil, and Chelsea Metals for inviting us this evening. We have all learned a lot from Yamagazi-san about the way the LME is regarded in the Far East, and Japan in particular, and this is a dialogue which I am sure can only be beneficial to all of us. We are very aware, as members of the Board, that the LME began life as a market to bring together consumers in Europe with the metal production of the Americas. To that extent, our Market has in the past tended to reflect interests from both sides of the Atlantic. Business with the dynamic, newer economies of the Far East has come to us relatively recently - with the exception, of course, of strong historic links with the tin producers of south-east Asia. Yamagazi-san has demonstrated to us this evening how important it is for the continuing health of the LME that we increase our dialogue with major non-ferrous metal market participants in the Asia/Pacific region. I can assure him on your behalf that we intend to take full account of this, as the LME continues to pride itself on its international nature. Gentlemen, may I propose a toast of thanks to Chelsea and Kanagi for this evening, coupled with a desire to see links between us beginning to grow." They all stood and drank. As they sat down again, the Chairman was happy because he'd got a theme he could develop in his speech to the LME Dinner in a few weeks time, Harris was happy because he'd presented the whitewash he wanted, and Yamagazi was happy because Harris and Edwards were taking him on to Stringfellows club later.

Harris got a phone call early in the afternoon of the following day.

"Phil, hi, it's Mack," McKee boomed down the earpiece at him. "How was your meeting last night? Did all my friends behave themselves?"

"Yeah, hi, Mack. It was good. We covered a lot of ground in explaining the Far Eastern business to them. Jamie originally had suggested inviting you along, but you already know Yamagazi and Kanagi Corp pretty well, so I didn't really want to teach you to suck eggs. I was thinking of suggesting that you and I and Hiro get together before he heads back off to Japan next week. How does that sound to you?"

McKee thought or a moment. "OK, I'd like that. But I tell you what. Instead of the usual lunch or dinner, I've got a box at the races on Saturday. Why don't you both come with me? Give Yamagazi a chance to punt with his own money, instead of Kanagi's."

"I'd like that, and I'm sure Hiro would too. It'll also mean Jamie and I won't have to drag round a golf course with him again. We played last weekend, and he is seriously the worst golfer I know - even worse than you, at that last Commet golf day when we played together."

"Yeah, well you know I'm more into shooting than golf - that way, any Japanese who get in the way, you can just give 'em both barrels." He laughed at his own joke. "Anyway, I'll get my secretary to call later with details for Saturday. See you then." And Harris was left holding a dead phone. The big man was obviously piqued that his competitors had been somewhere he'd been excluded from, and this invitation to the races was his way of trumping them. Never mind. Harris was confident his hand was on the controls.

And out in the dealing room, it looked that way too. Edwards was sitting in front of his screens, watching the copper price gradually tick up, as the market followed through the buying Commet had been doing over the previous days. He was sitting on big profits, and seeing them get bigger with each upward move. The day-to-day technique at the moment was just to sit tight, and let others do the work. Chelsea would only get involved if the price started slipping, and needed support. The next two months, of October and November, would see them busier. That was the so-called "mating season", when copper producers and consumers got together to thrash out the details of their annual supply contracts for the next year. They knew Yamagazi was going to need to play the market during this period, so he could fix the contracts as he needed them to be; then it would be a question through the next year of pushing the market to levels which would maximise their benefits from those contracts. Edwards was becoming convinced that by the end of the next year, Kanagi was going to have a huge hole in its accounts - probably matched by a corresponding profit in Chelsea Metals. Whether the game could go on into the year after that would depend on Yamagazi still having sufficient borrowing power to disguise that hole. And that was the one number Harris kept very much to himself within Chelsea. It was ironic, mused Edwards, that in the old days, his addiction had given him a bad reputation, even though his trading had been serious and above board. Now, when the world and his wife was beating a path to his door to beg to trade with him, it was all a house of cards, a scam. Ah well, the power of perception over reality. Probably just as well to begin planning how he might get out by the end of next year, just in case it did all come to a head. One thing he was sure of was that Harris's interests were Phil Harris, first, last and every time. In the end, he was going to have to take care of himself.

Chapter Twelve

The chauffeur-driven Mercedes McKee had arranged to take Harris and Yamagazi to the races picked the American up from his house in Chelsea, and then continued to Brown's Hotel in Mayfair to collect Yamagazi. They had about an hour and a half's drive from there down the M4 motorway, heading westwards to the racetrack at Newbury. McKee had actually borrowed the box for the day from some friends of his at a merchant bank, who owned it. The other guests - according to the list McKee's secretary had faxed across - were mostly senior men from a number of major copper mining companies. Apart from McKee himself, Rory Davis was the only one from Commet scheduled to be there.

Newbury is one of the prestige courses in England, and McKee's banker friends had not cut the cost when choosing their box. As they looked through the window, the guests could see the winning post directly opposite them. The early autumn sun shone brightly on the green of the course, with the track itself stretching away in the distance. Colourful flags fluttered from their poles along the home straight, and aeroplanes and helicopters littered the infield. Although they were early, with lunch to come before the serious business of the day started, crowds were already beginning to pour onto the flat ground in front of the stands. As soon as Harris and Yamagazi had walked in, McKee had welcomed them, and with his arm round Yamagazi's shoulder, ushered them across to the bar for a glass of champagne.

"Yamagazi-san, my friend", he boomed, "let me offer you a glass of Krug. I know Phil hardly drinks, but I'm sure you'll enjoy a few glasses this afternoon." Hardly giving the Japanese the time to reply to his greeting, he continued, "you probably know some of these gentlemen - I guess you buy copper from some of them. Anyway, let me make the introductions." And he led him out onto the balcony, where the group of seven or eight others were drinking and chatting. Harris was left standing by the bar table, a glass of orange juice in his hand. This was going to be interesting. McKee would presumably try to leverage his undoubted close relations with the miners to demonstrate how strong Commet was - and therefore by extension, that Yamagazi should be working with them, not Chelsea. As Harris was smiling at that thought, Rory Davis wandered in from the balcony.

"Hi, Phil. What's amusing you?"

"Rory, good to see you. Nothing, really. Just smiling at watching your boss at work. He is a unique guy, and I mean that positively as well as negatively."

It was Davis' turn to smile. "To be honest, Phil, he's a pain in the arse at the moment. Since he got back from his last trip a week or so ago, he's become impossible. He won't leave anything alone - even more than normal. Hey, you know him and the company well enough to know how we work. Mostly it's short-term, reaction trading. Let's be honest, we bully the market, 'cos we're prepared to take more of an aggressive punt than most of the others. That's why it suited when we were doing more with you - Jamie thinks like I do. But since Mack's been back, we're in meetings all the time about long-term strategy. What's our view for the next twelve months, and how are our positions set up to accommodate that view. That kind of stuff. Shit, Phil, I don't know what's going to happen next year. I just buy the market to make it go up, and sell it to make it go down. More often than not, I get it right. That's why we make a lot of money. But I think we may be getting into water that's too deep for us now. We're not long-term players, we're punters. But Mack's got a real bee in his bonnet." He looked briefly concerned. "I didn't say any of this to you, OK?"

"Sure, Rory, I understand. It stays between you and me." But Harris's mind was racing. He knew McKee had been banging on the miners' doors, because it was common gossip in the business. He also knew there had been some meetings with investors in New York. But why should that have got into McKee's mind like Davis was describing? He needed to get Yamagazi alone, to give him the nod that something else was going on. He didn't let on to Davis that he was particularly interested, and changed the subject. "Have you got any tips for us today?"

"Not really. One of the clients told me yesterday that his uncle had a horse running here, I think in the four o'clock, which he says has a good chance." Davis paused and grinned. "Other than that, at horse races I'm the sort of guy who picks them by the names. I really know nothing about it. But Mack's keen and I'm sure he'll have a few tips. He's got quite a lot of friends in the game."

"OK," said Harris. "Let's go outside and join the others, and see what the word is." And they walked through the glass door, into the sunshine on the balcony.

The guests were an eclectic mix, mainly Australians and Canadians, with one or two Europeans from Commet's parent in Luxembourg. Harris recognised most of them, actually knew about half of them from doing business over the years. From the way Yamagazi was chatting and laughing with two of the Australians on the corner of the balcony, it was clear that he knew them well. Not surprising, because Australian mining companies sold a lot of copper concentrates to the Japanese smelters. McKee was standing with a man Harris recognised as the head of concentrates trading from Luxembourg and two Canadians from rival mining companies in Toronto. He beckoned Harris over. "Phil, come and meet some of our very good friends from the copper mining business. These are guys from the real world, not the paper-trading one we live in. We were just talking about the way the market's been behaving lately, and I'm having difficulty explaining why the price keeps going up. Perhaps you can help?" Harris smiled as he introduced himself to the others.

"I don't quite know why Mack thinks I may be able to explain things more than him. I'm just a small-time broker - he's the one at the top of the big trading company. And you guys produce the stuff - you must know more about it than I do."

The older of the two Canadians - a tall, grey-haired man, chief executive of a powerful group with mines in Chile as well as western Canada - took a long swig from his glass of champagne and said "Frankly, I don't really care too much why, I'm just grateful the price is still so strong. My shareholders are heading for a good return on their investment this year. But tell me, Phil, Mack has been recommending to us that we should sell into this rising market for some time now. We haven't gone along with that, and so far we've been proved right. But we're beginning to wonder how much longer this can go on. I know you've got a lot of contacts in the Far East; what's your thinking?"

Harris paused for a moment. This could be the right opportunity to move forward the next step, even though he hadn't really discussed it with Yamagazi. Still, in his mind, he was running the show, and the Japanese had to follow on. "Well," he began, "there may be something in what Mack says, but I think his strategy is going to cost you money - or at least stop you earning as much as you might do. Instead of selling, I would suggest that you look at the opportunity to buy put options." He held up his hands towards them, "I know. You and your boards don't like the word option. You don't like something you can't control. It creates a risk profile inappropriate for a mining company. I've heard all the arguments before, and in one sense I agree with you. I don't think it makes sense for you to sell options, because that is precisely creating an unknown for you to manage -

if you've sold the option, you have the exposure to whether somebody else exercises it on you or not. So you don't know where you are. But I'm suggesting you buy the options. That way, you decide whether or not to exercise them, so you are in control of your position."

O'Hagan, the Canadian who had spoken before, interrupted. "Yeah, sure, we understand that much about options. But if we buy them, then it costs us money, because we have to pay an option premium up front. So to me, your scheme costs me money. And my Board don't like paying out, except for solid assets in the ground and the kit to mine them out with. They don't want to pay for your paper." The others in the group were nodding their agreement, except for McKee, who was smirking at Harris, waiting for his reply.

"That's a fair point," answered Harris. "But you have to look at the relative price levels to see if it's worth it. And you have to consider the timing. You see, Mack's right. The price of copper isn't going to keep going up for ever. It can't. We all know that that can't happen in a rational world. So one day, it'll hit a peak, and then it will drop - maybe quickly, maybe slowly. But you can be sure that one day it'll go all the way back down to where it was a year and a half ago. And when that happens, then gentlemen, the question your shareholders are going to ask is, why didn't you use the LME to sell five years production forward, while the price was high? Why are we watching the value of our investment drop, every day as the copper price goes down? Why didn't the management protect us? D'you think they'll care that you had to pay for option protection then? Or will you be the one who keeps his job, because he spent a bit of money now to protect the long-term?"

McKee was confused. This shouldn't have been the speech Harris made. Why was he talking about a price drop? Was McKee missing something? Harris continued, "Anyway, you can buy some pretty cheap options, if you choose a low enough floor price. That way, you don't spend too much money, but you've got protection against a catastrophic drop in the price. I should think most Boards of directors would be ready to go for that. And for you guys, it gives you a better chance of keeping your jobs when the downturn comes." He could see from the thoughtful expressions on their faces that the two Canadians were pondering his words. Enough of a hint to stir their minds for now. Let them mull it over, then it will be time to come back to it again. Seeing Rory Davis wandering over to join them, he changed the subject. "Have you put any bets on yet, Rory? Or are you guys going to give us the inside track?" And the conversation drifted off onto the racing.

McKee was, as ever, a good host, and the party swung on through the afternoon, so it was not until they were in the car heading back to London that Harris had a chance to talk to Yamagazi alone. He needed to explain to the Japanese why they were going to become the biggest sellers of options in the business. The way the relationship was developing, he no longer felt the need to make the pretence that it was Yamagazi's idea. The time for that approach was over. Now, he just outlined the game, and trusted that he would sweep the Japanese along with him. As they settled back into their seats for the drive back up the M4 to London, he started speaking. "Hiro, you know with the way we are beginning to push the market into backwardation we will soon need to start drawing down on the Union Hong Kong credit line to pay some of the LME cash requirements the Kanagi accounts will begin to need."

Yamagazi nodded. "Yes, Phil. We have always known this point would arrive. That is why we arranged the facility in the first place. So that however much copper we have to pay for and hold, we will be able to finance it." He grinned. "Until there is no more money, of course, because it has appeared at Chelsea."

"Yeah, that's the point. There's a way of making the money last longer, and getting some extra leverage on the positions. That way, we can make the game last longer." He paused. "Kanagi are gonna start selling put options to the copper miners." As Yamagazi started to protest, he held up his hand. "Let me finish. I know you're gonna tell me that Kanagi, like every other Japanese company, doesn't sell options, that it's not a strategy you're familiar with and you don't want to do it. Well, I can go along with all of that, but it's gonna create a lot more money, and it won't increase our risk, as Chelsea, at all. Look, we know that at some point if the price keeps going up, the miners are going to start selling, because the price will be so far above their production cost that they won't be able to help themselves. They would be crazy not to take advantage of guaranteed profits by selling forward. That's a danger for us, as we've always known, because in the end they can swamp us with the volume they can sell, even though we control the Japanese smelters. OK, we've known this, and we've been looking at cashing out and running when they start. What I'm saying is that instead, we start selling them put options. That way, they can still have a floor price to protect themselves, but they'll also benefit from the price still going up. For us, we'll take the premium they pay us, and use it to pay some of the costs of maintaining the backwardation. And as long as we keep pushing the price higher, there's no danger in us selling as many puts as the miners want to buy. It lets us keep control for longer; sure, when the thing finally does collapse, it screws Kanagi up even more, but you and I are gonna be long gone by then."

Yamagazi was nodding thoughtfully. "Yes, it is interesting, and what you say makes sense. It may be difficult, though, to secure internal approval in my company. I will have to make a presentation to the Board to obtain their agreement. But it may be possible; they trust me totally with the copper trading, they know I am an expert." His face broke into a broad smile. "Yes. We can take this policy. But I must have some time to gain approval."

"Sure. Time is not a problem; I've still got some work to do to get the guys wound up to buy the options. We don't have credit lines for most of those companies, so what I intend is that we sell options via Commet. That'll make McKee think he's involved at the centre of the business, and stop him ferreting around too much otherwise. You're heading back to Japan the day after tomorrow, aren't you?"

Yamagazi nodded. "Yes, so I will begin discussing with my top management the new scheme. I think I can secure approval within two to three weeks, so maybe you will begin on your side as well."

"Yeah. I'll plant the seed in good old Mack's head again, and wind him up and let him go." He grinned. "It's been a good day. I won a couple of hundred on the races, you know. My luck keeps running."

Yamagazi looked seriously at him. "Do not joke about luck, Phil. We need it to remain with us for some time still."

Longer for you than for me, my friend, thought Harris. But he said nothing.

McKee was alone at the wheel of his BMW 740, heading north up the A34 and then west into Gloucestershire, where he was spending the Saturday night and Sunday with some friends. He was still puzzled by Harris' conversation with the miners - he still couldn't understand why he'd suggested prices could fall. He above all was the one who had such a huge vested interest in the market climbing. Unless McKee was wrong in his interpretation of what was happening. He dismissed that thought as soon as it came into his mind. He *knew* he was right. So where did that leave them? He pondered as he drove along, as always enjoying the power and speed of the big car. Well, if he couldn't get to the heart of it alone, maybe he'd confer with his colleagues.

Reaching for the carphone, he dialled Rory Davis' car number. Davis was heading back around the M25 towards his home in Westerham in Kent when the phone rang. He picked up the handset. "Rory," boomed McKee's voice "You on your way home? Listen, did you hear that stuff Harris was feeding the guys about how he can see the market coming down? I don't see why he's saying that. He needs to stop them from selling, not encourage them."

"Yeah, I was thinking about that. I think there's two possibilities. Either he's bluffing because we were there, and he'll spin them another story on Monday morning, or he realises that they're going to sell anyway, and he's trying to get some control over it by getting himself in with them."

"No, he's smarter than that. And how would that really give him any control, anyway? Wait a minute, though. Think about this. He's talking about them buying put options. Suppose his intention is to sell the puts himself. If he does that, and doesn't hedge any of the options, then he can take in the premium money, which gives him a nice positive cash flow, and at the same time, it will delay any selling, because the miners will have protected their downside, and so will be happy to let the price keep running up. And as long as it goes up, Harris has got no risk being short of put options."

"Because with a rising price, the options will never be exercised," Davis finished for him. "That's not a bad idea, Mack, although it's a pretty high-risk strategy, even for Harris."

"Yeah, but he's never been averse to risk, provided the reward is there. Look, I'm in late on Monday, but I'll be in time for the strategy meeting we're having at lunch time; I want you to get hold of Jamie first thing, and tell him you've got some customer interest in buying puts. See if he's keen to offer. Shit, there's a cop car up ahead. I'm going to have to hang up. See you Monday."

Davis put his own phone down, smiling. With the amount McKee had drunk during the afternoon, using a phone handset while driving wouldn't be the only thing the police wouldn't like about his boss if they stopped him. But he had to hand it to him. The picture he'd just painted sounded like a good shot at understanding what Harris was up to. But where did that leave Commet, and their putative short-selling plan with Jason Serck? Not for the first time, Davis wished they could just go back to their traditional, market-bullying trading methods. He was much happier as a tactician than trying to be a strategist. The problem was, deep down, he thought McKee was too. He prayed they weren't getting out of their depth, playing with people used to much bigger games. Ah well, time would tell. He still had quite a few miles to go, and he put his foot down and pulled out into the outside lane, revelling in the blaring exhaust note of the Porsche. Well, if it all worked out and they made all the money McKee was predicting, he'd buy himself the new Ferrari that had just been announced. As he'd said before, there had to be some compensations for working for Mack McKee.

Slowing down and passing the police car at a more sedate pace than he had been doing, McKee was more and more convinced that he had hit the target. If he was right, then how could Commet profit from it? It would make sense to talk it over with Serck on Monday, to see what ideas he may have. He drove on, musing. Through Oxford and onto the A40, he cleared his mind. It was time to concentrate on the rest of the weekend. The friends he was visiting were some old shooting acquaintances, with a substantial estate out beyond Burford. It was the close season for shooting at this time of year, but they'd promised him that amongst the other guests were a couple of aspiring models, and he had high expectations of their accommodating natures. The car surged forward with his enthusiasm. A good dinner, with plenty of classy wine, a few spins of the roulette wheel and shoes of chemin de fer, and he would be set up to take advantage of whatever the night had to offer. Not for the first time, he congratulated himself on staying single to enjoy the fruits of his money. He chuckled. Not like Rory Davis, back to semi-suburban respectability by now.

That Sunday, Harris, Edwards and Yamagazi met for lunch to discuss progress. They sat at the back of the restaurant, while Harris outlined the current position, and then began to run through what he saw as the next logical stage of their game, the selling of put options to mining companies. Yamagazi had had the chance to think it over overnight, but it came as something of a shock to Edwards.

"We've always looked to go for low risk, Phil. We're making good money at it, why change?"

"Jamie, listen to what I say. I'm not going to change the risk profile of Chelsea at all. I am increasing Kanagi's exposure." He grinned wolfishly at the other two. "And since when have we been concerned with that, as a problem to us?"

Yamagazi grinned back. "Only problem is for me, to keep explaining to my Board why we have such big LME position. But the bigger the position gets, the more they have to rely on me. No-one else in Kanagi can begin to understand where we are. Jamie, look, I am very happy with this latest idea of Phil's. I can sell all the puts the others want to buy, and still I keep pushing the price up. That way, they will never declare the options, so I just keep the premium; it's like another source of cash for paying to keep backwardation on LME. Gives us more room with bank lines." He nodded emphatically as he said it.

"Yeah, Hiro, I understand that, and I'm not questioning that it tightens our grip on the market. But what I am saying is that if we do this, then when we can't hold the market up any longer, the collapse will be quicker and much, much bloodier. We may destroy the entire copper market and bankrupt a lot of people - and that's without thinking about the effect on Kanagi. I just wonder if you've really thought about that."

"Jamie, said Harris, patiently, "there's an English saying I'm sure you're familiar with - you can't make an omelette without breaking eggs. We've always known that at some point it was gonna get tough for somebody. Don't tell me you're beginning to worry about other people's problems."

"No, it's not that. Sure, I've always had a pretty clear idea that somebody'll get hurt. It's just that this way, it's going to be a huge hurt. We're going to be very unpopular people. The regulators will be just the beginning. For heaven's sake, Phil, there are some pretty hard guys in this business - for the amount we may cost them, we maybe should be expecting some retribution."

Harris' eyes narrowed, and took on the hard, flat look Edwards had seen a couple of times before. "Jamie, you're gonna be a very, very rich man. That buys a lot of security. Don't get soft on me now." His eyes flicked for a moment towards Yamagazi and then back to Edwards. "Don't forget what I've said before, about where we get out. This isn't the time for this. I'm telling you the strategy we're gonna use, not talking about business ethics."

Edwards recognised the signs, and just nodded. "OK, you're the boss. How do you want to start?"

Chapter Thirteen

McKee walked into the office in the middle of the following Monday morning. It had not taken much persuasion by the two models for him to stay over in Gloucestershire for Sunday night as well as Saturday, and he was feeling particularly pleased with himself, after his exertions with the pair of them. As he walked in, he passed Rory Davis and the rest of the trading team on their way down to the floor of the LME.

"Mack, good of you to drop in," said Davis, grinning. "Guys, you carry on down, I'll see you later. I need to talk to Mack. You know my position for the first copper Ring. I'll call down to let you know if I'll be there for the second." And he followed McKee back into the trading room.

"Come into the side office, Rory," said the big man. "There's a few things we need to talk about." It was a feature of Commet that no-one, not even McKee himself, had a separate office. Private conversations happened in the two or three small conference rooms opening off the dealing room. McKee liked it that way, because he thought it gave him a better control of what was going on – if things were said in the public of the dealing room, he reckoned he could hear them, and if people went into the glass-walled side rooms, he could always see who was talking to whom, out of his earshot. The fact that others could also see who he had private conversations with could also be turned to his advantage, to keep them all guessing about what was going on.

As Davis closed the door behind them, McKee started speaking. "I've been thinking about what we were discussing on Saturday afternoon, about what Harris is up to. The more I turn it over in my mind, the more I'm sure we're on to something with this idea of him selling puts. We know the risk is high, but we also know that Harris is a risk-taker, and for sure selling them himself is going to be more attractive to him than letting somebody else get into the action."

"Yeah, I go along with that. And you realise the opportunity that creates for us?"

McKee just looked at him, so Davis went on, "When you sell something, what happens? The price goes down, right? More specifically, when you sell options, what happens?"

This time McKee interrupted: "Effectively, you sell volatility, so the price of the options goes down. So I guess what you're saying is that we shouldn't be in a rush to buy puts ourselves, because we'll get them cheaper if we wait."

Davis nodded emphatically. "Exactly right. If we let him bash the hell out of the volatility, then we'll be set to buy when the price has dropped."

McKee looked dubious. "That's all very well, but how are we going to know how far they're going to push the price down, and when they're going to stop? If we wait too long, we'll miss the chance completely."

"True. I guess the only thing we must be able to be sure of, is that eventually they'll decide the price of copper has to stop. They know it can't go up for ever, even, or especially, since they're the ones who are rigging it. One day, they are going to have to take the money and run. We have to aim to buy puts the day before they execute that decision." He grinned at his boss, and continued, "Piece of cake for a man of your talents."

"Yeah, but that's the problem, isn't it? How do we know when to act? How much do you still speak to Jamie?"

"On and off. They aren't as friendly as they used to be – I get the feeling Phil has told him and his boys to be a bit more circumspect with us. Let's face it, they know we're not in business to chase after the commission, and some of the other brokers just bend over for them, with the amount of business they see. But I did have a brief chat with Jamie about options this morning, as you suggested. He implied that they would be happy to trade with us, 'cos I guess not many of the others will have the liquidity he's looking for. I didn't push it particularly, because we needed to have this conversation first and I didn't want to preempt whatever we might decide."

"Mmmm," mused McKee. "I wonder if it's perhaps time for me to have another little dinner with my buddy Phil. Maybe I could get some kind of feel for what he's thinking. He's the most difficult man I know to read, but it might be worth a shot."

"Can't do any harm, I guess. Meantime, wouldn't it make sense to talk to Jason Serck about it? We are supposed to be working together, after all."

"Yes." McKee looked at his watch. "Still a bit early, though. Why don't we give him a shout at around two thirty? That time, he's probably been in for an hour or two, got rid of the immediate stuff he has to do, and should have time to talk." Not for the first time, Davis was struck by the deference his boss had for the fund manager. It wasn't normally Mack McKee's way to bother about anyone else's convenience if he wanted to talk to them. "OK," he said, "then I may as well go down to the floor. I'll see what the guys are doing, and be there for the Kerb. I'll be back in time to call him, anyway. See you later." And he got up and walked out of the room, leaving McKee.

Rory Davis and the floor team arrived back in the office around a quarter to two, the morning sessions having finished pretty dull. McKee was in his position at the end of the dealing desk, with the back office manager sitting next to him, talking over some improvements they were aiming to get done to the computer system to speed up the settlement process. Davis went over and sat down with the floor clerks to go through the business they had done during the morning, making sure that all positions agreed, and that customer trades were allocated to the correct accounts. At other broking houses, the chief trader wouldn't normally do such mundane tasks himself, but part of the success of Commet was based on the way they meticulously checked things, and the trader was not allowed to sign off the trading sheets until he was satisfied every deal was reconciled. It was one of the reasons why Davis and his Commet team had never been amongst the group of traders Jamie Edwards used to mix with in the pubs and wine bars all lunchtime. Another of the little things that set Commet apart from their competition. McKee, of course, was in the habit of going out to lunch most days.

Today, though, he stayed in, and around two thirty he and Davis went off into a side office and dialled up Jason Serck in New York.

"Jason, hi, it's Mack. I've got you on a speaker and Rory is here with me. We wanted to talk a little bit about the copper market."

"Yeah, hi Mack, Rory," came the electronic voice back out of the speaker in the middle of the table. "The market seems a little dull to me right now. We've been concentrating on currencies; got a few nice little plays on there, but nothing major. Just waiting for that copper to really start to work for us. So any words of wisdom you guys have got will be gratefully received."

"OK, well we spent last Saturday with Harris and a gang of copper miners: we took him and Yamagazi to the races with us. It was quite an interesting afternoon. Our friend Phil, the man in the world who most wants copper to go up, made a speech to a few of the miners telling them it won't last forever, and that they should buy put options to protect themselves. We all know that's true, but it's a bit of a surprise Harris talking in that vein."

"The thing is, Jason," Davis interrupted his boss, "we think we see the reason why it's going to help Harris' case if he can persuade some of the big boys to buy puts."

"OK, I'm ready to hear it."

McKee spoke again. "We think what he is aiming to do is to

grant the options himself, or actually get Kanagi to do it. That way, as long as they keep control of the market, and keep pushing the price up, the options won't be declared, and they'll get to keep all the premium. Incidentally also helping them with their funding cost."

"Kinda risky, though," interjected Serck. "I don't think that's a game I'd be too keen to play. It could go horribly wrong."

"It could," agreed McKee, "but my guess is that's a risk Harris is prepared to take, given that we think he's got Kanagi's money to play with. Yamagazi didn't bat an eyelid through all this. Mind you, it's always difficult to know what they're thinking."

"Alright, let's suppose for a moment that you're right. What does that do for us? Does it move us forward any? We've gotta concentrate on what we want, not what Harris and Yamagazi want."

Davis mused on the fact that more and more they were focussing on Phil Harris as the ringleader, not the Japanese. What was the relationship between the two?

"That's true," McKee said, in the direction of the speaker, "but we also have to consider how we use what *they* want to get *us* what *we* want. At the moment, they don't realise that there is anyone ranged against them with the financial clout to take them on. They can control the mining companies - we know from our own experience that that's not too difficult, 'cos they don't understand what you can do with the market. And they know that none of the traders or brokers has got the money to do it. Let's face it, even if they think Rory and I have an inkling of what they're trying to do, they know Commet alone doesn't have the capital to see them off. They think they're sitting pretty, and that's what we've got to keep in their minds. They've got to think they're still in control. They mustn't realise that you're in here with us, and that we've got the patience and the resources to take them on."

"Okay," said Serck. "I've been talking to a few people at some of the banks. No question, Kanagi have been drawing down loans in the last few weeks, more than normal. All collateralised against

LME copper warrants. It looks like things are beginning to move, and that ties in with what you just said - option premium is good for them, it helps the cash flow. We gotta find that weak point, where there's the maximum strain on that cash flow."

"We can't be too eager to buy puts from them," Davis broke in, "we need to see volatility pushed lower before we want to step in."

"Yeah, I agree," McKee put in. "For now, I think we get the customers to buy options, always less than Kanagi or Chelsea want to offer, so they're always left as sellers over, that'll force them to push the price down to sell the next tranche."

"I'm gonna be relying on you guys to pick the moment for us to come in ourselves. That's where you get to be responsible for my money - you better be good, because I don't like losing, especially when it's outside my control. Keep me informed." And the speaker box clicked as Serck hung up.

"Rory, I'll arrange to see Harris tomorrow evening. The way I'm aiming to play it is to suggest in general terms that we could be buyers of reasonable volumes of put options on behalf of our mining company clients, and especially for our own guys in Luxembourg. I won't directly ask him if he's going to be a seller, but I'll indicate that I'm looking for one; that way, if he wants to grab the hook, it's up to him. I'll encourage him to think the guys have been on to us since they heard his comments on Saturday. Flatter him a bit, and see where the hare runs."

Davis smiled and nodded. "Yeah, there's no need to mention the conversation I had with Jamie this morning. We don't want to make them think this is a big deal for us. They need to believe it's just a piece of customer business we have to do, not something we see as interesting from a proprietary point of view." He stood up. "I've got work to do. The rest of the business still goes on, even though this stuff may be important." In truth, Davis felt more comfortable with the regular business, as he feared they were getting more and more out of their depth. He walked back into the dealing room, leaving McKee sitting gazing out of the window, lost in thought. Somehow, the big man mused, he had to get a handle on Harris's timing of the game; if he could do that, he was sure that it would open the door to a big heap of money for Mack McKee, and possibly, though this was a secondary consideration, for Commet.

Chapter Fourteen

McKee and Harris met the following evening in Annabel's, the fashionable night-club on Berkeley Square. Once again, Harris watched McKee in action with the maitre d', getting them a quiet corner in one of the rooms away from the dance floor. Another tribute to the heavy spending of Commet's money. On the way in, McKee had greeted various of the glitterati as they pushed their way through the throng; even on a weekday evening, the club was heaving. Lots of money around to be spent.

"So, Phil, how's the world treating you? I didn't get a chance to speak to you much on Saturday. I hope you enjoyed it."

"Yeah, it was good fun. I won a bit, which always makes it good at the races. Hiro enjoyed himself. I think he was trying to get a bit of early guidance out of those Australians about their terms for next year. Their sales campaign in Japan will start in a couple of weeks."

McKee laughed. "Come on, Phil, this is me you're talking to. He's got so much control over the Japanese market at the moment that he's just going to tell the miners what they're getting. No point in them trying to force the issue with him."

"To an extent you're right. But even so, I guess he's got to be fair, because he still needs the physical tonnage, even if he can dictate the price terms. He's got himself into an interesting position." This last bit was said with the beginnings of a smile.

McKee looked at him for a moment, before speaking. "Ye-es. Interesting is a good word. Can it last? Or were you hinting at something on Saturday, when you were talking about the price not being able to just keep on going up?"

"C'mon, Mack, I was just making an observation. You know as well as I do that it's true. Nothing can carry on in one direction for ever." He grinned. "If it could, you and I wouldn't have jobs. Hiro's clearly in a nice position right now, but we can't expect it to last ad infinitum. That's one of the things you and I need to discuss."

McKee didn't say anything. However much he liked the sound of his own voice, he was smart enough to realise when keeping quiet might help him to learn what he really wanted to know.

Harris continued: "Mack, I've got to think about my next move. It's been a good 18 months or so, but I need to see the next turning. I think you and I can help each other here, providing we're both gonna be honest with each other." That an outsider would have given very long odds on the likelihood of these two even knowing what being honest with each other meant didn't seem to cross his mind. Everything has it's own perspective. The waiter approached discreetly and put the inevitable orange juice in front of Harris and a glass of champagne in front of McKee. As he stepped away, Harris continued: "Look, let's be frank. We both know we're the only two people in the broking business who really understand how to make money. Without you, Commet will just blunder along like all the others. And MacDonald and Thompson have already shown that without me, they're nothing. They're making less than half what they used to now. And though I love Jamie like a brother, without me there, Chelsea is nothing."

McKee held up his hand: "I think the relationship with Yamagazi counts for something."

"Yeah, right, and that relationship depends on me. I need to make enough money out of it to get out for ever, and to know I'll never have to worry about money again. Isn't that what you come into the office for?" McKee nodded. "So is that ever gonna happen at Commet? Or are you kidding yourself, because you're worth a couple of million? I'm talking about hundreds of millions, Mack, insulation from every hassle in the world." He paused. "I know how to get it, but I need to work with someone, and you're the best candidate."

"I thought you already worked with Jamie and Yamagazi." McKee spoke just to buy time. "Surely the three of you have a deal all worked out. Why do you need to involve anyone else?" He couldn't for the life of him see where this was heading, but it sounded promising. "But of course I'm interested in making that sort of money, everyone is."

"Yeah, but very few people have the opportunity. And not many are prepared to do what it takes to get there." Harris gestured towards the people standing around in the club as he spoke. "Half these guys inherited it - they don't know they're born. The other half are like you - they're rich in Joe Blow's terms, but they've still got to play the game. They still can't do what they want, when they want to - and that's what I want. And I'm very close." Harris paused. Going any further would tell McKee exactly what he was intending to do, what his escape was. He had no illusions about trusting the big man; but was he right in his assessment of how greedy he was? There was only one way to find out, and a very expensive way if he was wrong.

"Mack, you know that Chelsea and Kanagi are a scam. You've been trying to work it out since we started. I don't think you've got to grips with more than half of it, and you're way ahead of the rest of the market. What I guess you do understand completely is that it can't go on for ever - the house of cards has gotta come tumbling down. When that happens, I wanna be out - with my money." McKee sat silently, not wanting to interrupt what he was sure finally would lead him to the centre of the puzzle.

Harris continued: "You know we're getting very long of the market, and that the way we're pushing the price up means we've got a big unrealised profit, in both Chelsea's and Kanagi's accounts. The original deal that Yamagazi brought to me, right back at the outset, was that we would carry that on, and over a period of time, we would gradually transfer the longs - always leaving the profits in Chelsea - to the Japanese smelter accounts and the Chinese, who were the ones gullible enough to let Hiro trade on their behalf, or at the very least trade on his advice. Kanagi would obviously have been left with the long they are building up as well. Nice, straightforward deal, and we can keep it going as long as Kanagi can borrow money to finance the position. Technically, Chelsea's not doing anything illegal, although Yamagazi probably is. But that's *his* problem - I guess he intends to be out of Japan before the storm breaks, so he can pick up his share from Chelsea."

McKee interrupted: "So you and he are the owners of Chelsea?"

"Let's just say we are some of the shareholders." Harris saw no need to go into any more detail. "But that doesn't matter. What does is that I can see a different way out of this, a better one for me, and for you, if you want to play. I meant what I said to your buddies at the racing - copper can't go up for ever. It can go up as long as we keep pushing it, and as long as we've got more money than the people who want it to go down, including you." McKee smiled to himself - Harris had no idea that Commet had access to Leopard-Star's coffers. It was a moot point right now as to who had the deepest pockets. No need to mention that, though. Harris continued, "OK, look, what's gonna be the best position to have once the storm breaks?"

McKee looked hard at him. "Short, obviously," he said.

"Short, right," agreed Harris. "But for me personally, short somewhere completely outside the Chelsea/Kanagi circle. Somewhere where nobody will even look for traces of good old Phil Harris - or at least not look immediately. Chelsea can't be short. That would ring too many bells for the regulators and the LME. Chelsea has to be square and effectively out of the equation, with it's profits taken back home to Liechtenstein. No, there needs to be another vehicle that's short, not in any way associated with me or trading through my brokers."

McKee smiled. "Let me guess, Phil. You've got a new client in mind for Commet. One that's going to start building up a short position in copper."

"Kind of. But I was thinking of one that might be a bit more to you than just a client. Look, let's not play games, Mack. You won't open an account for me - even though it's clearly not in my name - unless there's something pretty good in it for you, right?" McKee nodded. "Well, I've got a little company, registered in Panama, that just might want to start buying copper puts. And I've got a client of Chelsea, Kanagi Corporation, that is ready to start selling puts like it's going out of fashion. But I can't just put them together, I've got to put the trades through someone else, so there's no connection."

"And you want Commet to be that someone else," McKee finished for him.

"Yup, in return for which you get to own a third of the Panamanian company." He paused, and looked hard at McKee. "That means you get to make a third of the profit when the market goes, as we both know it's going to. But as long as nobody knows you have any connection with the put buyer, you're clean. You have one client who wants to buy puts, and you know that Chelsea - on behalf of Kanagi - will be a seller of those same puts. And in the end, you have no contract with them, because it goes to BancSud through the Clearing House."

McKee stared at him. "You're a devious bastard, aren't you," he said, almost admiringly. "But you would know I had a connection with the buyer, so that's my risk."

"Yeah, but you also know enough to tie me into it. Our knowledge of each other's involvement is our protection from each other."

McKee considered this, then called the waiter over and ordered another bottle of Krug. "OK," he said. "It looks like we're partners in - what's it called?"

"Kestrel Aviation and Trading, of Panama City, Panama. Sounds a million miles away from a scam on the London copper market, doesn't it?"

McKee signed to the waiter to pour them both champagne this time. He raised his glass "To Kestrel Aviation and Trading - may it have a short life, but a happy one."

Harris also raised his glass; his face gave away nothing, but inside he was exultant. He had all the parts in place; now he was ready to play the game through to the end.

"You realise how bloody this is going to be, don't you?" said McKee. "If you keep pushing the market up until Kanagi runs out of money - or the ability to borrow any more money - it's going to crash so far that it will take years to recover. It risks making the tin crisis look like a storm in a teacup" (he was referring to the collapse of the tin market in 1985, when a group of governments had walked away from the liabilities of their creation, the International Tin Council, and left an industry in ruins). "The copper market won't recover easily, and that will mean mine shutdowns, lost jobs, a kick in the teeth of the third world countries that depend on copper exports - you know what'll happen."

"Two things, Mack. One, I'm just using the market to get what I want. Just like everybody else who's involved. The only difference between me and all the others trading copper is that I'm better at seeing opportunities. Hiro brought me the first idea of this - he brought it to me as a way, frankly, of defrauding his employers and their allies of a lot of money. And all those guys running the LME: do you see any concern there for the poor third world miners? If they'd thought of it, don't you think they'd be doing the same as me?" McKee's silence was an eloquent testimony to his agreement. Harris went on, "Second point. All those copper miners at Newbury the other day. I told them to be careful, I told them it couldn't go on for ever. They know how to protect themselves. But will any of them do it? No they won't, and you know why. They're too greedy even to use some of what they know is unreasonable profit to protect the future. Just like you and me, they want it all now, and let the future go screw. We're not the world's moral policemen, Mack. The opportunity's there. We just have to decide whether to take it or not." He grinned. "You're not getting cold feet already, are you?"

McKee grinned back. "No, I'm just getting to grips with the scale of the whole deal. I knew Chelsea wasn't kosher, but I really didn't grasp how far you were going to go." A thought struck him. "How much does Jamie know about the real picture?"

Harris looked hard at him for a moment. "Frankly, Mack, that doesn't concern you. Jamie knows as much as he needs to know, and he will learn - when it's relevant - anything else he should know."

So he's in the dark, thought McKee. That could be interesting. "Is he going to run the option sales programme for Kanagi?" Because I'm going to buy for Leopard-Star, as well as Kestrel. McKee already saw the extra opportunity opening up.

"Yeah," said Harris, "I'll give him the overall instruction, but day-to-day, he'll be looking after it. In conjunction with Hiro, of course," he added as an afterthought, "Obviously, he won't sell exclusively to you - that again might look suspicious, so we'll have to sell to the market as a whole." And they chatted on, until around 1:30, when they were joined by some other friends of McKee. Harris stuck around for another half hour or so, and then made his excuses and left. McKee stayed until the club finally closed, then left, taking the extremely drunken wife of a member of the House of Lords with him.

Chapter Fifteen

A couple of weeks later, there was a meeting held by the Chairman and Chief Executive of the LME and two representatives from the European copper consuming industry, one from a semi-fabricator in northern Germany, and one from a French tube manufacturer. These two were both in their middle fifties, and had seen unpredictable and unexplainable gyrations in the LME copper price countless times during their careers. This time, however, they were complaining officially to the Market's administrators that the sustained high price, and more particularly, the continuing backwardation, was beginning to cause serious damage to their industrial businesses. They pointed out that the spot price of copper, which was what they had to pay their suppliers, was continually the highest price, and that they felt they were subsidising a market manipulation which the LME had a duty to investigate, and, if they were proved to be correct, to control. The LME representatives defended their position of non-intervention by maintaining that it was a free market, and that they could see no signs of irregular activity.

The meeting was acrimonious, and the Europeans left with a strong feeling of dissatisfaction. However, they would have been happier had they heard the conversation that continued after their departure. Almost unknowingly, they had used the phrase that set off alarm bells for the LME men. "Market Manipulation", and the responsibility of all Exchanges to police it, was the hot potato that the UK's new City regulations had thrown at the markets to hold. The LME was already under scrutiny by the regulators, who did not like the potential for abuse created by the unique ability of LME brokers to transact business on behalf of customers, while simultaneously trading their own proprietary books. The so-called "Big Bang" of 1986 had outlawed this in the stock market, but the LME, being so much smaller and lower profile, had slipped under the net. A scandal of manipulation would destroy the cosy world, and, more importantly to the Chairman, would scar the memory of his time at the helm - and he was a man desperate for history to think well of him.

So, up in that panelled boardroom above Fenchurch Street, the two of them debated what to do. They knew Chelsea was behind what was going on, although they didn't understand it. But Chelsea wasn't a member of the Market, and was therefore not directly susceptible to their discipline. So they decided to do the next best thing, and invite Ronald Waverley, as Chairman of Chelsea's clearing broker, in to have a chat about the state of the market.

The call to BancSud didn't particularly concern Waverley at first. He didn't really understand Harris's business, but equally he didn't feel he needed to; his only concern was that BancSud themselves were doing nothing illegal. What his client did - in the regulatory environment of the time - was not his responsibility. Anyway, that's what his compliance director told him, when consulted. But a little worm started stirring in his brain, the more he thought about it. That ownership option that Harris had granted him would not please the regulators. He would have to be sure to avoid any knowledge of that becoming public. At least he could control that, since nobody else in the company was aware of it, as he had kept the relevant correspondence with Harris strictly confidential. And he was sure that Harris wouldn't have seen any need to publicise the arrangement. To be on the safe side, though, he elected to see the LME alone, rather than taking his compliance officer with him, which would have been more usual, in the circumstances.

So the next day at ten o'clock, he was a little bit tense as he was shown into the LME Boardroom, and asked to wait a moment while the secretary told her bosses he had arrived. And then they came in, smooth, smart, every inch the City establishment. The Chairman, Tom Lubbock, came from a successful family of midlands scrap traders, who, in the go-go post-war market with it's huge demand for metal for the reconstruction of Europe had expanded to become LME ring-dealers, a business which under his guidance in the sixties and seventies had outstripped its humble scrap dealing origins. Now his concern was in being seen as a true leader of the LME, not the compromise candidate the Board had elected him as a couple of years earlier. He wanted to be remembered as the man who had turned the quaint old LME into a fully-fledged international financial market - with all the implications that had for being at the forefront of consumer-friendly regulation. His partner in this project was the Chief Executive, Donald Thresher, who was an accountant by profession, and who had been appointed to his role shortly after the Chairman took over. Their joint fear was a public scandal, exposing the cosiness of the LME world before they had had a chance to push through the reforms they wanted to modernise the Market. All three of them in that room that morning had a vested interest in ensuring that the market was seen to be clean.

"Ronald, good morning," began the Chairman. "We see a lot of activity in the copper market these days, and BancSud seem to be one of the main participants. Obviously, we're very pleased to see good volumes and we're pleased that your business is expanding. I wonder if you could give us a brief overview of what sort of business you're doing, and what you perceive to be its origin."

"Certainly. As you know, we are a commodity broker, not historically a metal trading house. We've been building up a portfolio of metal clients in the time we've been members, but our clearing operations, which are more akin to our traditional business, are of much more relevance to us. So you will see in the Clearing House daily business reports that we, on behalf of our clients, hold substantial positions, but by far the greater part of these positions are cleared to us by our clients' executing brokers, rather than actually traded on the floor by our dealers. So although we hold quite a big position at the Clearing House, in general it's not made up of deals we have traded. In fact, we try to keep the trading to quite small limits, because we prefer not to have the exposure; we work as a broker, but on the LME more and more business seems to be done on a market-making basis, and we don't really like that risk. We find we can make our money without too much risk exposure." That was more a reflection of making a virtue of necessity. It was the public face BancSud liked to present; the truth was that he would have liked his dealers to be more active traders, but they had not proved to be very good at it, and right now the income from Chelsea was pretty much all they had to rely on in their metals business. No need to go into all that now, though.

"Ye-es," said the Chairman. "What we really are slightly concerned about is the very large long position built up by two or three of your clients. In particular, Kanagi Corporation and Chelsea Metals both appear to be holding very large longs, both in the cash and forward dates. We know that they are two separate entities, but we are not naive, Ronald, and we know that those two companies have extremely close links when it comes to LME trading. Add to that the fact that we see other Japanese interests also holding long positions through BancSud, and you can perhaps see where our concern lies."

"I don't really see any cause for concern. It is true Chelsea and Kanagi work together in some operations, but as you rightly say, they are quite separate companies. I recall you were both at a meeting hosted by Chelsea a short while ago, where the Kanagi copper trader, Yamagazi-san, indicated that he envisaged at times holding large LME stock and long positions in order to facilitate physical copper supply to his customers. I have no reason to suppose that the current situation is anything other than a manifestation of that."

"Have you discussed this with either Kanagi or Chelsea?" This was Thresher.

"Not specifically, recently, no. As I said before, our interest in this business is as the clearing broker, so as long as our clients remain within their credit limits, or deposit sufficient margin to cover their exposures, we do not really get too involved in their trading strategies."

"You realise that if they were working together it could be construed as collusion to distort the market, don't you?"

"Yes, but the onus cannot be on BancSud, as purely the clearing broker, to police the trading. If you think there is something untoward going on, then surely you should be speaking to Phil Harris and Hiro Yamagazi, not me."

The Chairman spoke again: "Ronald, we as the executive of the LME are in an invidious position. We do not want to disturb the legitimate business of our member firms - indeed, we want to encourage it, and we want to create an environment where that business continues to grow. However, we have another function as well, imposed upon us by the regulatory authorities. We have an obligation to preserve an orderly market. Now, that phrase is clearly open to interpretation, and different people will take a different view of its meaning. I must tell you - in confidence - that yesterday morning we had a visit from two of the largest copper consumers in Europe, and they protested very vigourously that the current copper market was not orderly, and that they were being disadvantaged by the operations of an unnamed party or parties. From our point of view, that looks like a direct pointer in the direction of your clients. Those clients are not members of our Exchange, and therefore in order to establish what they may or may not be doing, we feel it reasonable to ask you, their clearing broker and provider of credit, since, in that function, you must have done your own due diligence on their operations before granting them the facilities you have given them. All we want, therefore, is for you to share with us the results of that due diligence, which, we trust, will demonstrate exactly what Yamagazi said before, namely, that he needs to trade in this particular way in order to protect his physical trading position."

"Which is, after all," added the Chief Executive, "the traditional function of LME hedging."

Lubbock nodded thanks to his colleague, "Exactly. So our stance, prima facie, is that we assume users of the Exchange will be behaving correctly. We expect that you will be able to confirm to us that that is the case. Then we can be sure that we have done all the regulators could expect of us." Did he have to spell out to Waverley that they all wanted the same result?

Waverley could see what they wanted, but it did create a problem for him, since any examination of the facilities granted to Chelsea would demonstrate that the credit line given bore no real relationship to the background and financial information BancSud had. As Harris had intended, tying BancSud into Chelsea's fortunes meant that Waverley had to protect Chelsea.

"Well, I understand your approach, but frankly the relationship we have with our clients is a confidential one, and I don't see how I could disclose any information to you without discussing it with them first of all. Obviously we have our criteria for dealing with people, and these are a matter for our own Board and credit committee."

The Chairman sighed. "Ronald, we know that such information is confidential. What we want, however, is to avoid a major investigation of something which really shouldn't warrant it. All we need to be able to demonstrate is that the Exchange and its members are working in such a way as to avoid the possibility of manipulation. To do that, we need your co-operation."

Waverley pondered. He could not afford to have the details of the relationship with Chelsea explored; however, he might be able to buy some time which could give him the chance to blur the water a bit, and maybe regularise things. "Well, I see what you're looking for, but I think you will understand that I have to refer to my co-directors before I can give you any details of confidential matters. Perhaps we could re-convene this meeting when I have had a chance to discuss it with them. And perhaps you could be more precise in what you want to see," he added as an after-thought.

The Chief Executive nodded imperceptibly to his colleague. "OK," said the Chairman, "we can agree that you need to confer. However, by tomorrow morning at this time, we need to see your full client files on Chelsea and Kanagi Corp, and we need to see your credit policy document. Obviously, we shall expect the former to reflect the latter."

Waverley agreed to the schedule, and left. As soon as he was out of the door, the Chief Executive said: "There's something not quite right there. We didn't ask for anything he should find difficult, and yet he was clearly uncomfortable with the whole idea. We really need to keep this within the Exchange, you know. We don't want the regulators trampling all over us, telling us we don't know how to regulate ourselves."

"I know. If there's a problem at BancSud, we need to discipline them quickly and hard. Let the world see we come down tough on our own members, if they're misbehaving. But I don't get it. What could his problem possibly be?"

Waverley was straight on the telephone to Harris when he got back to his office. He outlined the course of the discussion, which didn't seem to ruffle the American's calm. "That's very interesting, Ronald, but I don't see what it's got to do with me. It's your rela-tionship with the exchange - Chelsea aren't members. Whatever you see the need to discuss with them about our relationship is up to you. I've got nothing to hide."

"But what about the option on Chelsea shares we have? How can I explain that? The regulators won't accept that we could have an interest like that in what is supposed to be an arms-length client."

"I guess they won't. But it's not my problem. Tell them what you like. We've done nothing wrong - but if I'm asked the question, I can't deny the existence of that agreement. I have to be honest."

"So if you're not asked the question, you won't say anything?"

"Yeah, that's OK. If I'm not asked, I have no need to volunteer any information. But really, Ronald, I'm totally indifferent to the whole thing. I mean it - relations between you and the Exchange and your regulators are nothing to do with me." And he hung up.

That left Waverley in a quandary. His choice was to tell everything or nothing. If he exposed detail of the relationship, it would all come out, because they would have enough to ask Harris the right questions to get the detail. But if he refused to co-operate, they wouldn't know what to ask Chelsea. But could he get away with pleading client confidentiality, and simply handing over a general document on credit and compliance procedures at BancSud, claiming that the Chelsea relationship fitted with the bank's internal rules? He called in his compliance officer, and asked him to bring a copy of the internal rules for review.

At ten o'clock the next morning, going in to his scheduled meeting with Lubbock and Thresher, Waverley was apprehensive. He had poured over BancSud's internal policies and the LME Rules and Regulations long into the evening with his compliance officer, and was of the opinion that his approach was defensible, even if it was more a question of complying with the letter not the spirit of the rules. Nevertheless, he had his concerns that the Chairman would not agree.

Half an hour later, his worries had proved to be justified. Lubbock and Thresher were adamant - they demanded to see the full details of the relationship between Chelsea and BancSud. Waverley was equally firm, that they were welcome to see BancSud's internal process documents covering all customer relationships, and he would give them his verbal assurance - as Chairman of the company - that Chelsea complied with it. What he was not prepared to acknowledge that they had a right to see, however, were the actual Chelsea files. The stand-off was just the same as the previous day. Lubbock and Thresher asked Waverley to wait, while they considered their position. They left the Boardroom, and stepped next door into Lubbock's office.

"I'm not sure what we can do, if he simply refuses. It is a grey area, we don't *really* have the right to see his confidential files. But on the other hand, we can't be seen to let a member just flout a request from the executive of the Exchange. Frankly, while we're just between ourselves, we need a threat that will bring him back into line. Any ideas?"

"Well, a financial threat is the best one. Losing money is what will hurt him the most. Can we fine him?"

Lubbock considered. "We probably can't actually *fine* him, but we could probably dress it up and insist that if he doesn't co-operate, then the Exchange may run into the cost of an investigation, and we feel that we should be able to recoup those costs - or part of them at any rate - from BancSud, given their reluctance to co-operate with us. How does that sound?"

"Frankly, it sounds to me like a real lash-up," said Thresher, grinning. "But maybe we can get it past. I guess he's making a hell of a lot out of that business, on the clearing side. In fact, from what I gather from the others, without that business, BancSud might as well give up metals business. And let's be honest, sleazy little man that Waverley is, we don't want to lose them as a member - the outside world only sees the prestige of the name on our exchange, not the reality of the business." He sighed. " Why is it that our members are such a bunch of greedy, unprincipled bastards?" He realised what he had said. "Present company excepted, of course."

Lubbock smiled. "It's the nature of the business. It's been so loosely regulated for so long, they've forgotten what integrity is. And that includes my family's interests. Look, we've talked about this before. We can straighten it out, but a public dispute with Waverley now will set us back a long way. Let me have a private word with him, and see if I can't persuade him of the right course to follow."

And so he went back into the Boardroom. "Ronald, we both know, strictly, I can't force you to tell me what I want. However, cutting all the crap, we also know that the only reason you wouldn't tell me is because you have something to hide." He waved aside Waverley's beginnings of a protest. "Don't give me any rubbish about principles. You've got something you don't want to show me that makes you money. Fine. Right now, I don't need a public spat with a member, so we both want to keep the dispute quiet. However, I'm going to have to respond to the criticisms that the market is being rigged at the moment; so I'm going to have to announce that the Executive of the Exchange are undertaking a review of the copper market. As the holder of the biggest long positions, you're going to be central to that. You are going to pay the exchange a contribution to its costs in making that investigation. That's the price, Ronald, for not pushing what our discussion is really about. The position is non-negotiable, before you even think of arguing. The amount will be one hundred thousand pounds." Now, nothing is actually non-negotiable, and by the time Waverley left the exchange and Lubbock went back into his office to give Thresher the detail, they had agreed that BancSud would pay the Exchange an amount of £75,000, as "a contribution to it's costs in investigating the unexplained price movements in the copper market." No suggestion given as to why BancSud should have co-operated in this way. Insiders just smiled and shrugged their shoulders, when it was announced.

Back at his office, Waverley wasted no time in picking up the telephone to Phil Harris. "It helps us both, Phil, despite what you said before. Neither of us want to be looked at too closely. So I don't really think BancSud should be the only one to pay."

Frankly, Harris couldn't care less about £75,000; he was playing for the big time. "Yeah, you've got a point. Look, I'll make sure Jamie gives your boys something that'll pay you back, OK? I can't be seen to be contributing openly. I'm sorry, Ronald, but I'm a bit tied up in something here right now. Let's get together next week, huh?" And he hung up, with characteristic abruptness.

The money meant nothing; but the fact that the Exchange were rumbling about looking at the market was a serious concern. Timing, timing and timing - the keys to making money out of any market. Harris was getting to be more like a juggler now, and he had to make sure that when the balls finally fell down because he couldn't catch them all any longer, he was fast enough to be out of the way. Time to crank up the stakes. "Jamie," he yelled through the door into the dealing room. "Can you come in here for a moment. Close the door," he said, as Edwards walked in. "Now, Jamie, where do we stand at the moment? How's the position looking - not just Chelsea, but all the associated Japanese accounts as well?"

"Pretty good. We're all long, of course, and we keep getting the ammo from Japan to push the market up, so valuations all look good. Excluding realised profits, valuation for Chelsea is probably about 40 mil. About the same as we've realised over the last year. The total for the Japanese accounts is about the same - the position currently is split roughly half in Chelsea, half in Kanagi and associated smelter accounts. The Chinese stuff is insignificant - Hiro's not really getting that moving."

"OK. That's good. I'm not really that concerned the Chinese haven't started yet. They soon will. Now, we need to start to get Chelsea out." Edwards just stared at him. " I mean, Jamie, I want Chelsea to realise it's profits, make it real money." One of the peculiarities of trading futures is that the value of an open position can swing hugely from profit to loss and back as the market price of the open contracts fluctuates - only when the position is closed out is the profit real. "But look, I don't want you to close them with the market, I want you to sell to Kanagi, the smelters and the Chinese. I'm gonna call Hiro shortly to discuss it with him, to make sure he understands he's got to give you discretion to buy for those accounts. When we've closed Chelsea out, then we're gonna be in a position to pay you and me some serious money." He grinned. "It's getting near pay-day, Jamie. You're gonna be a seriously rich boy. But we've gotta make sure we get out cleanly. No loose ends left lying around. OK? So, we have to crystallize Chelsea's profits, and then act purely as a broker, because there's gonna be a period after Chelsea's own positions are finished when we are still active on behalf of the Japanese companies - particularly when it comes to selling their put options for them."

Edwards frowned. "But if we're out of it, why do they need to keep selling puts - that's just going to increase their exposure if the price finally does drop."

"That's true, Jamie, but we need to try and get them out. To do that, we need to keep the pressure on the price. Nothing will change in what you're doing, except that Chelsea will become a pure broker; no more position taking, that's made us our money, but we carry on with the plan as Hiro originally outlined it."

Edwards was confused. He knew he was missing something, but he couldn't see what. Something felt wrong, though. "Is there something you're not telling me about this?"

"Jamie, there's a raft of things I'm not telling you. Remember our original conversation. Trust me; I know what I'm doing, and you're on the right side." At the beginning, of course, Harris had been able to reassure his colleague that what they were doing was not technically illegal. Now, he no longer knew if that were true or not; and for sure, by the time it was over, he would emphatically not be able to give that assurance. Still, no point in him bothering himself or Edwards with that little issue right now.

Edwards shrugged. "You're the boss. You're going to speak to Hiro, agree the new line with him, yeah?"

"I am. I'll call him overnight. But I'm going to Japan next week, so we'll have a longer talk then. In the meantime, don't increase our own long position, and if you get the chance to realise any profits, take it."

"This isn't a rush job, is it?"

"No, take your time. Nothing to worry about, but I just want to get Chelsea out to pay some of the big bucks to you and me. We've been doing the work, we deserve some of the fruits of our labour. But take it easy."

Harris sat at home that evening, thinking. The pace of the game was picking up. He had two vital meetings, to settle the way it would finish. First, in Tokyo next week, to bring Yamagazi up to date - or as far as he wanted him to be - and secondly, with McKee, to get the Kestrel trading under way. He was still as calm as he had ever been, but he could feel that pressure was increasing, and a false move now would destroy everything. In all his planning, the only thing he hadn't accounted for was this sense of building towards an explosion. But, handle this one, and the goal was tantalisingly close.

Chapter Sixteen

Phil Harris woke in the upstairs seat of the Virgin 747 as it began its descent. Opening his eyes and looking through the window, he saw the unprepossessing flat brown landscape around Narita. The engine note changed, and the plane banked out over the sea, before lining up for its final approach into Tokyo's airport.

Arriving at Narita is only one stage in getting into Tokyo. The airport is around 60 kilometres from the city, and although those 60 kilometres are virtually all freeway, it's usually a solid traffic jam most of the way. Not for nothing does the driver normally warn you the journey could be anything between one and three hours. Harris was relatively lucky this time, arriving to check in at the Imperial Hotel in about 90 minutes. Once he got into his very luxurious - but by most standards rather small - room, he called Yamagazi and arranged to meet in the lobby of the hotel at around six thirty that evening. As it was only two o'clock, he stretched out on the bed to doze away the jet-lag.

The lobby of the Imperial is one of *the* meeting places in central Tokyo. It is a huge area, with coffee lounge and bar off to the sides, and seats flanking the central space. The seats are hideously uncomfortable, as they have no back to lean against. Harris came down the huge double staircase from the mezzanine lift and saw Yamagazi sitting uncomfortably off to the right. As he approached, the Japanese stood up, and his face broke into a smile. "Phil, my friend, it's good to see you again. How was your flight?"

"Are flights ever anything but a means to get somewhere? I slept OK this time, and the stewardess didn't keep on pestering me to eat or drink something, so I guess it was fine. Anyway, how are you? You're getting to be more and more famous in the London metal trading community. Virtually all of them now call you "the mad Jap", even the ones who don't know who you are or what you do. Jamie tries to make people believe we do business other than yours, but nobody believes him." He grinned. "Well, we always knew we'd create a high profile."

Yamagazi looked seriously at him. "It's not good that it should be so well known. You know the Japanese way is not to be so obvious, and I have to keep things in perspective for my bosses. But anyway, let us go and have a drink, some food and some more drinks this evening. We have time for serious talk tomorrow." And he led the way to the side entrance of the hotel, and out into the bright-coloured neon lights of the Ginza.

As ever, Harris broadly stuck to his orange juice, while Yamagazi racked up the beers, before they headed off to a sushi bar he knew. There, with the fish, he launched himself into the sake. "Phil, it's so rare for me to have a real friend to go out with in Tokyo. Most of the time, I must spend my evenings with the brokers who are desperate to secure some of my business. It's sometimes difficult to be so controlled, not to say what's really going on, what we are really trying to do." So he's feeling the pressure as well, is he, thought Harris. We need to finish sooner rather than later.

The sushi was excellent, and Yamagazi managed to coax Harris into a sake tasting session, carefully explaining to him the differences in each bottle, caused by different rice, or the special water of whatever prefecture it came from. Not a drinker, not a sake expert, Harris could nevertheless taste some of the nuances - that evening, at any rate. Like every other westerner who has done it, though, when he awoke the following morning, it was with a fervent desire never to see the stuff again.

It had been a relaxing evening, even though they both knew that the following day, when they met, they had some serious talking to do, discussions which would shape the future for them both.

They met at lunch time at the Jade Garden Chinese restaurant, a few minutes walk from the Imperial. It was one of Yamagazi's favourite lunch time haunts in Tokyo, and he used it often enough to be sure to get a genuinely private room where whatever they discussed wouldn't be overheard.

"Phil," he began, "how much longer are we going to be operating as we are?" As ever, with people he knew well, his English was impeccable. "We are close to the position where we have used all the finance we can get from the Union Hong Kong and the other credit lines. We are holding virtually all the LME stock, and we have huge long futures positions on the markets. My bosses have now asked me many times what is happening, am I sure we are following an appropriate policy for a Japanese trading house. So far, I can reassure them, because the valuation of the position always shows a profit, and fortunately they are not aware of the bank loans that are financing it. However, the time when I can no longer keep the two things separate is getting close. We must make our final plan now."

Harris nodded. "OK," he said, "but just a couple of things first. How are the smelters handling the situation, and where are your Chinese friends in all this?"

"The smelters clearly are very happy. You know their under-standing of the LME market is very limited. So all they see is that they have a long position in a rising market, which is protecting their physical sales, to me and to other traders. Besides" - Yamagazi grinned as he said it - "they always trust me to take care of their business. With the Chinese, we have not done so much. I understand from your call last week that you believe we should start to involve them more?" It was inflected as a question.

"Yes, that's necessary. But before the specifics, let's just be sure we both agree we need to start to get out. I have instructed Jamie to start liquidating Chelsea, so that the money will be free to go back to Liechtenstein - waiting for us. To do this, we have to pass all of Chelsea's position to Kanagi, the smelters and the Chinese. You need to give Jamie your instruction to go ahead with that, as we discussed, again last week. When we have done that, and when Kanagi run out of bank lines to keep the price up, then the liquidation that will follow will be bloody." And, although there was no way he would tell the Japanese this, exacerbated by the activities he and McKee would have been putting through Kestrel - in order to facilitate which, Yamagazi had another function to fulfill. "Before we let it all finish, though, to help keep an even keel while we liquidate Chelsea, it's gonna be time to start serious, aggressive put option selling. I've been priming various sources who will be keen to buy, so I think we must do as much volume as we possibly can. The broker credit lines Kanagi have with BancSud will be big enough - until it's too late, of course. So you need to keep giving Jamie the orders and the discretion on price to get them filled. So that means we'll be taking in option premium to help out on the financing." He stopped and grinned at his friend. "It's gonna work, Hiro. Between us, we got it planned right, and we're gonna execute that plan. It's real close."

Yamagazi also smiled and nodded. "I believe you are right. But I have one more point. When all falls down, Kanagi see the size of their losses, you are going to be gone - in your Liechtenstein, or Monaco, or elsewhere. I, however, have to be staying in Tokyo virtually until the end. How will I get out, because the Japanese establishment will not be very happy with me?"

Harris had recognised this point long ago, and knew there was no certain answer. Still, no reason to let Yamagazi see he had a doubt about it. "Well, we will know when it will be. The problem won't be seen until London time zone, when BancSud ask for margin to cover that day's LME stock position, and we will already know that the money won't be there. So when we reach that stage, you leave Tokyo before it becomes clear that they have not been paid and that there is no more money left. It doesn't really matter where you go initially - I guess somewhere in south-east Asia - Malaysia, probably, and from there you can come on to join me in Monaco in your own time. We've always known timing at the end would be vital." Harris thought to himself it sounded reasonable, and, to be fair to him, he genuinely hoped Yamagazi would get out of Tokyo before somebody had the bright idea of taking his passport away while they had a closer look at what had been going on.

The Japanese nodded slowly. "I suppose there has to be some risk in what we are doing. But please, make sure I know really when to go. I don't want my trip to Monaco to be delayed by a spell in Yokohama jail."

"We'll look after you, Hiro. And the money will be safe - Chelsea's bank in Liechtenstein has truly old-fashioned, traditional European views on maintaining the confidentiality of its customers. There'll be enough for you, me and Jamie." Particularly since the real big money for me will be in there too, courtesy of Kestrel, he added to himself. "What do you think Kanagi will do," he asked, out of curiousity. "Do you think they will pay up and try to keep it as quiet as they can? Or will they really take it through the courts?"

"That is a difficult question. The world in Japan is changing. In the past, they would have covered up, paid back to the smelters - and maybe the Chinese, but they are foreigners, so not so sure - to keep face and relationship intact. Now, I can't say. Many younger generation executives will be ready to let the smelters suffer their own loss. We are becoming more like you, my friend. We no longer always value face and honour above money. It is a shame how the traditional Japan is being left behind, being forgotten, in the rush for western materialism." Harris nearly choked on his mouthful of food at that one, given that the man opposite him regretting the passing of a more spiritual Japan was the man ready to execute one of the biggest frauds there had been against a pillar of the country's establishment. No point in going down that road now, though. So he just nodded.

They finished the meal companionably, chatting generally as they had effectively resolved the serious questions. As they got up to go, Yamagazi said, "Phil, let's finish this quickly now. We have come so far, we must not fail at the last hurdle. I can keep the Tokyo end going still, but it starts now to be more difficult. I feel the dogs may soon be snapping at our heels."

Harris nodded his agreement. "I know. But we are so close, just hold your nerve. As long as we can keep the facilities in London in place, the house of cards stands up. It's the time that tests our trust in each other." And within the bounds of the conversation, he meant it. His arrangements with McKee were in a different compartment of his mind, at that moment.

The following day, he took the early afternoon flight back to London. He had a meeting to set up with Mack McKee.

Chapter Seventeen

"Mack. It's Phil Harris. We need to have a little quiet private meeting." It was Friday morning, and Harris was on the phone, back in the office after his trip to Tokyo. "Can we get together later today, or Monday?"

"I've got a better idea. We need this to be private; I've got a little cottage down on the coast that I use when I'm sailing. It's out of season now, but I haven't been down to close the place up yet, so why don't you come down tomorrow - stay the weekend, if you like."

"OK. Sounds good to me. Why don't you get your secretary to fax me over some directions?"

So late the next morning, Harris found himself in his Mercedes, heading along the A27 to Chichester. McKee's cottage was in the harbourside village of Itchenor, deserted at that time of year under a grey drizzly sky. He carried on virtually down to the water's edge before he saw McKee's BMW outside a row of what had presumably been fishermen's cottages, before the boom in leisure sailing priced them out of range. McKee came to the front door as Harris stepped out of the black 500SL.

"Phil, come in," boomed the big man. "I'm just having a cup of coffee. Same for you?"

"Thanks," said Harris, stepping into a large room that seemed to occupy the whole of the ground floor. It was filled with light from a big window at the back, giving a view onto what seemed to be a boatyard. Everything was finished in light coloured wood, including the open-tread staircase. They sat at a long wooden table in the kitchen/eating end of the room.

"What do you think, Phil? I had all the internal walls knocked out down here so I have one decent size room rather than three pokey ones. I've done the same upstairs - just two bedrooms, both with shower-rooms. I don't use it for big entertainments, but I've been keeping my boat down here for years, and it seemed a good idea to have a base here as well."

"I didn't know you sailed. We used to do a lot when I was a kid in California, but I've never really got to grips with weather and the bad-tempered seas over here."

"It sorts the men from the boys, Phil. I sail with a lot of different people, quite a few from the business. It's how you find out what their real thresholds of fear are, in a force eight bashing down the Channel to Guernsey. You'd be surprised to find who's got the balls and who hasn't. I've been using it for some team-building for the guys from the office as well, recently. Get 'em on board with a professional skipper - I steer clear for those weekends, they don't need me breathing down their necks - and make them work together. It's been quite an interesting exercise. Look, if you're interested in boats, we'll go round to the boatyard later and you can have a look. It's out of the water for the winter - maintenance, anti-fouling, all that sort of thing." He looked hard at the American. "But first, I guess we've got some important talking to do, haven't we?"

"We have, but it's not going to take all weekend. I'd be keen to see the boat. Why don't we do that first, and then after lunch we can get all our discussion done in one shot."

"Suits me," said the big man. "let's go."

And so they walked round behind the cottages, to the boatyard, where McKee proudly showed off the features of his boat. It was bigger than Harris had expected, a 44-footer, with every conceivable piece of navigation kit and electronics on it. No wonder McKee was proud of it. Idly, Harris tried to estimate what it must have cost him.

They lunched at the Itchenor Sailing Club, alone apart from the few dinghy sailors who had braved the late autumn weather to take part in a frostbite series. The food was good, the clubhouse a traditional place of dark beams and pewter tankards. Good old England, thought Harris. McKee was in good form, retailing a stream of sailing stories, most of which illustrated his megalomanic way of skippering his boat. Reading between the lines, though, Harris guessed he was a pretty knowledgeable, skillful sailor.

They finished their leisurely lunch around three thirty, and strolled back the few hundred yards to McKee's cottage.

"OK, Mack," began Harris, once they were settled in a couple of easy chairs, "we're getting very close to needing to set Kestrel off on its flight. The account is all set up, isn't it?"

"Yeah, that was done after our last conversation about it. You still intend it just to buy put options?"

"Paying cash for the premiums, yes. There's no need to think of credit lines."

"Phil, even the way I run the company, I couldn't give Kestrel a credit line. If you want to start soon, you'd better wire in some money to get started."

"That can be done on Monday. It'll come in from Liechtenstein - I can give you details of the remitting bank before I leave this weekend. There'll be enough cash."

"Liquidating Chelsea to pay for this?" McKee said with a question in his voice.

Harris' eyes took on the hard, cold look. "With respect, Mack, you don't need to know where the money comes from. Just be grateful you're gonna benefit from it big-time. But the most important thing is timing. Jamie is getting instructions from Tokyo on Monday to begin the aggressive phase of the option selling. You need to make sure that Kestrel gets to buy - I don't want to hear about copper producers getting in first, or anything like that. I know how much we can buy, and don't forget I also have a big say in how much comes from the seller."

That's a hell of an admission, thought McKee. And a problem for him, because Jason Serck was expecting to be in pole position when the price couldn't hold any longer. Something to get his mind round once Harris had gone.

Out loud, he said, "OK, I can make sure we get the trades before anybody else steps in, but I'd like to know how long you intend the programme to last. Are we going to do it all in a week, or a month or six months?"

"Certainly not six months. Probably not even one. In a way, we just have to suck it and see, wait until we see how the market reacts. We need to get as much as we can before we push the price over the edge, and reality comes back to copper. The longer we can keep it propped, the more we're gonna make. But the other side is that we can't risk the collapse happening before we're ready. We're juggling facilities in London and Tokyo. But anyway, this final phase can't last long. You'll know where we are."

They batted the technicalities back and forth for the rest of the afternoon, before heading off for the White Horse Inn at Chilgrove, just north of Chichester, for dinner - McKee promised "one of the best wine lists in the country." And he was right.

The next morning, it was a perfect late autumn day - clear blue sky, a light, low sun, and a soft south westerly breeze. McKee suggested a walk along the harbour to a pub in Dell Quay for lunch; Harris happily agreed.

Chichester Harbour is one of those special places, and that morning it was at its best. The blue-grey water contrasted with the reds and golds of the trees, and the white sails of those hardy enough to brave the cold scudded across the waves. The path took them right along the waterside, with big houses on their right. McKee was relaxed. "You know, this is really where I'm happiest. I love the sailing, the Channel may be an evil-tempered bit of water, but I enjoy the challenge. Who knows, maybe when we're through I'll retire down here."

"At least you understand you're going to be through with the business by the time we've finished," replied Harris. "But I'm heading for Monaco. I need the sun and the warmth. I've had good fun down on the Cote d'Azur since I've been in Europe. I guess it's the closest I'm gonna get to California. And however much my countrymen like entrepreneurs, I have a feeling that I'm gonna need a more benign tax and legal framework than the good old USA can offer." He paused. "Seriously, Mack, we're gonna be persona very much non grata. And there's no point in pretending we can be anonymous - we can't. We're gonna be plastered all over every newspaper in town. You said it yourself last time we met - the end of this will leave blood on the floor. The industry won't recover for a long, long time. Still wanna play the game?"

McKee looked at him. "Look, I won't pretend I like that thought. But you know me well enough after all these years. I'm not proud of it, but Mack McKee is my first priority. The metal business isn't some kind of sacred trust, it's a means to an end, and the end is to make Mack McKee a rich boy."

They walked on a while in silence. Then, "Phil, where does Yamagazi come out of all this? And before you go all coy on me, I'd say it's too late for that. I guess I'm the only one who really knows what you're going to do, because you need me, sure, but you might as well tell me the whole truth. Your future and mine are thoroughly tangled by now."

Harris nodded slowly. "OK, I'll buy that. The truth is, I don't know. Timing in this thing is critical. If it all works like it should, Hiro should have sufficient time between the end game and the enquiries to get out of Tokyo, into south-east Asia somewhere. From there, he should join me in Monaco, or go wherever the hell else he likes, that's got a friendly regime. What he will have done is gonna be actually illegal, whereas I think I - and you," said with a thin smile - "are probably only being total shits, not criminals. And if the timing doesn't work, then it's tough for Hiro. But still, a Japanese jail is probably better than a western one, US or Europe."

McKee was taken aback. The business was all about turning over the competition, but here was Harris frankly talking about the fact that it was a real possibility that his co-conspirator would end up in jail - while he enjoyed the benefits of their game. "Jesus, Phil, remind me not to get on the wrong side of you, if that's where your friends go."

"Mack, this was Hiro's scheme in the first place. I've refined it a bit, to make it a hell of a lot more profitable, but in essence it's the same thing he brought me all that time ago. He's always known there's a real risk for him. He obviously thinks it's worth it. Look, I don't really know what drives him. He's a friend, in a way, but ....look, you and I know the Orient better than most. Do you claim to understand what drives them? Hiro wants the money, and the freedom, and he looks across the gap at us in the west, and thinks it's his goal. Would you or I risk years in jail? Probably not. We've got the easy bit, where the worst that can happen is that we don't show our faces here or in the US for a while. But eventually the indignation of our peers will die down. And I'll tell you what," he finished, "I guess Hiro won't even be comfortable here in the end."

The walk had taken them past the yacht marinas at Birdham, and they were approaching the pub across the pebbly foreshore. The wind had brought up clouds from the south west, and the day was turning grey and cold. Harris spoke again. "You said you might retire down here." McKee nodded silently, sensing what Harris was going to say. "I'm sorry, Mack, but I guess you know now as well as I do that that ain't gonna happen. We're not gonna be able to stay, at least not for a while. You'd better start thinking about it. Hey, you like the social whirl, you should join me in Monaco. Grand Prix time, that's where all your buddies from Annabel's hang out. Lots of young girls there for you, and notoriety's a hell of an aphrodisiac." He started laughing. "The world's not perfect, but we just got one of the few chances to make it fit us better. It may not be in character, but I want a drink now. Let's get in that pub."

McKee followed him in through the door, only half joining the American's laughter. For the first time in his life, he wondered if he was getting in out of his depth. And he still had to address the problem of how to get Jason Serck off his back, while he and Harris made their fortunes.

Harris was in the mood to drink for once, and the pub had good food and wine, so it was late afternoon by the time they called a cab to take them back to Itchenor. He'd also drunk far too much to drive himself back to town that evening, so they sat in the cottage long into the night, swapping reminiscences of their parallel careers, particularly in the Far East. The next morning, leaving McKee to clear up some details with his boatyard, Harris took off early in his Mercedes for the drive back to London.

In fact, dealing with the boatyard had been an excuse on McKee's part; what he actually needed was some time to himself to think about the problem of Jason Serck and Leopard-Star. At the time, the deal with Serck had been ideal, a way for Commet to profit from Harris' market manipulation. But now, the game was different, and the profit opportunity was for Mack McKee, not Commet, which was clearly more important. He sat for a long time at his breakfast table, a pot of coffee at his elbow. There didn't seem to be simple way out. He would have to juggle Serck's ambition against what he knew he had to do. And increasing the pressure would be Rory Davis and Stu Benson, both of them expecting him to act with Leopard-Star in the way they had planned together. In the end he knew he would have to do as he always did, and trust to bluster and bullying. He sighed to himself. Maybe he was getting too old for it; perhaps the opportunity to get out had come just in time. He left the clearing up for his weekly cleaning lady to do when she next came, and got into the BMW. As ever, there was something therapeutic about the power of the big car. He mused to himself that when this was over, perhaps he'd do what he'd never bothered with before, and buy himself a truly self-indulgent car. An Aston Martin, that was probably what would suit him. The closer he got to London and the office, the more the game enervated him, so that when he finally walked into Commet at around lunch time, he was back on form, ready to take them all on, the depressing thoughts of the morning pushed to the back of his mind.

Looking at his Reuters screen, he saw the copper market was rampant again. He had to take his hat off to Harris - and presumably Yamagazi - for the way they were managing to keep pushing the market higher. But, then, if you don't care how much damage you do, maybe it's not so difficult. Rory Davis was out that day, visiting a customer in Germany, so he called directly to Stu Benson in New York. "Stu, good morning, my friend, how are you? Anything going on over there yet? I've been out this morning, but copper looks very strong again. Any word from Jason?" Might as well get straight into it.

"Nah, it's just watch them push that price up at the moment. Last time I spoke to Jason, he was happy to leave it to us. You know he takes next month off, don't you. Some kinda retreat he does every year. One month with absolutely no contact with the office or the outside world at all." McKee didn't listen as Benson wittered on about retreat being a subjective term, and he wouldn't regard a month on a private Caribbean island as any sort of penance. Halleluyah, he was thinking. The way out of his predicament had just revealed itself. Thank you, whatever God protects corrupt, cynical men like me.

"OK, Stu, I guess I'd better call him and get some plan in mind in case it all kicks off while he's out of contact. I'll let you go, and we'll talk again later."

He went into one of the private offices, and sat thinking about how he was going to handle what could be one of the most significant calls of his life. Play it right, and everything would be done by the time Serck got back. He wouldn't be pleased, of course, but McKee thought he could handle an unhappy hedge fund manager - especially when he knew he was going to be right out of the business.

Over in New York, Serck was finishing his morning briefing with his closest aides when the phone rang. Waving his staff out of the room, he picked it up. "Jason, it's Mack McKee," came the voice down the line, "how are you?"

"Good, Mack, and you? How's our favourite market treating us? We've been watching this rally and it sure looks like there's some pressure there. My technical guys, the chartists, are pretty unanimous that it's overdone, and we should be starting to get some action going. But you know, you guys are the experts, we're in your hands. What are thinking?"

"We can see the price still higher. The mining companies we speak to are pretty much all of the view that they can afford to wait a bit longer. And you know our strategy: we don't want to be the ones who start the drop. We want to pick the moment when it's just turned over the top, we need to go in on a market which has already turned."

"Yeah, sure that's what we agreed, but we gotta make certain we don't let it run away from us."

"Relax, Jason," boomed the confident voice out of the earpiece, "this is our business, we know how to do it. Between us we've got the firepower, and that's what matters. Your guys are probably right from a technical point of view - this market is overbought, in conventional terms. But we know that conventional terms don't apply. Harris and his buddies are still on course." Out of curiousity, he asked, "How about the banks - any sign that they might be stretching their bank lines?"

"Not really, or not in the US, anyway. I'm heading off to the Far East when I get back from my retreat, maybe I'll pick up some vibes in Hong Kong. But keep your ears to the ground, anyway, Mack, we don't want to miss it. I'm out of circulation for a bit, on my annual retreat, starting next week. If you're OK with it, I think we sit tight while I'm out, unless you need to take control yourself."

"Yeah, sure, I'm happy with that. I don't really expect it to go wild just yet," McKee lied happily.

A bit more desultory conversation, and they hung up. Both were sure they'd agreed what they wanted, but McKee knew he was left with the upper hand.

Chapter Eighteen

It began quietly enough in early December. Pushed on by Harris, Yamagazi started giving Edwards orders to sell put options. Edwards found that the best buyer around was his sparring partner Rory Davis at Commet. At first, Davis didn't think anything of McKee's new customer, Kestrel Aviation and Trading. Over the years, the big man had unearthed all sorts of people who traded with him, people who on the surface had no earthly reason to trade LME derivatives. Mostly, after McKee had finished with them, they wished fervently they'd never heard of a market so volatile. So Davis put the trades through, always scalping a bit for Commet. It was meat and drink to the dealer. If he was curious that Kestrel only ever spoke to McKee, and never questioned the prices, he didn't show it.

The dialogue between McKee and Harris - always on mobile phones, with no risk of the tapes on the land-lines - went on constantly. Harris was also co-ordinating their actions with Yamagazi. Despite Jason Serck's lack of information, the truth was that the bank lines in Hong Kong were getting stretched, and they were virtually at the point where Kanagi was meeting it's daily margin calls from BancSud purely with the money generated from option premium. As Edwards was also liquidating Chelsea's positions and the money was being repatriated to Liechtenstein, so it was recycled by Kestrel to buy the options. If it had been a house of cards before, it was now more like an inverted pyramid, that one push out of equilibrium would send toppling down and down.

Once again, the LME authorities looked nervously at what was happening. This time, there was no real credit concern, since Chelsea itself was not a principal to any of the trades - as Harris had insisted, they were now purely a broker. What was exercising Lubbock and Thresher was the way the open interest - the number of contracts traded - was soaring in those early days of December. From one point of view, it could have been interpreted as a vote of confidence in the exchange they ran. Their worries, quite rightly, as it turned out, focussed on the fact that so much of the business consisted of put options. That meant, in the light of their experience, that somebody was making an enormous bet on a decline in the copper price. That was all right - why not? But the other side of the bet began to frighten them, since they had no way of judging the solvency of the counterparty if the price did collapse. The roads all led them back to BancSud, since it seemed to be their client - or, Lubbock fervently hoped, their clients (spread the risk and make it all safer) - who were so keen to sell options.

So, again, Ronald Waverley was summoned to the LME's panelled Boardroom to explain what his clients were doing, and why they might be doing it. The LME business, which before the relationship with Harris had been a marginal activity for BancSud, had come to be far and away their most profitable activity. Waverley was riding high, paying himself enormous bonuses, and reluctant to concede that anything could be wrong. He easily admitted the names of his customers this time, since Kanagi and the Japanese smelter companies were blue-chip. Everybody wanted to deal with them, and Waverley, conveniently forgetting that he owed the success exclusively to Phil Harris, was happy to lecture the two LME executives about the Far Eastern copper business, and how the trading all fitted into a logical pattern.

"What you have to understand, gentlemen, is that my clients are amongst the biggest participants in the copper market. Kanagi needs to have physical copper available to deliver to customers, and although they are at risk of taking delivery against their puts if the market comes down, they have analyzed the risks fully. First, they believe the market at present will keep rising, since copper is by no means over-valued at current prices." The crazy thing about this was that there were indeed metals analysts with most of the investment banks who had been so hoodwinked by events that they were actually publishing research notes saying precisely this - they were completely ignoring the genuine economic cost of copper production. "Secondly, even if the market does fall, they are confident that their market share of the physical business will hold up, and they will in any case still need the physical metal. As you know, the smelters rely heavily on the expertise of the head of copper trading at Kanagi, Yamagazi-san, and they are following his advice, based on his experience of the market. And frankly, up to now, they haven't done too badly on that policy, have they?"

Lubbock had a lot of faults, and some of the blame for the debacle that followed can legitimately be laid at his door for not acting sooner, but he wasn't a complete idiot. He *knew* that what Waverley was telling him was basically drivel, that the man was deluding himself, blinded by the money he was making. However, his agenda was to make the changes he believed to be necessary for the market at his own pace, and so he weighed it up, and decided that although he knew the risks, he could comfort himself with the thought that the Japanese companies involved were massive, and could support their positions and the losses they might incur.

So they agreed with Waverley's analysis of the situation, and did nothing. The promised investigation of the market, to which BancSud had reluctantly contributed, had been conveniently forgotten, almost as soon as it had been announced. A phone call to McKee satisfied them that his client, who was buying options, was paying up prompt cash for the premium, and therefore there was no financial risk involved, since no credit was being given.

Why the client should be speculating so aggressively on a drop in the market was not really discussed.

Within Commet, though, that question was being asked. Stu Benson in New York was beginning to wonder why somebody appeared to be getting in ahead of Leopard-Star, with precisely the game-plan that they had previously agreed with Serck. He'd been raising the subject with Rory Davis daily; but Davis, genuinely rushed off his feet by the increasing flow of business going through his copper book, had been too busy to take much notice. Late one evening, however, just as the market closed, Benson tried again.

"Rory," he called down the open line squawk box to London, "have you got two minutes? We really need to talk about what's going on. I know Jason Serck's away, but his guys are watching the market nevertheless. I gotta know what to tell them."

Davis picked the phone up off the open line, "Stu, I'm sorry. We've been incredibly busy. Give me five minutes to finish checking today's biz, and I promise I'll call you before I go home this evening. I know it's important."

The five minutes stretched to more like fifteen, but finally he finished, and, stepping into a side office, called through to Benson.

"OK, Stu, so what's your concern?"

"It's simple, Rory. Who is this Kestrel that's buying all the puts, when that was the strategy we all put together with Leopard-Star? Until recently, I'd never seen the name, but right now they seem to be huge. And where's the other side coming from? I assume we're not just booking them to ourselves." Benson saw a daily list of customer business, but he didn't see trades with other brokers, which were clearing house matches, so he didn't see the Chelsea side of the deals, as they were matched as BancSud, Chelsea's clearers.

"No, we're not booking them. That's far too much risk, even for us. I'm able to buy them all from Jamie Edwards, so it looks very much as if we were right in our scenario about what he and Harris were up to. I guess their customer is Yamagazi; he obviously wants to take in the premium, and keep ramping the market up. But to be honest, I don't know much about Kestrel. It's one of Mack's, and he keeps it pretty close to his chest. I did wonder if it was actually a front for Leopard-Star. D'you think it could be?"

"Unlikely, I'd say. I know hedge funds over here are pretty unregulated, but even so, I think they'd have difficulty operating through an offshore company like that. What is it, Panamanian?"

"Yes, that's what the details I've seen say. But I haven't looked far into it. Hold on, let me just get the details up on the screen here." And he tapped the customer code into the PC on the desk in front of him. "Yeah, seems to be a Panama address.... hold on," he said, as the lines of print came up, "mmmm, interesting, seems the bank payment instructions are to Liechtenstein and....." another pause, as he scrolled down the page "that seems to be where the money comes in from, as well."

"Rory, I know you guys in Europe love your little tax havens, but a Panamanian company paying and receiving money through Liechtenstein, that stinks. You know what it says to me? Sounds like a washing machine."

"Doesn't look too straightforward, does it. But you know Mack. Maybe he's put together a deal with some of the mining companies to run a price protection scheme, and structuring it that way keeps it off the balance sheet and away from the shareholders' eyes, in case it all goes wrong."

"Maybe. But I don't think you believe that any more than I do. If that were true, I think he would have told at least you what was happening. He couldn't keep that to himself. I think this is something nasty, and I think we'd better get to the bottom of it before it swallows us. We're senior officers of this company as well, don't forget. It's our asses on the line."

"Yeah, you're right. You better come over here and we'll make Mack tell us what it's about. But, to be fair, it's unlikely he'd be involved in anything seriously wrong. He's got too much to lose, as well."

"True. But there's still the other problem, that Kestrel's doing what Leopard-Star should be." He started laughing. "Our client list is beginning to sound like a zoo. Look, I'll get over at the beginning of next week. Mack's not travelling, is he?"

"Not as far as I know. I'll make sure he doesn't. And don't worry, Stu, I'm sure it'll be OK."

After finishing the call to Benson, Davis called McKee at home, catching him just as he was going out to dinner. McKee confirmed he'd be in to talk to Davis and Benson, and then spent most of his dinner date pondering how he would deflect their questioning, with the result that he was too distracted for the liking of the girl he was with, who left straight after dinner, refusing his invitation to go on to Annabel's. Unusually, he went straight home himself. At least he had a few days to mull over the story he was going to tell them. Anyway, he thought, things were going his way; bluffing his own colleagues would be much easier than bluffing Serck. It was one of the things he'd had years of experience doing.

The only one of the main players without any major worries was Jamie Edwards. He was sitting in the middle, unaware that his boss was actually the source of both sides of the business that was keeping him, too, probably busier than he'd ever been. All he saw was his constant stream of orders from Yamagazi, which he was able to place with no more than some relatively easy price haggling with Davis. He assumed that Davis was acting on behalf of his mining company customer base, seeing them take protection against the possibility that the current high price could not be maintained. He'd pretty much closed out Chelsea's positions by now, and most of the money they'd made had flowed back to Liechtenstein, where, as far as he was aware, it was waiting for him, Harris and Yamagazi. He may have been more concerned had he known that that same money was being recycled to pay for the options he was selling daily to Commet. If it had all got a bit incestuous, the reality was that by this time, the other participants in the copper market had become completely peripheral, and all those earnest brokers and traders assuring their clients that they knew what was happening, that they understood the logic of the market, were talking so much rubbish. The only factor of any significance in the market was when Yamagazi would run out of the funds he had borrowed on behalf of Kanagi. And the *only* ones who knew that were Harris, Yamagazi and McKee. And only Harris and McKee knew what Kestrel was up to.

As it turned out, it was a week before Benson could get out of New York, as freak snowstorms closed both JFK and Newark airports. During those few extra days, the trades between Kestrel, Commet, Chelsea, Kanagi and BancSud hit a peak in volume. Kanagi finally hit it's maximum borrowings, and any dip in the price would from then on trigger a collapse, as the Japanese would be unable to meet their margin calls, which would result in BancSud forcibly closing positions to cut the risk, thus feeding selling into the market. When he finally got a flight, Benson came into the Commet office direct from Heathrow, and he, McKee and Davis went straight into a meeting room.

"Stu," began McKee, "I understand from Rory that you've got some concerns about some of the business that's going through at the moment. You know you two are the future of this company, after I've gone, so I'm always happy to listen to any problems you have. Tell me what it is, and I'll do my best to answer any questions there may be."

"OK, Mack, you know I've always appreciated your openness. I'm worried about two things, which I think are pretty closely related. First, I thought the put option buying strategy was gonna be a joint venture between us and Leopard-Star, but right now it seems to be a completely separate company that's getting all the action. I guess that concerns me because it's limiting our own profit potential, and it seems to be a direct conflict with the relationship we are trying to build with Jason Serck, which going forward could be one of our most lucrative. Second problem, I don't like the sound of this Kestrel company. Panama company, paying and receiving through Liechtenstein. To me, and I would guess to any regulator looking at it, it screams money laundering. And as you say, you're gonna quit one day, and I guess Rory and I will take over - I want to take over a company without those sort of problems clinging to it."

"OK, Stu, those are two fair points to make. Before I answer them, though, what's your view, Rory? Do you share Stu's concerns? Do you think I may be taking us down the wrong road?"

Davis thought for a moment before answering. Then, "Yeah, I guess I do. But it's not a question of you taking us the wrong way. Nobody's suggesting you're doing anything wrong. I think we just need to understand what's going on, so we can make a decision, all three of us, about it."

"Right. OK, let's address the two issues. We'll take the second one first. You know over the years I've brought in some pretty big speculators, who we've made good money out of. They're not always the most straightforward of corporate entities, but that's the nature of the business. This one is a bit more secretive than some of the others have been, but I can categorically assure you that these guys are not money launderers, they have no association with organised crime, and they are not trying to wash the proceeds of drug running or racketeering, which I guess are your primary concerns." He held up his hand, as Benson started to interrupt. "Just a minute, Stu. I am not free to tell you who they are, because they made me promise to keep their identity confidential. Although what they're doing is not technically illegal, they would not like all their associates to know about it."

"They're some of the executives of the mining companies, aren't they," Davis broke in. "I knew it! They don't trust the price up here, and rather than hedge their companies, they're trying to make money personally."

Benson looked at McKee. "Is that right, Mack? Are we helping these guys put one over their own shareholders? A little bit of personal account trading?"

This was precisely the impression McKee had wanted to create. To be fair to him, he didn't want to have to lie to these two, who he'd worked with for a long time. He'd much rather they drew their own conclusions from his hints and allusions, than that he actually had to make untrue statements.

"I repeat. I am not at liberty to disclose the identities behind Kestrel. But your logic is not bad, Rory. I will say that they are people intimately connected with the metal business in their mainline occupation." That was true, anyway; he and Harris were exactly how he'd described them.

Davis looked relieved. He didn't want this argument. He just wanted to get on with the trading. Benson looked sceptical, but said, "OK, let's let that one go for the moment. I can see you're not going to be any more forthcoming on it right now. But what about the other problem? Why are we stitching up Jason Serck, after we made an agreement with him? I gotta say I really don't like it."

McKee frowned. "I don't particularly like it, either, Stu, but we have to do what makes most sense for us. Serck's away, uncontactable, and he's always had a slightly different view on the time perspective than we have, as you'll remember from our first conversations with him. On the other hand, the other guys came to me a short time ago, ready to go, cash in the bank to transfer to us to cover everything. I had to make a tough decision. But anyway, nothing's happened yet, so we've still got every chance to go with Serck while the market's still up here. I made the judgement that in the long term, we were better supporting the guys involved with Kestrel as a first priority."

"Don't you think that was a decision we should have been involved in as well?"

"Not really. I run this company, and I have to choose the direction it goes in. Until the shareholders want to replace me, that is. Look, Stu, you know I respect both of you for your professionalism, and I give you a lot of latitude in how we operate. But there are some things I have to do alone. And this kind of decision is one of them."

"And that's all you're gonna say about it?"

"Yes it is. If you have a problem with that, then I'm sorry, but you've got to live with it."

At that moment, there was a knock on the door, and one of the clerks came in. "Mack, Rory - oh, hi Stu, I didn't know you were over - there's a headline just appeared on Reuters I think you may want to know about. It says Yamagazi's been suspended by Kanagi Corp, pending an investigation into the company's copper trading and LME positions."

"What!" exclaimed Davis. "That's going to move the market, Mack, we'll have to finish this later. I've got to get out there."

Davis, Benson and the clerk dashed out, leaving McKee, who, as soon as they'd gone, pulled out his mobile and dialled a familiar number. "Phil. It's Mack. What's going on? I just saw the Reuters news. How are we placed if it all blows up now?"

"Relax, Mack," came Harris' cool voice, "I'm not quite sure how it happened, but it looks like Kanagi got suspicious for some reason, and somebody started looking a bit deeper into the position. They'd got Hiro's passport in their travel department, getting him a visa for somewhere, and one of the managers there seems to have been smart enough to hang on to it."

"So he's still in Japan?"

"Yeah. Look, I'm trying to find out the details. But we're OK. We've got a big potential short position through the options, so we just wait and see. Nothing ties Kestrel into what Kanagi's been doing. I'll get back to you later." And the phone went dead in McKee's hand. Slipping it back into his pocket, he went through into the dealing room, where the volume of noise was increasing, dominated by Davis shouting at the clerk, "Look, just give me my full position now. Futures and options. I need to know where I am."

The telephone dealer boards were lighting up like Christmas

trees, as the calls came in from clients, anxious to talk to their account executives, to try and second guess what the market would do. But Rory Davis was in no doubt. He snatched the position sheet from the clerk, and started hitting the lines to the other market-makers, trying to find buyers of copper.

"Get me some bids," he shouted. We need to sell! Anything, this market's going down." He looked across at the client desk. "I'm not buying anything, OK, so if you've got clients who want to sell, we're not the place for them to come." McKee, even as Davis was speaking, could see the prices on the screens ticking lower, as the rest of the market came to the same conclusion.

Benson, standing with McKee at the end of the trading desk, looked hard at his boss. "So much for having time to get Serck in - this is what we were waiting for, and we've left him right out in the cold."

Davis overheard. "Fuck Serck," he snapped, angrily. "Get on to your US customers. Wake 'em up. Get me some buyers. We can make a fortune today, if you guys get me the ammo. Nothing else matters right now."

And indeed that morning was a bravura performance by Davis. Even though he'd said he wasn't going to buy anything, his quick wits kept Commet right in front of the market, as it yo-yoed, dropping, recovering a bit, dropping again as the morning wore on. Then around mid-morning, a huge wave of selling hit the market, smashing any thought that it might hold in the face of the uncertainty. McKee correctly guessed that was the moment Kanagi had formally told BancSud they would not be able to meet the margin call against their massive long position, and BancSud had no alternative but to begin to liquidate it. He smiled to himself; he'd never had much respect for Waverley, and he doubted his ability to manage the crisis.

Davis was smiling by now. "We're up big time, Mack," he announced. "I'm tempted to stop now, keep the money and just trade any orders that come in purely back-to-back. This morning's made sure we have a bumper year, already." McKee was only half listening. He knew how short Kestrel would be by now, and how much money he and Harris were making. Even for blasé, seen-it-all-before Mack McKee, it was an awesome amount. Harris had been right. This was real, never work again, I'm one of the rich boys, money. He needed to get out of the office, to talk to Harris about how they were going to close out the position and realise the money. "Yeah, sure, Rory. Play it how you want. I've just got to go out to see someone." Davis stared in disbelief. This was the biggest day of their careers, and McKee was going out. He shrugged, and went back to his phones.

Through the morning, Reuters had been updating the story as the news broke. It seemed that serious fraud was now suspected at Kanagi, and Yamagazi was being detained by the Tokyo police pending a full enquiry. Kanagi put out a statement that it did not have a serious liquidity problem but that it was as yet unsure of the extent of any unauthorised trading. Investigations were being conducted by senior officers of the company and it's auditors. A news conference by the chairman was scheduled for the following morning.

McKee and Harris met in a coffee bar in Chelsea. "What happened, Phil? Why did it all go off before we expected it?"

"It's always the little things that change your plans," said Harris, philosophically. "It doesn't really matter to us. We were ready, in terms of the position. I would have liked Hiro to get clean away, though. They're going to get their teeth into him over there, because he's a Japanese who's besmirched the good name of Japanese integrity in the eyes of the world. But anyway, before that, we gotta get Kestrel closed out. I bought some back this morning, but there's quite a lot still to go." Seeing McKee's puzzled look, he went on, "Sorry, I hadn't told you, I was able to set up a small account for Kestrel with M and T. Nothing big enough to make them curious, but it's just got us started. Now, I guess we need to get some buying in at Commet, so we're getting the profits realised. We both know this is not a storm in teacup, so we don't have to scramble, but the sooner we're out, the sooner we can take off for the sunshine." So, they sat and worked out what prices they thought they would have to pay to square out their position, and how long they thought they'd have to take over it. It was almost surreal to McKee. Sitting in a coffee bar in Chelsea, the week before Christmas, talking about the completion of a trade that was going to make them both massively rich, they were two - frauds? He still didn't actually know if what they'd done was legal or not. He knew it would spell the end of his metals career, though; but then the new possibilities it opened up were there.

He couldn't help himself. He just started laughing. "We've done it," he struggled to get the words out, "we've beaten the market. We're there." And Harris started laughing, too. Anyone watching would have been mystified at two well-dressed men in their forties sitting laughing hysterically. For the moment, they'd conveniently forgotten the cost to Hiro Yamagazi of their good fortune.

Chapter Nineteen

There were a lot of unhappy people around the world that day, and in the days that followed. Amongst the first to suspect problems were Union Bank in Hong Kong. They had in fact precipitated the whole affair, because it had been one of their overzealous clerks, who, when he couldn't get through to his normal contact at Kanagi to confirm a regular roll-over of one of the loans, had instead asked to be put through to the finance department. At first the Japanese he had spoken to had thought he was talking to a lunatic, but the man's insistence eventually made him look into what to him was a non-existent loan. As he delved into it, he didn't really understand what he was finding, but had the presence of mind to alert his manager to the fact that the copper department appeared to have dealings with Union Bank which were completely unknown to the rest of the corporation. The finance manager had started at Kanagi as a fellow graduate trainee with Yamagazi, and resented the way the latter's career had taken off, while he was stuck in a dead end, so he was ready to grasp at anything that might be to the other's disadvantage. It was he who had persuaded the travel department to make sure they hung on to the copper trader's passport, and it was he who followed up with Union the full extent of the indebtedness. Union were understandably very twitchy about the whole thing, and that, allied to what was being uncovered in Tokyo, had pushed the senior management of Kanagi to take the unusual step of suspending Yamagazi, and calling in their auditors and the police to begin an investigative enquiry. This had been the piece of news that Reuters' Japanese Bureau had picked up, which set the ball rolling.

BancSud were disturbed when they saw the news. Harris had told his people to head off any calls from Waverley for him, and in the absence of any firm information, Waverley had decided that they had to act mid-morning, just as McKee had surmised, when Kanagi had told him they would not meet their margin call pending the results of the investigation. It was the crass way BancSud's dealers had begun liquidating the position which had largely created the opportunities for Rory Davis to profit.

Stu Benson left the Commet office in disgust, later in the day, convinced McKee had broken a firm agreement with Serck; he felt he needed to get out to decide what to do. He was essentially a decent man, but his later actions would cause the worst effect of the crisis.

Jamie Edwards was in the Chelsea office, watching the mayhem hitting the market. He didn't really have a role to play as the game ran on. He'd done his bit earlier, and he just watched, almost in disbelief. The brokers were all clamouring down the phone lines to him, anxious to tell him their view of what was going on, convinced that he must be trading and desperate to get some of the business they were sure he was putting into the market. Needless to say, none of their interpretations, which grew wilder as the day wore on, had much connection with the truth, which Edwards himself only partly understood. He was puzzled as to why Harris went out mid-morning, but in truth he was shell-shocked by the viciousness of the market move that he knew they'd caused, even though he didn't really understand how. And, just like Harris and McKee, but on a smaller scale, half his mind was on his share of the Chelsea profits, as far as he knew waiting in the bank.

And meanwhile, back in Tokyo, the man at the centre of the storm sat quietly in a room at the police station. He had actually expected to get out in time, so he hadn't really considered what he would do in the event that he was caught. Nobody seemed particularly anxious to speak to him, since the regular police didn't know what to ask him. They didn't have a glimmering of what they were supposed to be investigating, and the Kanagi management and the auditors, who were beginning to understand with a horrible certainty what they were looking at, were far too busy trying to unravel things so they could reassure the markets of Kanagi's solvency. So he was left alone with his thoughts, in a grubby little room, with a lock on the door. He supposed they would discover the extent of the fraud soon enough - after all, once it started unravelling, there was no way any of it could remain hidden. He knew the Chelsea profits had been taken back to Liechtenstein, and he trusted his friend Phil Harris to have made sure from there that the funds became buried beyond the reach of any investigators. He supposed that he would go to prison. The fatalism of the Shinto he'd been taught as a child helped him to face that prospect; and that in turn helped him to believe that beyond the punishment would be the rewards of his efforts. There was no feeling of guilt; that was for weaker men. He knew he'd brought the scheme to fruition, and but for an unforeseen hitch, he would have been out and gone. All this meant now was that he would have to wait a little longer than anticipated.

Back in London, the day wore on, and the market continued to head downwards. McKee phoned some buying orders for Kestrel through to Davis, and if the latter was still amazed by how detached his boss seemed, he didn't show it. He was too busy making sure all Commet's risk was covered, making sure the company stayed in good shape. In some ways, it was that day that he emerged from McKee's shadow, and began to be a leader of the firm in his own right. McKee went home after he left Harris in the coffee bar, and sat in his study, numbed by the realisation of what they had done. Eventually, his mind started working again, and he began to realise that, actually, nothing tied him in to the affair. The origin of Kestrel, while he didn't really want to talk too much about it, was shrouded by secrecy laws in Panama and Liechtenstein. And although Harris had a problem, because the investigators would turn up the trading records of Chelsea and reveal that it had just been a way of washing money out of Kanagi, *he* had no connection at all with that side of the fraud. Harris would have to hide away in Monaco, or wherever, but if McKee just sat tight and kept his cool when asked about Kestrel, he was home and dry. He would have his money in the bank - somewhere - and he could keep it there until he was ready to quit, and go and live on it. He was the one in the whole game who had all the time in the world.

It was an invigorating feeling, to know that he could keep out of the line of fire. He needed to go out tonight, to celebrate at Annabel's. For sure he would find some like-minded spirits there; that took care of the end of the evening. But first, mid-afternoon, there was something else he had to do. He set off to Berkeley Square to have a talk with Aston Martin Sales of Mayfair. He needed to buy himself a present, just to prove to himself he wasn't dreaming. By the time he had finished with the salesman, he was back on top form. There was only one person he could have dinner with, who would be able to share his celebration, even if he, McKee, now thought himself in a better position. He picked up the phone and called Phil Harris again. It was a strange dinner, though. Both of them were still struggling to come to terms with what they had engineered, that for all the publicity given to the disruptive power of financial derivatives, they had actually harnessed that power to their own ends. They shied away from talking about what the long-term effects would be, in what kind of a mess they would have left the world's copper market. Harris basically couldn't care, and McKee had convinced himself during the afternoon that he would carry on as before, apart from a much, much bigger bank account. It was strange that he felt he wouldn't be able to let go of the business, that although he had the money now, he still needed the feeling of belonging.

Earlier in the day, at the LME, where McKee still wanted to belong, Lubbock and Thresher had stared in disbelief at the chaos in the market. They knew, after their last meeting with Waverley that there were some big, high-risk positions out there, but they had never really considered the possibility of fraud on this scale. Frankly, they didn't know what to do. They considered suspending trading, awaiting some outcome of the investigations Kanagi were undertaking, but in a conversation with senior Kanagi managers, they were told that the Japanese could give no indication of when they would have any conclusions. "And anyway, Tom," said Thresher, after they had finished the call to Tokyo, "I think we'd have serious legal problems if we suspended trading arbitrarily. You know our membership - they'd keep trading amongst themselves anyway, and then turn round and sue us for closing the market if it went against them. I've asked the lawyers for an opinion, but I'm pretty sure we can't do it. I think we have to tough it out. So far, the only non-payment of margin has been by Kanagi themselves, and you heard the man just now, he's assured BancSud, as his clearing broker, that this is not a real default, but just a temporary delay while they ascertain what's been going on. I think our line has to be that we sympathise with their position, and we will give them any assistance we can in trying to get to the bottom of what Yamagazi's done, but in the end, we have a market to run, and the issue is between them and Banc Sud. We *may* yet come out smelling of roses, if we keep our nerve; if it all settles down, we can then turn round and demonstrate that even in the most volatile trading conditions any of us have seen, we still managed to run an orderly market."

"Maybe," replied Lubbock, "but I wouldn't count on it. I've a nasty feeling you and I are going to be pilloried over this. When the regulators find out about our meetings with Waverley, and the compromises we made to prevent anything becoming public, they're going to roast us alive. I think we may be close to the end of our illustrious careers."

Thresher was silent. Despite his earlier confidence, deep down, he knew Lubbock was right. It was all so unfair; they'd genuinely been intending to reform the market, but events had just caught them out. As McKee and Harris, the traders, would have said, with no sympathy, timing in a market is everything.

As the day had wound through the time zones, Jason Serck's assistants at Leopard-Star had begun to see how big the crash on the LME was. They knew Serck had been looking at this market, and they knew he had been looking to get positioned for a big fall. But they also knew that so far, they had no exposure. It looked very much like they had missed their chance. There was no way they could disturb him at his retreat - it was the strongest rule of all, and breaking it, for *any* reason, would have spelt the rapid end to a career. They'd tried to get in touch with Benson, but all Commet New York could tell them was that he was travelling, and of the two people they had spoken to before at Commet London, McKee was out, with his mobile switched off, and Davis was too busy to return calls that weren't directly trading enquiries. So they were forced to rely on the other LME brokers, who didn't understand anyway, and their banking contacts, who were all panicking about whether they had an exposure to Kanagi. So they sat and watched.

In the first few days, as the market continued to tumble, and the copper industry learnt how derivatives *really* affect markets, it was only the specialist and financial press that followed the story. A couple of lecturing editorials in the Financial Times, and an article in the industry bible, the Metal Bulletin, about how this should have been seen coming, that was all it warranted. Most reports simply assumed that a rogue trader at a far-off Japanese company had run amok in a market that most of the population were barely aware of. But then, bit by bit, the name of Chelsea Metals began to leak into the public domain, and a week later the story suddenly exploded into the mainstream press. All at once, everyone was an expert in how the price of copper was critical to an industrial society, and how that price had been manipulated by —- but so far, they didn't really know by whom. The left-leaning journals reported on how tough life was for the miners, and in contrast how much money was made trading the now-pilloried copper derivatives. The more sober, capitalist element concentrated on how difficult it was to legislate for individual greed, and pontificated over how corporate governance should be reformed before systemic risk - as big a buzz phrase as derivatives - brought the whole free market edifice tumbling down. And still, Hiro Yamagazi sat quietly in his police cell in Tokyo. He hadn't actually been arrested, nobody knew quite yet what to charge him with, but Japan Inc saw no reason to let him go while they considered the details.

The speculation over the role of Chelsea obviously focussed on Jamie Edwards and Phil Harris. Their mantra was "we are a broking and trading company, with admittedly close relations with Kanagi Corp, but we are not responsible for the actions of their traders." At first, Edwards had been surprised when Harris had told him this was the line to follow. He had felt it was a betrayal of Yamagazi to cut him off and leave him to his fate. However, Harris had convinced him that there was nothing they could do for the Japanese, and it was better they stayed as uninvolved as they could, so at least they could safeguard their position for the future, for when he was again at liberty. The LME authorities called them in together with Waverley, representing BancSud, to try to get to the bottom of the mess; but Harris and Edwards just stuck to their story, and no proof could be found to implicate them or Chelsea. Waverley suspected a lot, but, as Harris had intended, his own private agreement over the shareholding in Chelsea was something he didn't want investigated, so he too said as little as possible. Anyway, he was concerned with his own negotiations with Kanagi to get all the payments made to his own company.

But none of this stopped the speculation about Chelsea, and eventually, first Harris and then Edwards decided enough was enough and headed abroad, on "holiday." The LME traders couldn't believe what had happened. After all, they had been taken in by the scam; but they were the experts, weren't they? So how could they have been so wrong in their assessments of the market? The popular view was that Harris and Edwards had just been the pawns of Yamagazi. After all, it was more comfortable for them to point the finger at a Japanese most of them had never met than to accept that some of their own number had been able to bamboozle them all for over a year. They felt vindicated when the Japanese police finally charged Yamagazi - with securities fraud, in fact, which they hoped was a broad enough catch-all to cover the fact that still no-one really fully understood what had gone on.

The one man who was determined to understand was across the Atlantic, in New York. Jason Serck had come back from his retreat at the beginning of January to find chaos in the copper market - the very chaos he and McKee had foreseen and had planned to exploit. However, it transpired that Leopard-Star had reaped no benefit at all from a correct reading of the market. Serck was a fair man; he didn't rant and rail at his associates, since he had established the rule of no contact during his retreat. He took the responsibility for the missed opportunity, but he vowed that if anybody had double-crossed him, he would make them pay. Inevitably, his first port of call was Mack McKee. McKee had had time to prepare his story. Fortunately, the LME were discreet in their dissemination of trading information, and Serck was not aware that Commet had featured in the clearing system as by far the biggest buyer of put options in the immediate lead-up to the crash. So when the call came through, McKee was ready.

"Jason, my friend," boomed the confident voice, "how was your break? I guess you were as surprised as we were to see the market crash when it did. Looks like we had the right idea, though."

"Right ideas don't make money, Mack, unless they're executed."

"Timing, Jason, timing is everything. We made a bit jobbing in and out as the price collapsed. Rory certainly earned his inflated salary in those few days." He couldn't resist giving himself flowers. "Of course, I was standing behind him to make sure we kept it all under control."

"That's real nice for you, Mack, but it don't help me at all. Last time we spoke, you were sure we were going to catch the market right. What went wrong?"

"Frankly, Jason, fraud," said McKee, breezily. "I don't think we've seen all there is to see with our friend Yamagazi. You know we expected the market to drop because he had bitten off more than he could chew, but we didn't reckon with a guy outright stealing money off his company. We were looking at economic realities, not a house of cards built by a criminal. I would still maintain that without the fraud, our timing would have been good."

"Without the fraud, who knows were the market would have been," said Serck. "I've got a bad taste in my mouth that we were taken for as much of a ride as everyone else." He paused. "Somebody made money here, Mack. I want to know who it was. It's an easy sum. Whoever had the big short position when the market lost fifty percent made a shipload of money. Some of that money should have been ours. We need to find out who it was because I don't believe it was all Yamagazi and Harris. Where is Harris, by the way? I guess you'd know. You two were pretty close."

Was that a veiled indication that Serck suspected something? Or was he just being paranoid? "I don't know. I know he's out of the country. Knowing him, if I had to guess, I'd say Monaco."

"Yeah. I'll be in Europe soon. I think perhaps you and I should pay a visit to Mr. Phil Harris."

"See if he's got anything to tell us, you mean?"

"Yeah." And Serck hung up.

In the weeks that followed, the market began to adjust to the new reality, as markets always do. The mining companies all cried foul to the LME, and as Harris had predicted back on that bright day at Newbury, their chief executives began to rehearse the excuses they would make to explain to their shareholders why they had failed to take advantage of the market spike, as it was now seen to be. Lubbock and Thresher spent days with the regulators, and did in fact save their positions, at the expense of much of the Exchange's freedoms. The anomalies that had allowed Chelsea to exploit its clients in quite such a blatant way were outlawed, and the market was made to toe the same line as London's other financial exchanges. The changes suited the regulators, but not the membership - or indeed many of the clients - but it was the price that had to be paid.

Business for the brokers was muted, in that period after the crash. Nobody really knew what to do. Chelsea's offices were largely deserted, although the company still existed, and it had been named very early on in a lawsuit begun by Kanagi to try and recover its money. BancSud was also named, and the litigation was poised to last for years. BancSud also counter sued, demanding repayment of the margin money it had paid to the Clearing House to avoid default. Union Bank, and those others who had lost far less, were busy suing Kanagi in turn to attempt to recover what they had lost in bad loans. There was an undercurrent of speculation that the chairman of Kanagi would take the traditional Japanese way of honour, but in fact he just resigned to go into early retirement. His successors declared their intentions to fight on through the courts.

Strangely, although the investigations had turned up the name of Kestrel, it was still seen as something of a side issue. The focus was entirely on the way Chelsea had laundered money stolen from Kanagi by Yamagazi. Mack McKee was in a kind of limbo. He was coming in to the office most days, but increasingly finding it difficult to concentrate on what was now just a game for him. His need to play the game was not as great as he had thought a few weeks earlier. Rory Davis was becoming increasingly annoyed with his boss's lack of interest, compounded by the sullen attitude Stu Benson was exhibiting towards McKee, and Commet in general. Davis' constant complaint was, "I have to make all the money, do I have to run the bloody company as well?" It was a fair criticism, and McKee knew he had to make a decision about where he was going.

He picked up the phone one morning, and heard a familiar voice. "Mack, how are you?" asked Phil Harris. "I'm sitting down here in the sun in Monaco, reading all about the problems in the copper market. Why don't you come down for a few days? We can talk about any opportunities it creates for us." They were both acutely aware of the tapes on the phone lines.

"That's not a bad idea, Phil. A few days out of the office might be a nice break. I can drive down in my new toy." They fixed a date a few weeks ahead; McKee strongly suspected that after being down there, he probably wouldn't want to come back. After all, between them, he and Harris had over $300 million in the bank.

Chapter Twenty

Stu Benson was getting to the end of his tether. He was a loyal servant of Commet and McKee, and he'd been well treated over the years. But he was an honest man, and the cavalier way McKee had ignored what Benson saw as a verbal contract with Serck rankled with him. He'd kept quiet in the immediate aftermath of the affair, but now the market was settling again, he began to question whether he could continue to say nothing. Rory Davis had noticed the change in him, but despite their friendship, Benson knew he couldn't confide in the dealer in London. Davis wouldn't do anything that would upset the Commet apple-cart. Slowly, Benson became convinced that he had to go to Jason Serck and tell him what had happened. He knew it would probably spell the end of his career at Commet, but nevertheless he felt he had to do it, or feel himself implicated in a double-cross for the rest of his life.

Getting in to see Serck was tough. The fund manager was not best pleased with Commet; he knew something had gone on, and McKee and his boys were the easiest target for his rage. At first, he assumed Benson simply wanted to try to persuade him the LME was still a market for him, and he refused to take the calls. Eventually, through one of Serck's aides, Benson managed to convey that he was prepared to talk about what had gone wrong before. They met for a coffee at the back of a dark diner on Third Avenue.

Serck was brusque and offhand, to begin with. "OK, Stu, you told Ed you'd got something to tell me about the copper business. What is it?"

"Before we go into that, you gotta know where I stand. I believe we had an agreement to work with you to bring about a collapse in the copper market which would profit us both. We agreed that we would both put our money at risk, and that we would share information to help us get our timing right. Is that also your understanding of what we all said?"

"Yeah, of course. We should have been working together."

"OK, well, look. I believe that Mack got hold of some other information and that he was working with somebody else rather than putting our partnership first."

Serck hunched forward in his chair. This was getting to where he wanted. "Who?"

"That I'm not sure of. In the weeks and particularly the days immediately before the price broke down, we were trading massive volumes of put options - effectively, what should have been our joint trade. But we were buying the options from Kanagi, via Chelsea, and we were selling them to a new client called Kestrel Aviation and Trading. Before you ask, I don't know who they are; it's a Panamanian company operating through Liechtenstein. Rory and I questioned Mack about it, but he wouldn't say anything definite. He gave the impression that it was set up by a group of mining company executives, to make a personal profit, while they did nothing corporately."

Serck sat motionless and silent for a moment. Then, "So you're telling me that McKee was operating our strategy on behalf of this Kestrel?"

"Yeah, I believe so. Look, I've worked for McKee for a long time, and it's been a good time. We've had a lot of fun, and we've all made Commet into the best. Sure, we're all trying to make money, but this time I think he's gone too close to the edge. We had agreed something with you, and he turned his back on that agreement. I can't let that go."

"Mmm. The question is, how do we prove it? And then, what do I do about it? We need to have a little conversation with some of our friends who have contacts in Liechtenstein and Panama." He grinned wolfishly. "One of the interesting things about running a hedge fund is that although our own operations are squeaky clean, some of our investors have very unusual pasts, and even more unusual connections. Stu, I'm grateful to you for telling me this. If it turns out there is something smelly in it, your position may become awkward."

Benson interrupted. "But there isn't really anything you can do. I mean, it's all over. The chance has gone."

Serck looked hard at him. "If someone has double-crossed me - and right now, that looks like Mack, then they'll pay for it. As I said, in our business you get to know some strange people. Antagonising us is not clever."

Although said quietly, in the middle of the sophistication of a civilised Manhattan afternoon, the words made Benson shiver. He began to wonder what he had done.

Serck went back to his office, and started making some calls. What he had said to Benson was true. Leopard-Star was as clean as a whistle, and he and his colleagues ran it professionally and honestly. However, the very nature of hedge funds, with their promise of high returns and their secrecy, attracted money that would not have been comfortable in more mainstream investment vehicles. Serck didn't pry too much into the pasts of his investors; as long as the money they put into his fund came from a legitimate bank account, that was fine by him - and by the regulators. He had, however, over the years got to know a little about the origins of some of his clients. So it was not too difficult for him to track down someone who could get him the information he wanted. In fact, for him using sources on the wrong side of the law, it was possible; for the lawyers investigating Chelsea and, to a lesser extent Kestrel, it was impossible to get the same information. The cynic may well say, therefore, that the secrecy laws had done their job.

So Jason Serck knew for sure that Mack McKee had managed to outwit him. He knew now that Kestrel was the true winner in the copper crash, and that Kestrel was owned by Phil Harris and Mack McKee. He couldn't care less about Harris; he'd had no agreement with him. But his anger with McKee was building to boiling point. Serck made another phone call, to somebody who made a call, to somebody who made a call, to somebody who made a call that resulted in a large bundle of French Francs being handed to an ex-Foreign Legionnaire in a dark, smoky bar in the heart of the run-down port area of Marseilles. Ex, because even the Legion frowned on some excesses of violence.

McKee didn't particularly want the world to know that he was off down to see Phil Harris in Monaco – in the circumstances, he felt it politic not to make their connections too obvious. But the legionnaire was a professional, so it wasn't too difficult for him to find out McKee's travel arrangements. It suited him fine; he'd much rather be able to finish his job at home in France, and not have to cross the Channel and operate in England.

Once he knew the big man had his Aston Martin booked on the cross-channel ferry, all he had to do was wait. McKee would have no option, certainly for the first part of his journey, but to take the A26 – the Autoroute des Anglais, from the Channel ports down to join the Autoroute du Soleil north of Lyons. So he gunned his motor-cycle northwards from Marseilles, then picked a suitable rest-area parking, with a clear sight of the cars heading southwards, and sat astride his bike to wait.

By the time he got to Lyons, Mack McKee was bored with the Autoroute. The Aston Martin was magnificent, big, brash and noisy, just like it's owner. He blasted past the traffic, with no regard for any speed limits, the racing green paintwork gleaming in the early spring sunshine. But he needed a road with some bends, a challenge, not the tedium of the long dual carriageway. He turned off left, heading towards Grenoble. He didn't notice the black 1000cc Kawasaki that had been tracking him since just outside Reims. Once through the traffic round Grenoble, he took the road winding it's way up into the foothills of the Alps, the Route Napoleon that the deposed Emperor had followed back to Paris when he escaped from Elba to head for his nemesis at Waterloo. Bypassing the plateau of the Vercors, where doomed Resistance fighters had held out for two bloody months in the summer of 1944, he climbed higher and higher. He revelled in the power of the big car, the booming V8 echoing back at him from the solid rock face on one side. Eventually, in the late afternoon, he found what looked to him like a sufficiently comfortable hotel for a multi-millionaire - that's what he was, wasn't it? - to overnight. He was right. There weren't too many guests so early in the year, still too cold for the walkers or the hordes descending to the coast, but the kitchen was open, and the wine list good enough even for his expensive tastes. He spent a quiet evening, mostly chatting to the girl serving in the virtually deserted bar after dinner; she was able to resist his charms, so he headed up to his room alone around midnight, after a fair few calvados' and a couple of Monte Cristos. He slept well.

Outside, in the black mountain night, a figure on a motor-cycle rolled quietly to a standstill next to the Aston Martin. The ex-Legionnaire dismounted, and lay down on the ground under the rear bumper of the car. He had a bag of tools in his hand, and whatever he was doing took him no more than ten minutes or so. Finishing, he stood up, replaced the tools in the pannier of the Kawasaki and rolled away a few hundred metres down the hill before starting his engine. The staff in the hotel, tidying up for the night, heard the bike roar away into the night and thought nothing of it.

Next morning, McKee was up bright, if not early. He only had a couple of hours drive down through the mountains to the coast, and then a short blast along the Corniche from Nice to Monaco. He took a leisurely breakfast, paid his bill and wandered out to his car, admiring it's lines as he approached it. He got in and started it up. As he drove away, there was a drying pool of fluid by where each of the back wheels had been. He picked up the car phone and dialled Harris' number. "Phil, morning, how are you? I'm up in the mountains. Should be not much more than a couple of hours, so I'll see you for lunch."

"Great, Mack, I'm looking forward to it. How's the new car, by the way?"

"Fantastic. You should dump the Mercedes and get yourself a real man's car."

Harris laughed. "I'll see you around lunch time." He hung up. McKee hit the button for the CD. "Money for nothing and your chicks for free," sang Dire Straits. He laughed to himself. You got it, Mark Knopfler, he thought, that's my life from now on. He turned the volume up.

The road, which had been relatively flat after the first slope down from the hotel, now began to steepen, with a sheer drop on one side, and McKee shifted the auto gears down a ratio. The engine was warmed up, and he put on a bit of speed downhill, enjoying the thunder of the exhaust mingling with the music. The first hairpin came upon him, and he hit the brake pedal. The car slowed, but the pressure of the pedal wasn't how it had been the day before. McKee made a face, but controlled the heavy car as it swung round the bend. By the next curve, the car was picking up more speed, and the brake pedal this time just flopped to the floor. Fighting the car now, he dropped a gear ratio and wrestled with the steering wheel to get round. The tyres screeched, and by the next turn, he had lost the fight. The front of the car couldn't stay on the road. It bounced over the edge, the big V8 screaming by now, and plunged down into the valley below. As it hit the bottom, there was a sickening *woof*, as the petrol ignited and a pillar of smoke and flame erupted from the wreck of the Aston Martin. By the time the first rescuers reached it, it was a burnt-out hulk, McKee's body crushed and blackened. Phil Harris didn't have a lunch guest that day, after all. The legionnaire on his Kawasaki was back in the same bar in Marseilles by that evening, ready to receive another fat wad of French francs.

What was left of the body was flown back to England for the funeral in London. There was a real sense of shock at his death amongst the metal trading community. Not everybody had liked the big man, but no-one had been left untouched by the power of his personality. Those who had been close to him, particularly his colleagues at Commet, were left with a genuine hollow feeling of loss. The funeral saw a huge turn-out, with the mourning led by his widowed mother; those who hadn't seen her before saw where he'd got his big, stooped physique from.

Harris and Edwards had made the journey together from Monaco. Neither of them relished going back to England while enquiries were still going on, but equally they were very sure that they had to pay their last respects to McKee. Jamie Edwards mixed awkwardly with the LME traders; until it had all started, he'd been one of their number, just one of the boys. Now, they all treated him with a reserve. Even Ferret, who'd been a close friend since their early days on the Exchange floor, was hesitant in talking to him. But in the end, Ferret couldn't stop himself from asking the question they all wanted answered.

"How much did you make, Jamie?" They all clustered round, anxious to hear.

"I don't know, Ferret." There were sceptical looks. "A lot. We've still got things tied up in Chelsea, a few properties, and some other investments." He grinned. "But, believe me, it's enough."

"And what about Yamagazi? He's going on trial soon, isn't he?" one of the others asked.

"You know as much as I do. I guess the Japanese authorities think he did something criminal. I don't know. We just took the orders from him. Phil had the closer links with him."

But nobody really wanted to talk to Harris, who stood alone; McKee had probably come to be the closest thing he had had to a friend. Now there he was. $300 million-odd in the bank, one friend dead, and the other person who could have become one looking at a jail sentence in Japan. All the money he wanted, but still a loner. Well, life could be worse.

Jason Serck had come to the funeral as well. He walked up to Stu Benson, who'd been chatting with Rory Davis and some of the other Commet staff, amongst them McKee's secretary, trying to blink away the tears she was crying for her boss. Benson nodded to Serck, and they moved a couple of steps away from the group. "A sad day, Stu. He was a well-respected man. I guess we've got all the great and the good of the LME business here mourning him. A real freak way to die. Have they discovered why the car went off the road? I guess he was just going too fast; maybe driving the car like he'd been living his life. What was it you said in New York? 'This time he's gone too close to the edge'? That was it, wasn't it?"

Stu Benson just stared at him, unable to believe the terrible thought taking shape in his mind. Serck went on. "I don't think there's any need for that discussion of ours to become public knowledge, do you? It would be better if the world didn't know he'd just pulled off a big double-cross." He gestured towards McKee's mother. "Much better for her - and all these other good people - to remember him as a bit of a pirate, but on the side of the angels, huh? We wouldn't want them to see him as a cheating bastard, right at the end of his life. You must excuse me, Stu, I need to go have a word with Phil Harris, while he's all alone over there." And giving Benson a conspiratorial squeeze of the arm, he walked off.

"What was that all about, Stu? You look like you've seen a ghost," said Rory Davis, approaching him as Serck wandered away.

Benson shook his head, to try and clear the thought from it. "Not a ghost, Rory, something worse."

Davis looked curiously at him. "No, it's not the time Rory," said Benson, "We're here to mourn Mack. Remember all the good times we had with him, not worry about our own problems." And it probably never will be the time to tell him, he thought to himself. Serck's right, better to leave sleeping dogs lie. All I have is speculation, based on two conversations and a horrible accident. And a frightening guilt.

Serck walked up to Harris. "I don't think we've met. My name is Jason Serck. I used to do some business with Mack McKee."

"Yeah, I've heard of your fund. My name's Phil Harris, by the way."

"I know that, Mr. Harris. You were the guiding force behind Chelsea Metals. I guess I gotta congratulate you on a great market manipulation. Relax," he said, as Harris' face stiffened at the phrase he used, "I'm nothing to do with the regulators. I'm congratulating you as one market player to another. Perhaps we should get together next time; my funds have a lot of clout if you want to move markets."

"It's a nice idea, but I'm not sure there'll be another time for me. I've got pretty much what I want. I'm aiming to relax and enjoy it now."

"That's a fine concept, Phil - you don't mind me calling you Phil?" Harris shrugged his approval. "But look at this fine gentleman we are mourning here today. I guess he was aiming to enjoy what he had, and look how short a time it lasted. One day a rich partner in Kestrel Aviation and Trading, the next dead in the burnt-out wreck of his new car. You never know what's round the corner."

With that, he walked off, leaving Harris stunned. Nobody should have known about McKee's involvement with Kestrel. And from the way he'd said it, Serck obviously knew Kestrel was the real source of the money. For the very first time since beginning the whole game, Harris didn't feel in total control. The sooner he got back to the security of Monaco, the happier he'd be. The veiled threat from Serck hung over him as he watched the coffin lowered into the earth, and he heard the words of the priest's homily, talking about trust and friendship.

Trust and friendship, he mused. Had he really gone so far down his lonely road that he had abandoned them forever? *His* funeral wouldn't be crowded like this. And yet, he'd been going to share the proceeds with McKee - it was just too late now. But Yamagazi was suffering for Harris's success, and Jamie Edwards had been an integral part of it, even if, at the end, he hadn't been fully aware of his role. McKee's death showed how ephemeral it could all be. Did he really want to live in isolation, with that threat of Serck's hanging over him?

Chapter Twenty-One

Harris and Edwards left directly after the funeral service – they didn't want to have to spend any more time mingling with the curious, the jealous or the vindictive. Their limo got them back to Heathrow, where they were glad to board their flight back to the haven of Monaco.

"So, Jamie," said Harris as they relaxed back into their first-class seats for the short flight to Nice, "It looks like it's back to just you and me, like it was at the beginning."

Edwards didn't understand. "You, me and Hiro, surely," he said, "and that's what it's been all the time, hasn't it?"

Harris had made his decision; he couldn't keep it all bottled up. McKee was gone, but he had to share his knowledge of what had happened with someone else. "Jamie, there were two games going on. You and Hiro knew about one, the original one, but you didn't know what part McKee played in it all."

Edwards just stared at him. "McKee?" he said, "Surely his part was just the way Commet were on the other side from us. That's why I could sell all the puts to Rory, to keep the pressure on while we were getting out."

"That's how it was gonna be at the start, but I worked out there was a better way out for me. And to take it, I had to work with McKee. All those puts you sold, the buyer was me. Or, more correctly, it was a company called Kestrel Aviation and Trading, that was owned by me and Mack McKee. We were the big short in the market, and we made more money than you can imagine."

Edwards looked hard at him, with cold, narrow eyes. "And were you going to tell me this, if McKee hadn't had his accident? Or was it just another case of setting me up as your pawn, like when you got me fired from Myerson's, just to suit your plans?"

Harris stared out of the aeroplane window for a few moments, lost in his thoughts. Then, shaking his head, as if to clear it, "Jamie, I honestly don't know the answer to that question. I hadn't even thought about it. I was tied up in the game, in the excitement of making the whole thing work. At the beginning, it was simple. You, me and Hiro were going to clean up however much we could wash out of Kanagi before the scheme collapsed. But then when I saw how much more there was there, how much Mack and I could make, I just grabbed the chance – like anyone else woulda done. How we would have split it, I don't know. McKee and I had about $300 million in Kestrel, plus whatever there is in Chelsea, which I guess would have gone to you and Hiro. I guess we all would come out pretty well. But now, what do we do?"

Edwards just waited, as Harris went on, "And there's another complication, one I don't fully understand. You know of a guy called Jason Serck?"

"Yeah, the fund manager. He was there today – some of the guys pointed him out when he was talking to you. I guess Commet do some business with them, so he knew McKee that way. Otherwise, why would he have been there?"

"I guess that's true. But he seems to know more than he should. He made it very clear to me that he knew about Kestrel, and McKee's involvement in it. How would he know that, and why should he care? I got a bad taste from it, Jamie, I think he may have had something to do with McKee's death."

"What? Why on earth would you think that? What could he possibly have to do with it? Mack had an accident, driving that car too fast on a mountain road."

"I hope you're right, Jamie, but I'm not sure. I think somehow

Serck was involved with Commet, and something didn't work out." He paused. "But then, maybe I just think everyone's as devious as me. Maybe it's all just as it seems, McKee had an accident and Serck meant nothing suspicious. We got all the money, so why should we care, anyway?" But he didn't believe that, and he knew for sure he was going to be very, very careful in future. He didn't want to end up like McKee, not for a long, long time.

"Yeah, we've got all the money," said Edwards, "but I've still got the problem that you want to treat me like a poodle. That first evening, in Brown's Hotel, you talked a lot about trust between us. But right now, from where I'm sitting, it looks like trust only goes one way. Why, Phil? Why didn't you let me know what was going on?"

Harris shrugged. "Jamie, I guess you just gotta take it the way it is. You can have a share in a big pot of money. Or you can take your injured pride and try and get a job to live some other way. Up to you."

Jamie Edwards looked hard at him. "You are one fucking bastard, Phil Harris," he said.

Epilogue

Four Years Later

It was a bright spring day in Yokohama. A black Nissan Infiniti with dimmed-out windows was waiting by the kerbside, outside an intimidating building. Yokohama prison. A small door in the gate opened, and a nondescript oriental came out, blinking in the sharp morning sunlight. In his hand he carried a small hold-all. He was wearing what looked as though it had been a fashionable suit, but it seemed to hang loosely from his frame, as if it had been made for someone a size bigger. Peering around him through his thick glasses, he spotted the Nissan and walked over to it. Without a word, the chauffeur jumped out, and opened the back door for him.

Slipping through the traffic, the black car picked up speed as it joined the freeway heading out of the Tokyo-Yokohama conurbation towards Narita. An hour and a half later, the Japanese man was sitting in the Virgin Atlantic lounge at Narita, a plate of canapés in front of him, and a glass of champagne in his hand. He almost had to pinch himself to make him believe it was real, after the rigours of four years in Yokohama jail. His sentence had been seven and a half years, but he'd behaved himself, caused no problems, and the parole board had decided to remit the balance of his punishment, releasing him three and a half years after the surprisingly low-key trial that had condemned him. The trial had been low-key, because Yamagazi had admitted to defrauding Kanagi by washing money through Chelsea. As far as anything else was concerned, he had simply said nothing. The loans he had arranged with the banks could not in the end be held against him. After all, Kanagi had deputed the authority to take those loans to him. Likewise all the trading on behalf of the smelters - he had had full authority to do it. As the time of the trial had approached, it had become blatantly obvious that Kanagi's internal controls were going to come under as much scrutiny as Yamagazi's own actions - and that scrutiny would create a lot of embarrassment. Japan Inc couldn't be held up to ridicule in the eyes of the westerners. So Yamagazi was allowed to keep quiet about much of what had gone on, and with a nod and a wink he was assured that his sentence would be far shorter in reality than was publicised. One condition was that when he was released, he should not expect to remain an inhabitant of his native land.

Kanagi's wish to avoid embarrassment was also the reason why in the end, they settled most of the lawsuits out of court. They took the losses, letting Union, the smaller banks and BancSud themselves off the hook. Waverley, once Harris had honoured his side of their bargain, faded into the background, his dreams of becoming a major City figure dashed - but then, he was a lot richer than his limited talent gave him any right to expect.

After changing planes in London, Yamagazi landed at Nice airport. An airline flunky ushered him across to the waiting helicopter for the short hop to Monaco. As he left the heliport on arrival, he was beckoned towards a red Bentley Turbo. In the back, with a bottle of Krug just opened and ready to pour, sat Phil Harris and Jamie Edwards.

"Welcome home, Hiro," the American greeted him.

About the Publisher

Twenty First Century Publishers is dedicated to bringing new authors to the market. We are interested in original manuscripts which we believe may be of appeal to our readership. Please contact us through our website at:
www.twentyfirstcenturypublishers.com.

OTHER BOOKS AVAILABLE FROM TWENTY FIRST CENTURY PUBLISHERS LTD

OVER A BARREL
From the moment you land at Heathrow on page one the plot grips you. Ed Burke, an American oil tycoon, jets through the world's financial centres and the Middle East to set up deals, but where does this lead him? Are his premonitions about his daughter Louise in Saudi Arabia well founded? Is his corporate lawyer Nicole on his side or against him? Does he have opponents in the Middle East?

As the plot unfolds his company is put into play in the tangle of events surrounding the invasion of Kuwait in 1990. Even his private life is drawn into the morass.

In this novel Peter depicts the grim machinations of political and commercial life, but the human spirit shines through. This is a thriller that will hold you to the last page.

Over a Barrel by Peter Driver
ISBN: 1-904433-03-0

THE SIGNATURE OF A VOICE
The Signature of a Voice is a cat-and-mouse game between a violent trio, led by a psychopathic killer, and a police officer on suspension. Move and countermove in this chess game is planned and enacted. The reader, in the position of god, knows who is guilty and who plans what, but just as in chess, the opponents' plans thwart one another. The outcomes twist and turn to the final curtain fall.

The Signature of a Voice by Johnny John Heinz
ISBN 1-904433-00-6

MEANS TO AN END
Enter the world of money laundering, financial manipulation and greed, where a shadowy middle eastern organisation takes on a major corporation in the US. As the action shifts through exotic locations, who wins out in the end? Certainly, the author's first hand experience of international finance lends the plot chilling credibility.

Means to an End by Johnny John Heinz
ISBN: 1-84375-008-2

RAMONA
How did a little girl come to be abandoned in the orange scented square of the Andalusian City of Seville? Find out, when the course of her life is resumed at age seventeen.

"Ramona" is a literary work that deals with Europe in transition and the relationships that form an ususual life.

Ramona by Johnny John Heinz
ISBN: 1-904433-01-4

Visit our website: www.twentyfirstcenturypublishers.com

Printed in the United Kingdom
by Lightning Source UK Ltd.
104627UKS00001B/187